SOUL CITY

ALSO BY RICHARD E. GROPP

BAD GLASS

SOUL CITY

RICHARD E. GROPP

ADAPTIVE BOOKS

AN IMPRINT OF ADAPTIVE STUDIOS
LOS ANGELES, CA

Copyright © 2018 Old Curiosity Shop, Inc.

Dialogue from "The Birds" courtesy of Universal Studios Licensing LLC

Visit us on the web at www.adaptivestudios.com

Library of Congress Cataloging in Publication Number: 2018956672
ISBN 978-1-945293-38-2
Ebook ISBN 978-1-945293-78-8

Printed in the United States of America.
Designed by Neuwirth & Associates, Inc.

Adaptive Books
3733 Motor Avenue
Los Angeles, CA 90034

10 9 8 7 6 5 4 3 2 1

FOR JIM

SOUL CITY

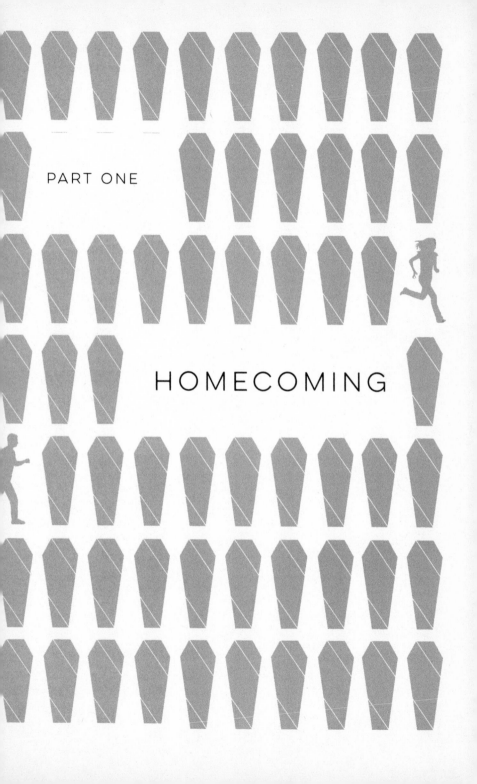

PART ONE

HOMECOMING

1

My dad will be dead by this time tomorrow.

I was nine years old when I first saw it happen. My sister, Darla, and I were sitting at the kitchen table. It was a hot summer day out, and we'd just come in from running through the sprinklers in the cemetery—up row A5, and back down A4, slipping and sliding through the wet grass. Our bathing suits were dripping wet, and we were leaving puddles on the linoleum floor. My dad had made us root beer floats. I was drinking mine, and across the table, Darla was playing with her straw and laughing her little girl laugh.

Then my dad walked up behind me. He put his hand on my bare shoulder—for just a brief moment—then continued on to the living room. He'd probably touched my shoulder like that a thousand times before, and I'd never seen a thing.

This time, however … this time was different.

The kitchen, Darla, and everything around me faded away to nearly black, with only the smallest pinprick of light in the center. Then, from inside that light, an image grew. It is an image I've lived with for the last eight years: my dad standing on a ladder, cleaning leaves from the rain gutter at the front of the house. He's wearing jeans, work boots, and a flannel shirt. His forehead's glistening with sweat, and his hair—longer and grayer than I've ever seen it—is matted to his head. I hear a woman's voice coming from a radio down below. *"… Monday, June the fourth, 2018, and this is All Things Considered."* I didn't recognize that voice until years later.

But that day, in my terrified nine-year-old mind, I saw plenty. I saw the vein in my dad's throat bulge as he gathered mud and leaves into a black plastic trash bag. I saw him wipe sweat from his brow with his sleeve. Then I saw him turn and lose his balance. He reached out to grab hold of the rain gutter, but it separated from the shingled roof, pulling away as if it had never been attached. And then he was falling through the air. The last thing I saw was my dad hitting the ground, his neck breaking with a terrifying *crack*—

"You look weird," Darla said.

And the vision faded away as quickly as it had come.

I was back at the kitchen table. Darla was pulling faces at me, trying to get my attention, and I looked down and saw that all of the ice cream had melted in my root beer float.

That was 2010.

That's when I first learned how and when my father was going to die.

———

"In preparation for landing at San Francisco International Airport, please make sure your seat belt is securely fastened, power off all large electronic devices, and …" Blah, blah, blah.

I ignore the flight attendant and gaze out my window, watching the city down below as we begin our descent. The skyline shimmers in the afternoon light. Sharp lines have turned hazy with fog, and the bay is reflected in the Transamerica Pyramid's thousand glass windows.

When I was little, Dad, Darla, and I would drive into the city from Colma, and in between errands we'd pretend the Pyramid was our own private rocket ship, ready to lift off someday and fly us all into outer space. We'd end up on a planet far, far away from our normal everyday lives, far away from school, and my dad's work, and all of the little things that drove us crazy. Like homework. And baths. And kale. I was the captain, of course, Dad was my first mate, and Darla was a badass grunt, shooting her way through a horde of alien monsters.

"Excuse me, sir."

I keep staring out the window as Fisherman's Wharf and Alcatraz swim into view.

"Sir, excuse me, but I'm going to have to ask you to put your seat into the full upright position."

I turn, confused.

There's a doughy flight attendant staring at me. I want to laugh. Is he calling *me* "sir"? I haven't shaved in four days, but I'm only a couple of weeks past seventeen, and I think I still look pretty damn young. He starts making an impatient hand gesture, like *get moving, put your damned seat in the damned upright position*, and then he reaches across the white-haired lady sitting in the aisle seat to push the button himself.

I quickly scrunch myself up against the window and make sure his hand doesn't touch any part of my skin. The last thing I need today—the absolute *last* thing I need—is to be forced to watch some random guy have a stroke thirty years from now, or maybe give up the ghost, exhausted and hairless, in a chemo chair just three months away. The flight attendant hits the seat button, retreats back into the aisle, and gives me a look that practically screams *freak*.

I shrug an apology. Sometimes it's hard to act normal.

I'm supposed to be studying for finals this weekend, but I faked an email message from my dad to the headmaster's office, saying that I had to come back to Colma for a family emergency.

And that's the truth—if just a little bit premature.

Eight years had seemed like such a long time when I first saw my dad's death. Almost the entire span of my life up to that point. I never imagined that tomorrow, June the fourth, 2018, would get here so quickly, or that I'd have so little time to stop my father's death from happening.

But time isn't my biggest problem here.

My biggest problem is the fact that my dad won't *want* me to stop it. He'll fight me every inch of the way.

———

The ability to see other people's deaths is a Cressman family power. Or curse. It passes down to every firstborn son in our bloodline, stretching back at least four generations.

And since the time of my great-great-grandfather—the first person to have this gift—every Cressman father has taught every first son that we don't ever, *ever* intervene. The consequences of telling people when or how they're going to die would be disastrous. Or so we're told.

From the time of our first visions, when we're around seven or eight years old, it gets hammered into our skulls time and time again: the universe has its own designs, and we mere mortals shouldn't get in its way.

The problem with this setup, however, is that eventually we see every death but our own.

We see time and place. We see the wide range of possible emotions—from pain and horror to exhausted relief—in everyone around us. But for us, there's nothing but a big, blank void. A huge, towering question mark.

And according to Dad, we need to enforce this self-ignorance. Otherwise, it would be too tempting to do something about it. We might end up meddling with the universe in order to save our own lives.

So he would never tell me anything about my death, and he expects me never to say a thing about his. I actually went to boarding school in Portland last fall because I was afraid I would give something away, because I wasn't sure I could look him in the eye every day and not tell him about the horrible thing that I knew was going to happen.

But I've thought it over for months now.

And I don't *care* what my dad wants anymore.

I can't let him go.

———

As soon as the wheels touch down at SFO, I check my phone. There's a silly text from my dad, a few from friends at school, and a notification for a funny cat video that Darla posted. She doesn't know anything about the death visions, and she definitely doesn't know about the horrible event that's about to rock her world.

Darla's just a normal, well-adjusted kid—a little snarky, maybe, but what fifteen year old isn't? It's amazing just how well-adjusted she is, given that her birth parents, who were best friends with my dad, died in a car accident when she was just four years old. That's when my dad, already her godfather, adopted her.

I can't imagine what losing Dad will do to her now. It will be the second time she's been orphaned, the second time she's had to lose the person who means the most to her.

I'm just looking at my first.

Or, rather, it *would* be my first, if I weren't about to stop it from happening.

As we wait to deplane, my white-haired seatmate turns toward me. "So, young man, do you live in San Francisco?" she asks. Her voice reminds me of my grandmother's.

"Nearby," I say. "I grew up in Colma."

"Colma?" She looks confused. "Is that East Bay? I've never heard of it."

I give her a small smile. "Yeah, most people haven't," I say. "We keep it a secret."

And I'm getting sick of secrets.

———

I grab my duffel bag from the luggage carousel and head out to the curb. This bag has a history: it traveled to Iraq with my uncle Roy twice, and if I press my face into the canvas, I swear I can still smell the sand, the oil, and the fire. He gave it to me when

I first left home, handing it over with a sad, complicated look on his face.

There's a little bit of daylight left as I board the South Bay Airporter, but it takes an hour of lurching and hissing for the bus to get to Colma. By the time it comes to a stop, the sky is a dark purple.

Pausing on the sidewalk, I close my eyes and take in the familiar smell.

As I walk home from the bus station, I recognize every crack in the sidewalk, every signpost and stoplight, every chain restaurant and mini-mart. It's only been three months since I was last home, but I feel like ten or thirty years could go by and this place would still be exactly the same.

A cold wind blows in off the ocean. The sky is clear, and the moon's rising over the mountains in the distance. A few cars drive past, but only a few, and the night stays quiet.

I cross the railroad tracks at the edge of town, hike up onto the ridge, and look out over the entire Colma Valley. There are rows of warehouses, clusters of three- and four-story apartment complexes, and a couple blocks of super-nice suburban houses stretching out beneath me. Then there are the cemeteries. Acres and acres of them, everywhere I look. The gravestones and marble statues are lit by the soft glow of streetlamps, and the mausoleums rise up from the ground, sturdy and unmoving. I'm home again.

I trudge past Woodlawn, past Olivet and Home of Peace, then past Cypress Lawn and Holy Cross. About two thousand people live in Colma, but—and here's the mind-boggling thing—over two million more are buried here.

Not that they all died in Colma, of course.

In the early 1900s, San Francisco outlawed cemeteries. City officials had been anxious to stop the spread of disease—this was back before penicillin or anything like that, and the city had had big sanitation problems—so they looked for places outside the city to ship their dead. They settled on Colma. Now, a hundred years later, the dead outnumber the living here a thousand to one.

Which explains our dueling town nicknames: "Colma, City of Souls," and "Colma, City of the Silent."

My boots make soft thudding noises as I walk up the winding gravel driveway that leads to my house. To my dad.

My heart is racing. I don't want to have to do this.

The old wrought iron sign for the Cressman Cemetery forms a perfect arch above my head. As a kid, I'd run up and down this driveway; I'd play with make-believe swords and guns, ride bikes, and throw water balloons. The cemetery had been one of the first professional, community-wide graveyards in Colma, predating my family's arrival by quite a bit, and the grounds stretch on for acres. Back when I was a kid, I always tried to avoid the graves whenever I strayed out into the yard—just in case the thousands of corpses could somehow reach up through the ground, grab my ankles with their skeletal hands, and pull me down into the darkness. I used to have nightmares about them turning me into a zombie, imagining my friends and family running away from my rotting flesh.

I'm not afraid of the dead anymore.

One thing I've realized after having to deal with dead people all of my life is that *they don't care*. They don't come back. They don't want to take the rest of us down with them. The dead are dead, and that's it. End of story.

At the moment, though, I miss my childhood fear. If I were a zombie, I wouldn't have to care anymore. I wouldn't have to face the fact that my dad is going to die if I don't stop it. As a zombie, I just wouldn't give a shit.

I climb the steps to the front door, put my bag down, take a long, slow breath, and deliberate for a moment. I have to do all of this just right.

I knock.

After nearly a minute, the porch light switches on, the dead bolt clicks back, and the door swings open.

My dad is a heavyset man—gray-bearded, chapped and sun-burned from working outside. Not all of my premonitions are date-stamped like my dad's was; sometimes it takes me years to figure out the timing of one of my visions, and sometimes I put it together only after the fact. But even if I hadn't heard Audie Cornish's voice on the radio, I would have known that this was the week. I would've been able to recognize the white hairs on the right side of his chin, the fresh bruise on his forearm, and even the grease stain on his jeans.

Dad squints at me, and then gives me a big, hearty smile. "Luke! What are you doing here? I didn't think you were coming home until next week."

I force a smile and pray that he doesn't notice my hands shaking. I stammer out, "Yeah … uh … my dorm at school's super chaotic and noisy right now, so I figured I could study for finals here. I thought I'd surprise you."

"Well, I'm surprised," he confirms with a nod. Then he hugs me and I catch a whiff of his familiar scent: plaster, cement, and ink.

"Are you okay?" he asks. He leans back to study me with a concerned look.

"I'm fine," I say, trying to keep the smile on my face. "It's just ... good to be home."

———

Our house is nearly a hundred years old, and we have furniture from every decade to prove it: wooden rocking chairs sit next to TV trays, molded neon end tables, and LED lamps. Every new Cressman generation has added to this collection, but I don't think anybody has ever bothered to throw anything away. The shelves in the entryway are lined with Waterford crystal, matchboxes from all over the world, taxidermied birds, binders of stamps (so many freaking stamps!), porcelain figurines, model airplanes, faux Fabergé eggs, and early Americana who-knows-what. You name it, it's here. And if it isn't here, it's probably crammed up in the attic.

"We could use a new picture of the four of us," my dad says as we continue back into the hallway. "It's been forever! Maybe we can do it tomorrow, if Darla will oblige. Although she doesn't seem to want to be distracted much these days."

"It's the first rule of *World of Warcraft*, Dad: do *not* interrupt *World of Warcraft*."

He laughs.

The walls are dotted with framed family portraits dating back to the early 1900s, when my great-great-grandfather moved the family here in order to take over the cemetery. As I follow my dad into the kitchen, I pause and spend a moment studying one of my favorites, one of the man himself, Aaron Louis Cressman. He has an angular jaw, cropped hair, and a mustache. His eyes look light, but I can't tell what color they are from the black-and-white photo.

Next to this picture is one of his entire family. Neither Aaron nor his pregnant wife nor their two daughters are smiling, and I can guess why: even if it had been a time when people smiled for photographs, Aaron Louis Cressman didn't have much to smile about. This couldn't have been very long after his first premonition, and he must have thought that he was going crazy. He was the first, after all, and he'd had no one to guide him, to tell him the rules and explain what was going on inside his head.

"There's some leftover pizza in the fridge," my dad says as we pass into the kitchen. "I can heat it up for you."

"That sounds good." I pause inside the doorway and watch as he moves about the room. There's a heavy grace to his movements, and it's comforting to see.

"Is Darla home?" I ask.

He shakes his head. "She should be back soon," he says, putting the pizza in the toaster oven and setting the timer. "She went over to her friend Liv's house. Said that they have a lot of studying to do."

"How is she?" I ask.

"Darla?" He shrugs. "She seems fine, I guess. Can you believe that she's going to be sixteen soon?"

"No, I really can't." To me, she's still that laughing seven year old desperate for my attention.

I glance out the window to see if there are any lights on in the guesthouse. "Is Roy home?"

"Of course Roy's home." My dad flashes me an amused smile. "Where's he going to go? A nightclub?"

I groan. "People don't say *nightclub* anymore, Dad. That's an old word, even for you."

"What do they call it, then?"

"I dunno. Just a club, I guess. Or a bar."

He laughs. "Well, you know your uncle Roy and me. We don't do too much … clubbing."

I walk over to the table. It's piled high with bills and junk mail. I take a seat in one of the ripped-vinyl chairs and press my hands flat against the tabletop, trying to keep them still.

"Maybe I can take you kids to the bowling alley tomorrow night," Dad says. "You and Darla used to love doing that. Remember the green ball that she always insisted on using? It was *way* too heavy for her, but she just loved the way it sparkled."

I nod, a cold feeling in the pit of my stomach. Who knows what we're going to be doing tomorrow night? It all depends on what I manage to change.

Before my thoughts can go any farther down that dark road, the toaster oven dings, and my dad brings me a couple of slices of pizza. He tells me about a difficult monument that he's been working on. "You should have seen it," he says. "The stone, to start with, was a monstrosity, like something cut for an Egyptian pharaoh. But I managed to class it up a bit: some decent calligraphy and embellishments, some nice, gentle curves. And I talked them into changing the text. They wanted John 3:16 in Latin. I convinced them to focus on the guy's life instead, the differences he made in this world."

"That's good," I say. I finish my first slice of pizza, but I don't think my stomach can handle the second.

"Actually, I took some pictures of it, if you want to see. I was thinking of adding them to the catalog. I'll be right back." And he heads into the living room.

I desperately want to go up to my bedroom and get through the night without having to talk to him anymore, without having to smile and pretend that everything's okay.

In all of the versions of this situation that I've played through in my head, we go to bed quietly tonight. I wait until tomorrow morning, go up on the roof, and show him that the rain gutter has rusted away at its attachments. Then we can get a professional in to fix it.

That's the plan, at least, but my shaking hands are threatening to give me away. I jump up, get some hot chocolate from the cupboard, and put the kettle on to boil. Then I take a deep breath and try to calm myself down.

The camera looks comically small in my dad's big, fleshy hands. Everyone's always surprised that a man with such big and clumsy-looking fingers can make such delicate carvings and inscriptions, but it's his art, his gift. For many people, the words on these monuments are the last memories they'll have of their loved ones, and everything my dad does is for them, the ones who are left behind. And it really *does* make a difference. It changes their lives going forward.

I hand a cup of hot chocolate to my dad and take a sip from my own. As I set it down on the table, my hand shakes, and the cup rattles.

"Are you okay?" he asks.

"I'm just tired," I tell him. "It was a bumpy ride home, and the flight attendant got a little too close for comfort. I wasn't in the mood to … to see any of *that*. You know?"

He nods, but I notice an odd look on his face.

He knows why I'm here. He must know!

My dad flashes me a gentle smile and launches into one of our stories. "You know about John Lennon's box of chocolates, right?" He glances around the house, making absolutely sure that we're alone. "Well, Yoko bought John a box of chocolates right before they had to head out to finish work on their new album, *Double Fantasy*. John was killed on his way home, so he never got a chance to eat even a single one. At least, that's what Yoko says."

I can't look suspicious, so I play along. This is our old morbid back-and-forth game. "How much do you think those chocolates are worth now?" I ask.

"That's not the important question," my dad says. "The important question is, what do you think those chocolates taste like?"

"Death?"

"Or eternal peace." He smiles. "Meanwhile, I just learned that Ernest Hemingway ate a bowl of Cheerios on the morning he killed himself. Can you think of a more anticlimactic last meal?"

It's my turn to offer a new bit of last days trivia, but all I can think about is my dad's last meal. Will it be tomorrow's breakfast? Will I cook it for him? Or will he have ten thousand more meals—chocolates and Cheerios and whatever the hell he wants?

"By the way," my dad continues, "do you know how John Wayne spent his final days?"

I shake my head. "I must have missed that one."

"Watching *Gunsmoke*," he says. "Isn't that just perfect? Apparently, he watched episode after episode until the stomach cancer took him."

I grunt. "What's *Gunsmoke*?" I ask.

He looks at me like I've just asked him what a headstone is.

"*Gunsmoke* was only the best western TV series ever made! I used to watch it every day when I got home from school."

I manage a short laugh. "How would I know about some old TV show?"

"For God's sake!" my dad says, sitting up straight in his chair, feigning horror. "What are they teaching you at that fancy private school, anyway?"

"Not that," I say. "All they're doing is teaching us not to use the word *nightclub*."

He shakes his head, then bounces up out of his seat. "I demand a refund!" he says, and he starts play-boxing with me.

Really, it's all an extremely embarrassing act, but I can't help but laugh.

"No son of mine is going to go through life ignorant, without a working knowledge of the classics. I'm talking about *Gunsmoke* here, and *Welcome Back, Kotter*, and … and *Cheers*! After all, I'm paying for this education, right? And that's like, what, fifty bucks a month for that place?"

It's actually closer to a thousand, even after the scholarship that Ms. Jenkins, my sophomore-year English teacher, helped me get. My dad throws a hook, and I pretend to stagger back. Then he raises his arms and takes a victory lap around the kitchen.

My smile fades as I watch him circle the room.

I want this to go on forever. I want him to continue embarrassing me for years and years to come.

Finally, Dad tells me he's tired, and I manage to escape. Somehow, I've made it through the first challenge of what promises to be a very long couple of days.

And I haven't even had to lie to Darla yet.

———

I don't think anyone has been in my bedroom since the last time I came home, back during spring break. There's a thick layer of dust on every surface, and the air smells stale and unhealthy. I push the window open, letting the scent of freshly cut grass and eucalyptus stream in. Uncle Roy's light is still on over at the caretaker's house.

As I stare out the window, tears start to burn in my eyes.

No matter what he says when I try to stop him, no matter what rules he tries to impose, I can't let my dad die. I love him too much. I'll tear down the gutter and break the ladder myself before I let him get anywhere near that roof.

There's a knock on the door behind me, and I turn, startled.

My dad fills the doorway. His eyes are fixed on me, and he looks intent. There's absolutely no hint of the jovial playacting from earlier.

"Hey," I say, giving him a weak wave.

His lips narrow into a bloodless line. "You didn't come home to study, did you, Luke?" he says.

"What … what do you mean?" I ask. "Of course I did."

He shakes his head. "No, you didn't. You came home to say goodbye to me."

My instinct is to step away from him, but in my current position that would send me tumbling out of the window. So I take a seat on the windowsill instead. "No. No, I didn't," I say.

He moves toward me. "Goddamn it, Luke. You're looking at me the same way you look at all of them—the doomed, the short-timers. You don't think I know that look?"

I've never been able to handle it the way that my dad does. When he knows that it's your time to go, when he gets a vision of your death, you'll never see a better poker face in your life, and you'll never see it coming. Me, I tend to flinch—even to cry, on occasion. *But I can't do that now,* I tell myself. *I can't let him know my plan.*

Never intervene—that's what he tells me. Never give anything away. Never play God.

"Fine," I say, trying to remember my contingency plan, the story I'd come up with in case this very thing happened. "I wasn't going to tell you about it, because I know what you're going to say, but I came home to say goodbye to a friend of mine."

"What friend?" he asks.

"Jared Blount."

My dad narrows his eyes, suspicious. "I've never heard of him," he says.

"We played soccer together in middle school. In a couple of days, he's going to hit his head really hard in a league game." The first part of this story is true; the second isn't.

Dad stares at me. He knows me better than anyone else in the world.

"No, Luke," he says. "I've never heard of any 'Jared Blount.' He doesn't exist."

"Check Snapchat!" I say.

"Or maybe he does exist," he relents, "but he's not a real friend of yours. You didn't travel seven hundred miles to say goodbye to a friend I've never heard of."

"Dad—," I start to say, but he cuts me off.

"Don't," he says. "Don't tell me, Luke. You shouldn't have come here. How many times have I told you? I thought I did a good job; I thought you understood just how dangerous this type of thing can be."

No. I open my mouth, desperate to say something that will make him change his mind, but nothing comes out.

No, no, no, no. I can't let this happen!

He's told me several times that he's going to get the gutters checked out by a professional. If I were a better actor, he'd never have known the difference. I could have woken up tomorrow, laughed with him at breakfast, and called the repair person myself. Or I could have torn down the gutters in the middle of the night. Or offered to do the chore myself. Or …

But now, if he won't let me stop him—

"You can stay the night, Luke," he says, "but you have to leave tomorrow morning. I can't have you here. If you let it slip, if you give me even the smallest hint as to what's going to happen, the results could be disastrous. And we can't do that. You and I have a greater responsibility here."

"But we've never even tried," I say, making my final plea. "We have no idea what'll actually happen."

"I love you, pal," my dad says, "and I know how hard this is. Believe me, I know. But this isn't a game we're playing, and this isn't a chance we should ever be willing to take. We don't intervene—that's what my father taught me, and what his father taught him. If we do, if we ever try to change fate, then the consequences could come back a hundred times worse. And we can't let that happen."

"But, Dad, please—"

He holds up his hand, cutting me off. "No, son. I'd take my own life if it came down to that—if you say one word, if you do anything to try to save me." I meet his eyes, and I know that he's telling me the truth.

I reach out to hug him, wrapping him in my arms. After a long, depressing moment, he finally squeezes me back.

I don't want to let him go.

2 Princess Diana, James Dean, Paul Walker, Sam Kinison, Jackson Pollock, Grace Kelly, and General George Patton died in car accidents. Aaliyah, Buddy Holly, and Ritchie Valens died in plane crashes. Natalie Wood and José Fernández died while boating.

My dad's accident wasn't nearly as interesting as any of those. It was just falling off a stupid ladder, on a stupid day, at our stupid house, thanks to me stupidly doing nothing to stop it. He sent me to the airport that morning, and I didn't even get the chance to cook him his final breakfast. The next time I saw him was right before we closed the coffin and put him in the ground.

A few weeks ago, I asked Darla if she knew how John Belushi died, or what he did on the last day of his life (inhuman amounts of cocaine and heroin, packed on top of ten lifetimes' worth of cheeseburgers and unhealthy living). She just shook her head and retreated back into the dark solitude of her room.

That's when I realized: there's only one thing worse than being one of two people with some messed-up magical power in a Po-dunk town.

And that's being one of one.

"Martha's grandmother gave me the biscuit recipe," Roy says, pointing to my breakfast plate. "And the starter, too. It comes from a batch that's been in her family for fifty years now."

"They're good today," I say. "They're always good."

Darla grunts her agreement, though she's just pushing a chunk of bread around her still-full plate.

Three months have passed since our dad's death, and it's the Wednesday after Labor Day, the first day of my senior year.

Over the summer, I transferred back to Mission Hills High here in Colma. Roy, my dad's younger brother, is taking care of Darla and me, playing legal guardian until we each turn eighteen. Roy's also—with our help and hard work—running the cemetery, trying to keep it in good shape until we're ready to take it over someday.

If that's something we ever actually want to do.

Frankly, I'm having a hard time thinking about the future right now, about where I want to go after high school or the life I want to live. I'm trying to keep it together and stay strong for Roy and Darla, but without Dad here, it's difficult to imagine what life is going to be like a decade from now. Or a year. Or even a week.

"When Martha died, her grandmother entrusted the recipe to me," Roy tells us. It's the same story he's told us a hundred times before. "She said that this way, I'll always have a little bit of the family with me." He grunts and smiles. "Connections—those are important in this world. Connections—that's life."

In 2009, Roy's wife had been thrown from a spooked horse in

the hills up near San Bruno. Her lung collapsed when she hit a boulder, and she died moments later. I'd seen her death coming a year earlier, when I was just six or seven years old, before I even understood what my visions were. It was actually one of the first premonitions I ever had. When I started to tell my dad about it, about what I thought was nothing more than a scary dream, he lowered his voice into a gentle whisper and told me that these dreams were so special that we had to keep them to ourselves. He didn't explain the truth until after my aunt's death.

"That's more than I'm going to learn at school today," Darla says, looking down at her plate. She's trying to be civil, but I can see that she's as unhappy as I am to be starting a new school year.

"Your dad used to protect me from bullies when we were in school together," Roy says. "He'd pull them aside and growl that he could bury a body out back without anyone ever finding out, easy-peasy. Are you going to do the same for your little sister, Luke?"

"I don't need that," Darla says.

And I believe her. Before I left for boarding school, she was a thin little wisp of a girl, always ready to laugh. She seems quieter now, more withdrawn and with a harder edge—stronger, and a little bit scary. I'm not sure if this has more to do with her growing up or her losing our dad. Darla and I have never been mistaken for biological siblings. She has light brown hair and freckles, while my hair is jet-black, thanks to my Japanese mother.

"Colma's changed since you went away, Luke," Darla says, pulling out her phone. She sets it on the table and stares at it while she's talking to me. It looks like she's messing around with some *World of Warcraft*–related app. "It's not like it used to be."

"What are you talking about?" Roy asks. He lifts a pan into the sink and starts scrubbing at a sticky film of scrambled eggs.

"Haven't you noticed, Uncle Roy? It's just … different now. Less relaxed. Everyone's on edge. Same with Mission Hills. It's more cliquey there. It's best to just keep your head down."

I smile, humoring her. "Since you're the expert, Darla, maybe *you* should be the one protecting me."

"That's good," Roy says. He's not always great at detecting sarcasm. "Just let me know if you two need any reinforcements. Maybe I can call in a drone strike."

I watch him as he works at the pan, scrubbing it down like he's polishing a new grave marker. Roy's wearing a terry cloth robe over a ratty pair of pajamas. He's got fur-lined slippers on his feet, and a red-and-black Elmer Fudd–style hunting cap on his head. He's always bundled up like this, as if it's the middle of winter. Soon, he'll be out mowing the grass under the bright South Bay sun in thick cargo pants and an army flak jacket, still wearing that same wool hunting cap, and absolutely drenched in sweat. He says it makes him feel like he's back in Kuwait, riding an M1 Abrams tank across enemy lines.

"I can deal with the Zimmermans when I get home," I tell him.

A couple of kids broke into the cemetery the other day and tagged up the Zimmerman family mausoleum. They wrote some pretty disgusting anti-Semitic things, and I can't stand the thought of having those ugly words junking up our cemetery for any longer than necessary.

Roy's a competent groundskeeper, but he gets distracted easily. He can't do the detail work that my dad did, and he gets overwhelmed and loses track of things if there's too much on his plate. So he needs our help now more than ever. Darla's been avoiding work for most of the summer. She says that it's still too painful, reminds her too much of our dad, but I'm starting to think that it's just an excuse for laziness—and a way to play more *World of Warcraft*. I actually enjoy the work. Dad's the one who taught me how to do etchings, how to dress up headstones and cenotaphs, and doing that stuff makes me feel close to him again.

"I want you doing your homework before you hit the cemetery," Roy says. "That should be your priority. They give seniors homework, right?" He turns toward me, genuinely asking.

"Nope, not anymore," I say. "Homework ends junior year. They want us concentrating on our college applications."

Roy grunts and turns away, seeming to believe me. Darla shoots me a look and shakes her head, a smile lurking at the corner of her lips. I hold a finger up to my mouth, telling her to stay quiet. I don't need Roy on my back, bugging me about homework when there are more important things he should be worrying about.

It's good to see Darla smile again. She's been so distant and withdrawn lately, it's like she's been lost in a fog. Roy and I have both tried to get her to talk about Dad, but she just shuts down each and every time. She looks away, then heads back to her room to listen to music and play *Warcraft*. Half of the time, she doesn't even eat with us anymore.

We've tried to give her time—it's not like I've been a cheerful bucket of sunshine myself—but she just seems to be drifting further and further away.

"Sophomore year, huh?" I say.

"It was enough to drive *you* away," she says. Then she stands, gathers up her backpack, and leaves.

If only she knew the truth. If only she knew *why* I ran away.

My phone dings. It's my oldest friend, Gael, asking me if I'm going to be at school today. I've gotten a lot of texts since I got home—from him and my other Colma friends—but I didn't feel up to responding to them right away. And then, when I did feel ready to talk, it seemed like I'd waited too long. So the messages just sat there in my inbox, awkward and unanswered.

I'm sure there'll be hell to pay today. There's nothing ruder than radio silence.

Ghosting. I've become a ghost, cut off from the life I once had.

———

Darla and I make our way through the dewy, tall grass, the legs of our pants getting wet as we cut across the yard to the main road. The sun's trying to peek through the clouds, but it's failing miserably, and the day remains steeped in gray.

I look toward the grove of cypress trees at the end of the cemetery drive. There are a pair of tall white angel statues back there, standing watch over my mom's and dad's graves. Hidden among the trees, those statues are always in shadow—still and serene, radiating a sense of peace.

Back when my dad was still alive, and it was just one angel, he used to leave small offerings at the statue's feet. It's an old Japanese tradition, he explained to me. Leaving food and money on the graves of loved ones is a sign of respect. I've seen pictures of the graveyards in Kamakura, the little town outside of Japan where my mom grew up, and indeed it looks like the headstones are nearly buried under offerings of sweet buns and coins.

Most of the time, I pretty much forget that I'm half-Japanese.

My mom died giving birth to me, so I never knew much about her or her life before meeting my dad. *The mother … did incubate in her own bosom the creature who would carry her off.* I googled "died during childbirth," and that Cormac McCarthy quote came up. It makes me feel like some type of murderous hell-spawn, but it's basically true.

I arrived and carried her away. My birth put her into the ground.

I scribble a note on my arm, reminding myself to leave a little offering for my mom and dad after I finish up work tonight. Maybe some coins. Maybe one of Uncle Roy's sourdough biscuits.

"You'll help with the Zimmermans after school, right?" I ask Darla.

"I won't be up for it," she says.

I grunt. "At least we're not making you talk to grieving family members." That's one of Darla's least favorite chores.

She just shrugs and looks back down at her phone.

Like Robert Mitchum and Steve McQueen, Darla will die of lung cancer. But not until she's ninety-five years old. I've found a couple of burnt-out cigarettes in the dirt outside her bedroom window, but if she's going to live that long, I figure what's the difference?

I just wish she'd try to do more with the life she's been given. I hate the way her face is always buried in her phone. It's probably just a way for her to escape reality, where there's so much sadness and death, but it seems like she's doing nothing but wasting time.

And if my powers have taught me anything, it's that there's nothing more valuable than time.

———

"Welcome back to hell," Darla says as we reach Mission Hills High.

She doesn't even look my way as she hoists her bag to her shoulder and trots toward the front door.

The parking lot is full of upperclassmen lucky enough to have snagged parking permits, which are given out according to need, seniority, and lottery. A pair of yellow school buses pull into the circular driveway, and everyone else comes pouring out.

I recognize at least half of the faces. Colma's a small place, and a one-industry town, so most of these kids have family in the business. They're the children of embalmers, funeral home directors, morticians, gravestone makers, coffin builders, gravediggers, and cemetery owners. Which makes the school mascot painfully appropriate: the California grizzly.

The California grizzly went extinct almost a hundred years ago. (And what was the last California grizzly's final day like? Maybe she ate a deer carcass, drank from a stream, took a shit in the woods... Elvis Presley died while taking a shit. So did Lenny Bruce.)

Some familiar faces smile at me, while others look confused, staring at me like, *hey, don't I know that guy?* as I make my way through the front door. I'm hoping for a slow reentry after my year away, but I stop abruptly in the entrance and cause a small pileup. Darla's heading down the main hallway toward the sopho-more lockers, but I can't seem to remember the way to the senior locker bay.

"Luke! Holy shit!"

My friend Gael Silva emerges from the crowd, smiling. Until I left for Portland, Gael was my best friend. We didn't really keep in touch while I was away, and I'm not sure where we stand right now, but it's a relief that he's the first friend I'm running into. He doesn't even seem to be too mad at me for not returning his texts.

He charges at me and wraps me in a big bear hug. My arms and legs are covered, but I know that Gael's death is nothing to be afraid of. He dies peacefully in a nursing home, surrounded by pictures of his children and grandchildren. He's at least in his eighties, and it's funny to see him shrunken into an old man, look-ing frail and very un-Gael-like. From the look of those photos, he's going to live a happy life full of family.

Gael pulls back. "Oh man, I forgot," he says, grinning. "You're not a fan of the man hugs, are you, Luke?"

"I'll make an exception for you," I say, returning his smile.

Gael has brown eyes and fairly long black hair that he keeps pushed back behind his ears. He's about my height—just shy of six feet tall—and there's a scar on his chin from back when we were kids and he flew over the handlebars of his bike while we were crossing a dry, rocky part of Colma Creek.

"I'm sorry I didn't text you back this summer," I say lamely. "I just—"

He doesn't even let me finish. "No sweat, man. I totally under-stand. How are you doing, anyway?"

"Okay, I guess. It's weird being back. I don't even remember where I'm supposed to go."

"Well, *I'm* definitely happy to see you," he says. "My dad was just asking about you and your family, and I started to feel like shit. I should have reached out more this summer. I mean it. I could have been a better friend."

The Silvas are one of the oldest families in the South Bay area—a founding family of Colma, moving here at the same time as my great-great-grandfather. We think that our great-great-grandmothers might have worked together cooking meals for vagrants during the Great Depression, and we know for certain that our grandfathers—both cemetery proprietors—drank whiskey together. And while they weren't exactly best friends, our dads did do business with each other on occasion. Gael's dad owns the Home Warehouse store in Colma and is one of the richest men in town. Unfortunately, I've seen his death, and it isn't pretty. It sucks to know that your best friend's dad is going to lose most of the family money to an out-of-control cocaine problem and then drop dead in the arms of a woman who is not his wife.

"Don't worry about it," I say. "You did more than enough. I just needed some time alone."

"Well, great," Gael says. "We've got to hang soon. My dad just put in a new entertainment system, and it's pretty cool. The whole house is online—wireless audio and video in every room, voice-controlled.... Oh man, do you remember our movie contests?"

"How could I forget?" I laugh. When we were young, we'd try to see who could watch the most movies in a year; I probably still have scraps of paper with our tallies on them. But always, inevitably, we'd lose track, and have to call the contests a draw. "You used to sneak downstairs in the middle of the night and watch those weird late-night movies. I could never get away with that."

"But you did watch *The Matrix*, like, what, a hundred times? And you insisted on counting each time as a separate movie." Gael laughs and shakes his head. "We were pretty weird kids, man."

"You still are," a voice says, directly behind me.

I recognize the voice immediately and turn to face another of my pre-Portland friends.

Heroji Pratt is one of the most popular kids in school. He's black and super handsome, with a slightly gap-toothed smile and freakishly bright amber-colored eyes. Heroji's family is one of the few in Colma with absolutely no connection to the cemetery business. His dad is an honest-to-God Black Panther, and he's been serving time in San Quentin for the last thirty-five years (a political prisoner, Heroji claims, guilty of nothing but being black). His mom moved up to Colma to be closer to him, and Heroji was conceived during one of their conjugal visits. We make fun of him for this constantly—quips about handcuffs, jumpsuits, and *Orange Is the New Black*, mostly—but he doesn't seem to mind, just rolling his eyes and laughing along.

"I called you, man," he says, "after the funeral. I'm sorry about your dad."

"Thanks, Heroji. I'm sorry I didn't get back to you, but—"

He cuts me off before I can finish my apology. "But nothing, man. Just fill me in on the important stuff—like, did you get any action up there in Portland? Were there a lot of hot girls?"

I laugh. "There were a couple of cute ones, I guess. But a lot of them were into crunchy granola-type stuff—not really my kind of thing."

"Is there even a cemetery up there?" Heroji asks.

"I never saw one. Hell, they probably send their bodies down here, too."

"Weird," Gael says, shaking his head like he can't even imagine a town that doesn't have eight cemeteries in it.

Amy Yoon, whose family owns the Korean cemetery, joins us, and welcomes me back with a "Yo, Cressman." She's with Erin Green, a blonde girl whose dad is known for doing some of the best facial reconstruction work in all the world. He once pieced together a man after his face had been ripped off in an industrial threshing machine, managing to pretty him up enough for an open-casket funeral. Only in Colma would something like that make you a high-profile celebrity.

"Hi, Luke," Erin says. She looks at me for a moment, then narrows her eyes. "You look different somehow," she continues accusingly. "Are you all fancy now? Is that it? Did you get to be too good for us while you were up there in Portland?"

Everyone pauses for a moment, taking a step back to stare at me.

"Yeah, now that you mention it, I think he did," Gael says, crinkling his brow and giving me a skeptical look.

Amy nods her head. "Totally."

"Just look at the way he's standing there," Heroji says. "He's judging us—I can tell. He's judging us with those piercing, judgmental eyes."

I raise my hands defensively. "Hey, I never—"

Erin smiles over at Amy, who chortles. "As gullible as ever," Amy says.

"Some things never change," Erin replies. Then she turns back to me and gives me a winning smile. "But seriously, Luke, it's good to see you again. Is it weird to be back? Is it weird to be home again?"

"It was weirder being away," I say.

"Did people freak out when you told them that you grew up in a cemetery?"

I shrug. "They didn't really get it. After a couple of weeks, I just kinda stopped telling people."

"Imagine if they knew what my dad does," Erin says. "The other day, at dinner, I had to tell him that he had a piece of someone stuck to his cheek. Then I went right back to eating my mashed potatoes."

Heroji clutches at his throat and fakes a dry heave, and Amy laughs.

The bell rings.

"What's your first class?" Gael asks.

"Calculus," I say, looking left and right. "Does anyone want to point me toward room 224? No, seriously, guys, I'm totally lost."

"You really did get weird up there in Portland, didn't you?" Gael says. Then he nods toward the stairs and gestures me along.

"Welcome back, asshole," Heroji says with a smile. Then he, Amy, and Erin turn to leave.

Amy and Erin both look back at me after a couple of steps. They flip me a pair of perfectly synchronized middle fingers, laugh uproariously, and hurry down the length of the main hallway. Heroji trails behind them, shrugging and shaking his head again.

Now that I'm back, I realize just how much I've missed these guys.

Plus, there's another benefit to being back in Colma that I'd forgotten about. Unlike in Portland, where it seemed like I was being assaulted by a new death vision every day, I've been in school with these kids since the first grade, so I already know how most of them are going to die. And fortunately—from all that I can tell—it seems like most of my friends are going to live long lives and die decent deaths. Heroji makes it to his seventies or eighties, as does Gael. Amy is in her nineties, at least. Only Erin dies young, crushed in a car accident in her thirties.

"Hey, man," Gael says, as we stroll toward the senior locker bay. "I was meaning to ask you something. Now that your dad's dead, are you guys going to be selling the cemetery?"

"What?" I say, surprised. "No. What made you think that?"

"My dad said that there'd been some people at the store asking questions about your property. Guys in fancy suits. Maybe lawyers. I don't know if you realize this, but a lot of people have been selling lately. Eternal Home changed ownership just last month. Home of Peace, too. I hear it's a Silicon Valley conglomerate, interested in the land."

"No one came by our place."

Gael grunts. "Yeah, well, maybe they're counting their pennies, getting ready to make you an offer."

I'm silent for a while as a loud group of freshmen stream by. "What would Silicon Valley want with a bunch of cemeteries, anyway?"

"Maybe they're just looking for land to develop. San Francisco's growing, you know, and the real estate market here's got to be booming."

"But there are ordinances," I say. "49B. The cemeteries are going to be here forever."

"Nothing's forever, Luke. Living in Colma, I'd think you'd know that by now." He flashes me a bitter, lopsided smile. "Someday, an initiative will pass, paperwork will be filed, and—*boom*—California will move the cemeteries somewhere else. At least that's what my dad says is going to happen. That's one of the reasons he got out of the cemetery business. There's just too much uncertainty, and too much money to be made off this land. Just imagine all of the condos they could put up here. Or expensive office space. Or maybe an Amazon distribution center or two."

"But ... all of those bodies," I say lamely. *My mother and father, resting beneath their angels. All of my ancestors, lined up side by side.* "What are they going to do with the bodies?"

Gael shrugs. "I don't know," he says, "but money has a way of making things happen."

———

Calculus is on the second floor, at the far end of the building. It seems like half of the kids at Mission Hills High are heading up the stairs at the same time, and I get caught in the rush of arms and legs and bodies—all moving together like one of the amoebas we studied in AP biology last year.

If Dad had heard about Colma being developed into a bedroom community for Silicon Valley, he'd be rolling over in his

"Solid Poplar Jewish Casket/With Cream Crepe Interior/Without Star of David" (he always did love how the Jews did their burials). When I was growing up, there'd always been some vague offer on the table, as corporate chains tried to buy us out. But I'd never heard of developers trying to build homes and businesses on Colma land. We'd learned all about Ordinance 49B in school, and it was supposed to stop that very thing from happening.

But things change, I guess, and if 49B falls, or is in the process of falling, then our cemetery will probably be one of the first targets.

Business in Colma is super competitive, but Dad always had an advantage. I wouldn't call what he did "ambulance chasing" exactly, but he was strategic and subtle about making people aware of the Cressman Cemetery in the weeks and months leading up to their loved ones' deaths. I, on the other hand, have always tried to avoid touching people, and as the second son, Uncle Roy doesn't have the premonitions my dad had. So all summer long, we've just been sitting around, waiting for the bodies to come to us. We've only gotten two since July, and we need at least *four* a month in order to break even.

Roy acts clueless a lot of the time, but I know that even he is beginning to worry. We can't be that far away from bankruptcy.

I've got to do something. Otherwise, the cemetery's going to die with my dad.

I turn up the next flight of stairs, and a blond jock with bad skin cuts directly in front of me. His arm brushes against the side of my wrist.

And my vision goes dark.

Shit, no! Not on my first day!

Sometimes, it takes a dozen skin-to-skin contacts before I get someone's premonition; it took thousands before I ever saw my dad falling off that ladder. I reach for the railing in the swarm of bodies and pray for the darkness to recede. But if there is a God, he's not interested in me today.

The noise and movement around me fade away. There is darkness, then a single pinprick of light. The pinprick expands, gradually, then explodes in a flash, and I see the boy standing on the white-sand beach of a tropical island. Maybe it's Hawaii, or somewhere in the Caribbean. He looks pretty much like he does now—maybe a couple of years older. His skin is sunburned, and he has a big smile on his face. Someone calls out to him, and he turns and waves at a pretty blonde girl in a bikini. I can smell the salt from the water and hear the cry of seagulls overhead.

Then the boy turns and runs out into the blue water. He dives beneath a wave, gliding smoothly and blowing out a long stream of bubbles before coming up for air. Then he treads water and smiles up at the sun. A swell builds around him. A wave surges, lifting him to the top of its curling lip, and he puts both arms out in front of his body. He soars majestically for a moment, like Superman; then the water disappears from beneath him and he's falling through the air. He looks around wildly as he comes crashing down to the sand.

He doesn't die immediately, but he can't move—his back is broken—and the waves pull him back out to sea.

He's facedown in the water, paralyzed, lungs burning and

mouth gulping for air. Then, slowly, his body stills and his lips stop moving. My view is just close enough to see the horror fade from his eyes.

"Hey, man, are you okay?"

And the stairwell swims back into focus.

A girl is standing in front of me. She's so beautiful, I do a double take and blink again, not quite sure if I'm back in reality. It feels like I've just jumped from one vision to another.

"You don't look so good," she says.

My hand lifts from the railing. I wobble and make a grab for it again. *God, I must look like a total spaz.* I feel my face turning hot and red.

Seeing my embarrassment, the girl flashes me a bright smile. She has dimples, and her eyes are a grayish brown, or maybe they're brownish gray. She's black, with short, natural hair that's pretty much all over the place, sticking up in artistic spikes. She's wearing a bright, summery dress over black Doc Martens, and her neck and wrists are wrapped in strands of mismatched jewelry.

If I was having trouble catching my breath before … I lose my train of thought.

"You need some air," she says, and she points up to the next flight of stairs. "Where do these go?"

"Uh … the roof, I think."

"Come on, then," she says. She grabs for my hand and starts yanking me up the stairs. Feeling my skin against hers, I can't help but get worried. *Not again,* I think. *I can't handle another dose of death. Not now. Not her.*

But thankfully, nothing happens. I'm still in the stairwell, not a vision in sight.

Except, maybe, for the one who's pulling me up the stairs.

———

"Thanks for the excuse to get out of there," the girl says. She walks toward the edge of the roof and peers down at the parking lot. "Sometimes I feel totally lost in crowds. Not that crowds can't be exciting, you know, but sometimes it feels like I'm melting away, becoming part of this huge, multiheaded animal. A crowd-beast, if you will…. Does that make sense?"

I nod, still standing halfway in the stairwell.

"Don't let that door close behind you, by the way. Prop it up with something; otherwise it'll lock and we'll get stuck out here. I learned that lesson the hard way."

I find a cinder block a couple of steps away and use it to hold the door open. When I look back up, the girl is standing closer to the edge. Her arms are raised up at her sides, and she's looking at me over her shoulder, a smile on her face. "One time in San Francisco, there was this guy bothering me on the street, so I ducked into this building real quick, you know? I figured I'd go up onto the roof and just climb down the fire escape on the other side. You'd think that would work, right? You always see stuff like that in movies."

She stares at me, and I'm sure I look dumb. It's like whiplash, going from the boy with the broken back to this beautiful girl talking a mile a minute and smiling at me with that warm smile, and it takes me a handful of seconds to get my bearings. Finally, I manage a nod. "Uh, yeah," I say. "Fire escapes."

"Anyway, it was a walk-up, and I had to climb, like, six flights of stairs, and when I got up on the roof there was no fire escape. Not up on the roof, anyway. And when I tried to go back down, I found that the stairwell door had locked behind me! I tried hopping from roof to roof a couple of times, but there were only three buildings close enough together. None of them had fire escapes, and *all* of the doors were locked. Man, I thought I was so screwed. I just headed back to the first building, praying for divine intervention."

She reaches into her bag and pulls out a pack of cigarettes: Parliament Lights. She fits one between her lips and holds the pack out to me. "Want one?" she asks, lifting an eyebrow.

"Uh, no thanks," I say. Will she think I'm uncool for turning her down? "I'm trying to quit."

"You don't smoke. I can see that." She fishes an orange BIC lighter out of her bag and lights up. "You're smart for not smoking. Me, not so much." And she takes a deep drag.

"So, did you get down off the roof?" I ask, mostly just wanting to hear her keep talking.

She lets out a loud, wild laugh. "Nope. I never did get down. I'm still up there. I made a tent out of a tarp, and I'm living off of rainwater and pigeon meat. It's a difficult life, but I'm used to it now. There's a Zen simplicity to the whole thing."

"Well, yeah, obviously you made it down," I say. "But how?"

"I knocked for a little while, but no one answered. Finally, just as I was psyching myself up to start screaming down at the street for help, these three guys just randomly pop through the door. They were surprised to see me, and I thought they were going to let the door close behind them, so I'm, like, *running* at them, yelling 'No, no, no, don't let the door close!' and they were just standing there. I'm sure they were confused—like, suddenly, they had this fourteen-year-old girl shouting at them. When I made it over, the first one says, all calm-like, 'No shit, little girl, we're not going to let the door close. This is the city. All of these doors lock.'" She shrugs and takes another drag on her cigarette. When she pulls it away from her lips, she's smiling. "But that's how we learn, right? We make mistakes. We get locked on roofs."

"Yeah, I guess so," I say. "But … well, who are you?"

The girl slaps the heel of her palm against her forehead. "Duh! Sorry about that. My name's Mia. Mia Chevalier. It's nice to meet you, Mr. … Mr. whoever-the-fuck-you-are."

"I'm Luke. Luke Cressman."

"One of the natives, I'd guess. It seems like everyone here is a native, and all of you have that distinctly Colma feel about you."

"I was away at boarding school last year," I say, "but yeah, born and raised here. Are you from San Francisco?"

"Yeah. I was living with my dad for a long time, but I moved here this summer, to stay with my mom for my senior year."

"Why?"

Mia shrugs and looks away, her smile dimming a little bit. "It's a long story, a long story full of boring, heartless characters and ridiculous plot twists."

"Tell me about it," I say.

"It's not the type of story I particularly want to tell, Mr. Luke Cressman." She fixes me with her gaze. "But what's *your* story? Just the CliffsNotes version is fine. Is your family in the cemetery business?"

I nod. "Have you heard of the Cressman family cemetery?"

"Is that the one with all of the dead people in it?"

She's funny. "Yeah, that's the one."

"Honestly, there are so many cemeteries here, they all just blend together. Colma's just one big cemetery to me. Is yours nice at least? Tasteful headstones? No big, gaudy mausoleums?"

"Yeah, it's tasteful." My mind goes to the little clearing wrapped around my parents' graves. Their angels.

She lowers her cigarette, and I get the sense that she's looking at me—really *looking* at me—for the very first time. Like suddenly there's something there worth paying attention to. "So," I say, trying to change the subject, "you're not worried about cutting class and smoking cigarettes up on the roof of your new school on your very first day?"

"Like you say, it's my first day. I can always just act confused and say I got lost. Besides, what's the worst they can do? Expel me?" She shrugs, giving me a far-too-cool *so what?* Then she takes one last drag on her cigarette and crushes it out against the roof.

"You really wouldn't care if you got expelled?" I ask.

"Maybe," she says. "But what I want to know is, what was up with you on the stairs? You looked like you were going to pass out there for a bit. Like you'd seen a ghost. Are you sick? Do you have cancer or something? Is that why you came back from boarding school?"

"No, nothing like that. It was just … just low blood sugar. I missed breakfast this morning, had a head rush, but I'm fine now. I've got a candy bar I'm going to eat in first period."

"That's good. I don't want the first guy I meet here to up and die on me." She flashes me that bright smile of hers, and I blush once again. "C'mon then, Mr. Luke Cressman. I'm sure our teachers would like us to make an appearance sometime today."

"What's your first class?" I ask.

"AP French. Room 203."

"Ah, French! You must be smart and classy, then."

"Of course I'm smart and classy," she says with a laugh. "But French is a blow-off class for me. My dad's Haitian. I grew up *par-laying le fran-çais*, as they say." She intentionally butchers the French, making it sound like something from the deep, deep South.

We make our way back down the stairwell. The second-floor hallway is empty; the fluorescent lights cast a sickly yellow glow on the scuffed linoleum flooring. We pass a case full of trophies and photographs commemorating the various Mission Hills sports teams, none of which have been particularly good. There are no state championship trophies, just a couple of surprise tournament placings and a lot of participation medals.

Then we stop outside room 203.

I manage a nervous smile. "Well, I wasn't expecting to meet anyone like you here on my first day back."

"Really?" Mia says. "'Cause you're exactly the kind of kid I was expecting to meet today. Very, very *Colma*."

I laugh. I can't tell if she's trying to be funny or not, but it seems like an uncannily appropriate observation.

"I'll see you around." Then she opens up the door and slips inside. Several rows of kids turn her way, and there's a glowering teacher at the front of the room.

Mia gives me a small wave, and the door closes behind her.

I jog off down the hallway, ridiculously late but happier than I can ever remember being on the first day of a new school year.

———

I open the door to calculus, hold up a hand to Mr. Ramirez—like, *I know, I know, and I'm sorry, I'm sorry*—and head for an empty seat near the back of the room.

"Do you have a late slip?" he asks.

"What? Me?" I try.

"Yes, Mr. Cressman. You're the only one sneaking in late on the first day of school. That's not a very auspicious beginning."

What the hell would you know? Meeting Mia Chevalier—I'd call that very auspicious.

"I'm sorry," I say, and start mumbling something about filling out transfer papers.

Mr. Ramirez takes a long, slow breath. "I don't need your apologies or excuses, Luke. I need a little slip of paper with an official signature on it. Next time, okay? You remember how things work around here, right?"

"Yes, sir," I say.

Mr. Ramirez is a tall, wiry man with a painfully scraggly goatee. He stops by our cemetery once a month to visit his mother's grave, and I haven't seen it myself, but my dad told me that he will die in a … well, in a very inauspicious fashion, trampled to death during a fire at a Kenny G concert about a decade from now. I'd put that near the top of the list of Lamest Deaths Ever. (My dad had to tell me who Kenny G was.)

As I take a seat between Haley Brown and Ian I-forget-what-his-last-name-is, I feel it: my phone's not in my pocket. I check all of my other pockets, then the compartments in my bag.

Nothing.

I'd been so mesmerized by Mia that I hadn't even noticed that I'd lost it.

I stand up and hurry back to the door. It has to be somewhere in the hallway or up on the roof.

"Where do you think you're going?" Mr. Ramirez asks. I don't stop to answer.

I search the stairs, the hallway outside of room 203, and the floor near the trophy case. Then I run back up to the roof.

Nothing. It's gone.

Not good, I think.

I have video of my dad on that phone, and the thought of losing it, of never seeing his face or hearing his voice again, makes my heart drop. Plus—and I feel a bit dizzy as I realize this—there are other things on that phone that no one should ever see. Incriminating things. About me. About my visions.

Really, really not good.

3

My dad and I never used to write anything down, for obvious reasons. We'd talk about the fates of people we knew, especially when I was feeling depressed or disturbed about something I'd seen. He'd counsel me and try to do his best to make me feel better. Then, when I went away to boarding school, we got a little bit … careless. Texting was the main way we stayed in touch for three-quarters of a year, after all. So buried inside the phone that I still can't find—and that wasn't in the school's lost and found—are messages like, *Saw Danny T. drinking Heinekens in his truck—yikes, can't be long now*, and, *Ricardo M. at Sunnydale sucking down bacon with almost no chewing—know it won't happen here, but still bracing myself. Need to run into his wife, remind her that we exist.*

I don't know if anyone besides us would be able to figure out what these texts mean, or if they'd even be able to get past my password, but I'm not exactly eager to try to explain it to any outsiders.

"Suck it, Jap hater," Darla mumbles. "I hope the maggots are eating you sushi-style."

She's staring out the window of Roy's pickup truck as I drive us past Holy Cross, the oldest cemetery in Colma, where James Phelan, mayor of San Francisco during the famous quake of 1906, is buried. The people who run Holy Cross are proud to have this notable historical figure interred on their grounds, but what they're conveniently forgetting is that Phelan had wanted to ship every Japanese American out of the country.

"Remember when we toilet-papered his grave, and you left all of those Pokémon figurines around the edge?"

"Yeah," Darla says, and she smiles slightly. "They were arranged in a holy circle, doing some type of revenge magic. I was, what, twelve?"

"Ha! Yeah, I remember you telling me about that as you set them up. You were trying to give his soul rickets or something." And I smile over at her, glad to hear her talking.

Unfortunately, it doesn't last long. She pulls out her phone and starts flipping through apps.

I let out a sigh. *Too much phone, too little real world.*

But maybe that's just jealousy. She has a phone and I don't, and the way finances are, I doubt I'll be getting a new one anytime soon.

"I met a cool girl at school today," I say, hoping to distract Darla from her phone and, really, just wanting to talk about that magical experience up on the school roof. "Her name is Mia. Mia Chevalier."

Darla glances up. Something in my voice must have piqued her interest. "I've never heard of her," she says, and she sounds a little bit skeptical.

"She just transferred here from San Francisco. She's funny and wild and gorgeous, and I'm afraid I'm going to screw it up. I want to go slow, not creep her out, but—"

And that's when I notice a commotion in the road up ahead, right in front of the Home Warehouse store, where we're headed. There's a line of cars and trucks stopped in the middle of the intersection. People are out of their vehicles and moving around, craning their heads and trying to get a look at something in the middle of the street.

"Is that … a *coffin* up ahead?" Darla asks. Her phone is in her lap, and as soon as I pull to a stop behind a red Prius, she opens up the door and slides out to get a better look.

After a couple of seconds, I put Roy's truck into park and follow her to the edge of a rapidly growing crowd.

There is, indeed, a coffin in the middle of the road. Its sides are cracked, but its lid is still shut. There's a five-foot trail of splinters behind it.

"There was a truck," someone is saying, "and three guys in the back just pushed it out. They almost hit me, but I managed to swerve; then they roared away."

"They were laughing," a woman says.

"And drunk, or high, or crazy," a man adds.

Darla leans over and whispers in my ear. "Someone stole six coffins from Lisa Epstein's mom's mortuary a couple of weeks ago. Maybe this is one of them. She said they think it was the bikers that have been hanging around. There was graffiti on the walls. Swastikas, that type of thing."

I give her a surprised look and she shakes her head. "I *told* you Colma is different now. It got darker while you were vacationing up in Portland." There's a definite anger in her words, but I can't tell if it's directed at the bikers or at me for leaving her and Dad and Roy behind.

A thin voice comes from the crowd. "Is there someone in the coffin?" the voice asks. I can't tell if it's coming from a man or a woman. "The way it fell from the truck, it doesn't look empty."

A bearded man in a trucker's cap and flannel shirt moves forward. I recognize him as the gravedigger from Eternal Home. "It's nailed shut," he says, studying the lid.

Slowly a thinner man in a suit and tie ducks into the cab of his car, comes up with a crowbar, and joins the gravedigger. Together, they slide the crowbar into place and start levering up nails. When they're down to the final two, the gravedigger grabs the loose lid and pulls it free with a massive, wood-cracking tug. The coffin's weatherproof lining rips free, half of it coming up with the lid, and immediately, bright red blood starts to spill from every crack, a wave of gore rushing out onto the street.

Darla reaches for my hand and grasps it tightly. I hear a woman retching off to my side, and everybody else stumbles back. But I don't move, don't react.

I can't tear my eyes away from the leaking coffin.

It looks wrong. Too bright, too glossy.

Then the man in the suit turns toward the crowd. "It's not blood!" he says, in a loud, reassuring voice. "It's just paint!"

And yeah, after the initial shock, it doesn't look like blood at all. It's too thick, moves too smoothly, and smells like astringent chemicals.

The coffin continues to drain. The level of the paint descends quickly, revealing a shape in the bottom of the container. It's not a human, but a crude mannequin made out of pieces of wood. The torso is a segment of tree trunk. The limbs are lashed-together branches. And the whole bizarre thing is coated in dripping red.

What does this mean? Is this a message?

The police arrive before the coffin finishes draining.

"Okay, people, clear the scene," one of the officers says, holding up his hand in a placating gesture. "It's just a stupid prank. We'll find out who did this. They'll be held accountable."

Slowly people start to leave, returning to their cars and driving away. Darla and I are among the last to go.

The last thing I see, as I start up the truck and pull away, is a half dozen police officers standing around the coffin. They are casting one another confused looks and shaking their heads. It's obvious that they have absolutely no idea what they should be doing.

———

Darla is on her phone two minutes later, as we pull into the parking lot of the Home Warehouse store. She's talking to her friend Liv, telling her about what we just saw. "It cracked open, and like, all of this blood came spilling out. Well, paint, actually—but still …"

I get out of the truck and she follows, still gossiping. There's more energy in her voice now than I've heard in a very long time, since before Dad died. Meanwhile, the whole experience—the sight of that coffin rupturing, spilling—has left me feeling sick and disoriented.

I'd always assumed that Colma would stay the same. The world around it might change, but it would remain a port in the storm—

an eternal resting place, always at peace. But now, with rumors of developers buying up property, with biker gangs and racist vandalism, it feels like it's starting to fall apart.

I'm lost in thought when Mrs. Rosen, my old piano teacher, waves at me as she makes her way out of the store. She's pushing a cart full of hydrangeas and smiling widely. I'm surprised at how old she looks. I guess she was old even back when I was taking lessons, but now she's got to be at least eighty, and she looks every minute of it. Her skin is like waxed paper, and her thin gray hair is cut into a short bob. *A pale prune,* I think. *Her head looks like a pale prune.*

"Luke!" she says, pulling to a stop in front of me. Darla, still on her phone, heads into the store without me.

"Hello, Mrs. Rosen."

"I just ... I just wanted to tell you that I'm so sorry for your loss. I heard about your father, and it filled me with such sadness." She gives me a gentle smile. "He seemed like such a good man."

Before I can even think to pull away, she reaches out and grabs my hand with her bony fingers. Her touch is light, with barely any strength behind it at all, but it still jolts the air out of my lungs. What follows isn't really a full-on premonition; instead, it's more like a powerful memory.

The first time I see someone's death is always the strongest, taking over my sight and senses, leaving me disoriented. But it diminishes each time after that, until I see only a faint echo. Sitting next to her on her piano bench once a week for a year and a half, I had plenty of opportunities to see Mrs. Rosen's death. But it's been so long, and I was so young at the time, that the scene is something I can barely recall. It comes flooding back to me now.

Mrs. Rosen is lying in her bed, a floral bedspread pulled up to her chin. Mr. Rosen is sitting in a chair at her side, reading aloud from the *San Francisco Chronicle.* The orange morning light filters in through the blinds. Mrs. Rosen starts to cough, but her husband, largely deaf in his advanced age, doesn't seem to notice. Her breath hitches as her lungs start to fill up with fluid. Her eyelids flutter, go wide, and there's a bloom of red as a capillary in the white of her eye bursts. She struggles for a moment, then falls still. Mr. Rosen just goes right on reading, unaware that his wife has passed away right there by his side.

As the scene fades out, Mrs. Rosen lifts her hand from mine, and I find myself back in the Home Warehouse parking lot.

She coughs loudly, and I shake my head, recognizing the thick, wet sound of that cough. I realize that she looks exactly as she had in my vision. Exactly.

This gives me an idea.

"That's nice of you, Mrs. Rosen," I tell her. "My dad always liked you, and I think he was secretly disappointed that I wouldn't practice the piano more, just because he didn't want me to let you down."

I reach out and once again take Mrs. Rosen's hand in my own, clearly surprising her.

This time, when I return to her bedroom, I try to pay attention to the details. The vision goes by fast—even hazier now than it had been just a minute ago—but I manage to make out the details printed on the front page of the *Chronicle*. It takes me a few moments, but I find the information that I'm looking for.

The date on the paper: September 6, 2018.

Tomorrow.

When I return to reality, I feel a bit faint, but satisfied. Even if it isn't particularly good news for Mrs. Rosen.

"Are you feeling all right, dear?" she asks, smiling weakly. "You look a little peaked."

"I'm fine, Mrs. Rosen," I say. *But you aren't. By this time tomorrow, you'll be dead.*

"Well, again, I'm sorry for your loss, Luke," Mrs. Rosen says. "Please know that I'll be praying for you and your family."

"Thank you, ma'am. I appreciate that."

Then she nods weakly and pushes her cart full of flowers toward her car.

As I watch her go, Darla sticks her head out of the store's front door and calls out, "Are you coming, Luke? I don't have all day."

"Let me use your phone," I say as I head to the store.

"Why?"

"Because I lost mine and I need to use a phone," I say impatiently. "Why don't you find a clerk and ask him if they have the sprinkler parts we need? I'll catch up to you in a minute, and I promise to install everything myself when we get home. That way, you can play *World of Warcraft* all night long. Deal?"

She lets out an annoyed grunt but slaps the phone into my hand.

I dial the number, feeling a bit shitty for what I'm about to do.

"Cressman Cemetery," Uncle Roy says.

How would Dad have handled this? I start out by asking Roy to repeat the sprinkler part number we need, pretending like I've forgotten, then oh-so-casually segue into my plan.

"You should call Mr. Rosen tonight and let him and his wife know that we're having a little gathering next week to celebrate our reopening," I say.

"Our reopening? But we were never closed."

"Yeah, I know, but it'll be like a reopening, since Dad died and everything," I say, scrambling for an explanation. "I just bumped into Mrs. Rosen at the store, and she said something about wanting to come over and bring us a pie. This will give her a chance. Plus, you know, it's important for us to remain in the public eye. Expand our network—that type of thing. Besides, her strawberry-rhubarb pie is the best." I pause for a moment. "But make sure you talk to *Mr.* Rosen. Mrs. Rosen seemed a little out of it when I talked to her, and I'm not sure she'd actually remember."

Uncle Roy is quiet for a moment. "Okay, Luke. If you think that's a good idea."

"I do, for real."

Thank God he's not the type to ask too many questions. Maybe that's a military trait, something they drill into grunts during basic training.

That's a good thing. If Uncle Roy wants the cemetery to survive, he's going to have to start listening to what I have to say.

———

Alfred Hitchcock died of kidney failure. He was eighty years old at the time, and he spent his final day caring for his sick wife, Alma

Reville, who was a talented editor and writer in her own right, and one of Hitchcock's favorite collaborators. She'd suffered a stroke, and he refused to leave her side. He died that night in a chair beside her bed, while Alma went on to live another two years.

My dad must have told me that story a hundred times when I was a kid. I think he wanted me to know what true devotion looked like. Plus, he loved Hitchcock's films. The dark ones, especially: *Psycho*, *Vertigo*, and, most passionately, *The Birds*. It was something he'd shared with his father. They'd gone to see each of those movies in the theater multiple times, and I can imagine them sitting in the back row, leaning in close and whispering about death, about their visions, my grandfather instructing my dad in "the rules" of the family curse.

"I like this part," Roy says.

"Shhh."

Roy and I are crashed out on the living room sofa, the lights turned low as we watch *The Birds* on DVD. Our TV is huge—my dad bought it nearly a year ago, back when things had been looking up businesswise and we could afford to splurge a little. Darla is upstairs, locked in her room, no doubt playing *World of Warcraft*. At dinner, while pushing a fork full of macaroni and cheese around her plate, she'd told us that she'd never watch *The Birds* again. "That's Dad's thing," she'd said. "We should have buried the DVD with him."

Those words had hit me pretty hard. I wish Darla could feel differently.

"Don't go in there," Roy says to the TV.

Tippi Hedren is walking up a flight of stairs. The little girl's bedroom is at the top, and she's about to find out that the evil birds have broken through the roof, that her hiding place has come under siege.

"She can't hear you," I say, shaking my head. "Besides, that'd make for a pretty dull climax if she just turned around right now."

The first time I saw *The Birds* had been with my dad at a little theater in Bodega Bay, where Hitchcock had shot most of the film. I remember the feel of the velvet seats in the theater, the taste of the popcorn we'd shared, the smell of the ocean breeze as we'd stepped back outside. But most of all, I remember the thrill in his voice as he'd driven us down there. This was special to him—a big, secret part of his soul—and he was happy to be able to share it with me, like his dad had shared it with him.

"Your grandpa used to say that all of the other Hitchcock films have reasonable explanations," my dad had told me as we threw stones into Bodega Bay afterward. "*The Birds* doesn't. It just … is. You can try to figure out why they attack, but when it comes right down to it, there's no good reason. It's an unsolved mystery. A quirk of the universe. Just like what happens to us. Maybe there *is* a reason why we have these visions, but we'll never know what it is."

My grandfather died about two years after I was born, and now that Dad's gone, there's absolutely no one I can have this type of conversation with. In the whole wide world, there's no one who can possibly understand what I'm going through.

I wish I'd never gone away to boarding school. I wish I'd spent the last year in Colma with my dad, talking to him, learning from him. But most of all, I wish I'd never let him die. I could have just yelled out, "You're going to fall off the ladder tomorrow." Would he have really killed himself? He would have been angry, sure, but I don't think he would have actually been able to go through with it. And he'd still be alive today. And the world, I'm guessing, would still be turning.

Right?

"Can I bring the lovebirds, Mitch? They haven't harmed anyone."

"Oh, all right. Bring them."

Tippi Hedren and Rod Taylor speak these final lines; then they drive off, putting Bodega Bay and the rampaging birds in their rearview mirror.

"I called Mr. Rosen," Roy says, sipping from his decaf coffee as the credits start to roll. "He said that they're leaving town next week, but they'll try to stop by this weekend."

Mrs. Rosen won't be going anywhere, and neither will Mr. Rosen. And now a seed has been planted in his mind. Hopefully, it's a subtle enough reminder for when the time comes to pick a cemetery.

It's a scummy thing to do—leveraging information from my visions in order to sell cemetery plots—but it's a necessary step, something I have to do to save the cemetery. I approached two more old people while Darla and I were at the Home Warehouse store, and I've started keeping notes in a journal. There's nothing imminent (other than Mrs. Rosen), but it's only a matter of time.

Anything to keep the developers at bay, I think.

The credits end, and Roy heaves himself up off the sofa, letting out an exhausted groan. He stretches and steadies himself against the fireplace mantel. A photo of my mom and dad wobbles next to his big hand. In it, they're standing at the base of an enormous tree trunk—they're on their honeymoon, vacationing in Redwood National Park. My dad had loved it there. It was a place where stuff seemed to live forever, he told me, where he never had to think about death.

"Did my mom like Hitchcock movies?" I ask Roy. "I never thought to ask Dad."

"No," Roy says, shaking his head. "She didn't like scary stories. She had to leave the room whenever your dad or I put something like that on."

"Why?" I ask.

Roy is silent for a moment, thinking about it. "Her parents were in Japan when we dropped the atomic bombs on Hiroshima and Nagasaki. Living with them, I imagine she heard enough scary stories to last her a lifetime. And those are the types of stories that you can't pause, eject, or return to Netflix."

I grunt. I've often wondered about that type of big, terrible event. Would I see it coming? Would I be able to piece it together from my visions? I imagine I'd touch one person, then another, and another, and see the same type of death speeding their way.

The good news about the future, my dad used to say, is that people still die for random, stupid reasons: cancer, car accidents, choking on a chicken bone, falling down a flight of stairs. Sometimes, there are deaths that I don't understand—it looks like there are going to be more robots in the future, and they'll occasionally be involved in accidental deaths—but as far as both my dad and I have seen, there's no extinction-level event looming on the horizon. If the big California earthquake is indeed coming, it won't be killing anyone I know.

"You were at Mom and Dad's wedding, right?" I ask Roy.

"Of course I was." And he smiles warmly, remembering. "I was your dad's best man. Heck, you were there, too, if you think about it."

My mom was three months pregnant at the time.

"Who else was there?"

"Everyone who could make it. Your grandparents. Even your mom's mom—she managed to fly in. You should send her an email, by the way. They do have email in Japan, you know, and I'm sure she'd love to hear from you."

I nod, suddenly feeling horribly guilty. I'm a terrible grandson, I know, totally unsuited to the job. I only talk to my mom's mother—my only surviving grandparent—like, once or twice a year. Birthdays and Christmas and that's about it. But she's all the way over in Japan, and ever since my mom died she's never wanted to come back to America.

"She's a remarkable woman, you know," Roy says, flashing me a smile. "She drank my dad under the table that day." He pauses, then his smile collapses. "Of course, happy drinking always beats sad drinking."

"Grandpa was sad on my parents' wedding day?"

Roy shrugs. "He didn't seem happy to me."

"I thought he liked my mom." Then I pause, and after a second my eyes go wide. "Oh, God! Please, please, *please* don't tell me that he was a closet racist."

"Oh no, nothing like that," Roy says, shaking his head vehemently. "Nothing like that at all! He *loved* your mom. He really did. He just … I don't know. He was just sad. Maybe … maybe he felt like he was losing your dad in some way." He grunts. And shrugs again.

I know Roy always felt a little bit left out when it came to my grandfather's relationship with my dad. He thinks that my dad got better treatment because he was the firstborn—special—and in a way, I guess he's right. Thanks to the family rules, Grandpa couldn't tell Roy his deepest, darkest secrets—the things that made him and my father and now me who we are. Dad always tried to make sure that Darla never felt this way, that she was included just as much as I was, but there was always that part of him that he just couldn't share with her.

"Your grandfather wasn't one to explain himself too much," Roy says. "At least not to me." Then he takes his coffee cup and heads into the kitchen.

I keep staring at the photo on the mantelpiece—my parents on their honeymoon, smiling, happy—when it hits me. Of course my grandfather was sad that day! The whole time that they were together, my dad never had a vision of my mom's death. He told me that he knew that it would probably happen, that at some point he'd touch her and suddenly know how and why and when her life was going to end, but that time had never actually come. In that respect, he'd been just like any other average, everyday schmuck, facing a bright, optimistic future with his new wife.

Grandpa, on the other hand, must have known. He must have had that vision. Hugging my mom, kissing her cheek, he must have seen her in the hospital, exhausted from childbirth, fading away, leaving my dad all alone with his newborn baby.

No wonder he was sad.

Did he wrestle with that knowledge? Was he trying to decide if he should tell my dad what was going to happen?

He stuck to the rules, I guess. He let fate take its course.

It must have been brutal.

Suddenly, a flash of light hits my eye. I get up from the sofa and move over to the picture window, getting there just in time to see a pair of headlights coming up our driveway.

After eight o'clock on a weeknight? These are *not* normal cemetery visiting hours.

For a moment, I've got the threat of motorcycle gangs and money-hungry land developers dancing through my head. Then I brace myself and open the door.

———

There's a blare of music coming from behind the headlights.

It's a Florence and the Machine song, "Cosmic Love." Loud, pristine vocals float over a harp, guitar, and banging drums. It's strange to hear such an ethereal song echoing out across the cemetery.

An old white pickup truck comes to a stop in front of the house. The engine sputters and then stalls, letting out a rattling sigh, and even from the doorway, I can smell burning oil and brake fluid.

After a moment, the headlights flicker off, and I can make out the person behind the wheel.

It's Mia.

I'm stunned and confused. Then I can feel my lips forming into a grateful smile. *Thank you, God!* And then, just as quickly, I'm overcome with an intense anxiety. Why is she here? What does she want? What do I say?

Mia kills the music, opens the door, and steps out. She's wearing the same flowery dress that she had on earlier today, but now there's a gray hoodie layered on top of it. I can see her colorful jewelry in the gap between her dress and her dark skin.

"Hey," she says.

"Hey," I reply, trying to keep my cool.

"I hope you don't mind me just showing up out of the blue like this," she says, "but I found your cemetery online, and I figured you might want to have this back." She reaches into her pocket and pulls out my phone.

"You found it!" I'm overcome with relief.

She smiles. "Yeah, I found it. I went up to the roof for another cigarette, and it was lying there by the door. I figured it was yours. But don't worry, I didn't peek at it or anything, and there's very little chance that I installed crippling malware."

I slip it back into my pocket, where it belongs. "I went back up and looked all over, but I must have missed it."

Mia shrugs. "It was by the cinder block you used as a doorstop."

Mia turns in a slow circle, taking in the cemetery. When she's done, she cocks her head and fixes me with that bright smile of hers. She looks stunning standing there, half in the porch light, half in moonlight, dark skin and light eyes.

"This place is pretty cool. It's got great … *juh-nay-say-quah*," she says, using that awful French pronunciation.

I laugh. "Yeah, I guess it does."

"Are you busy?"

"What, now?"

"No, last week, you dumbass," she says, rolling her eyes. "Yes, now."

"No … I'm not busy," I manage. "Not so much."

"Then how about giving me a tour?"

My heart is beating hard, and I feel a little bit faint. I try to imagine the coolest thing I could do—maybe saying something funny, offering her my arm like a suave gentleman, or kissing her right there and then—but I end up just stammering out, "Yeah … yeah, of course." Then, recovering a bit, I go for, "It would be my pleasure."

———

The wind has picked up a little, and nighttime fog has gathered around some of the taller family mausoleums. Some people would find all of this spooky and depressing, but walking next to Mia, hearing her footsteps alongside mine, I can't imagine anyplace more romantic.

We head down the long, paved path in the middle of row A4. When clouds pass in front of the moon, I use my phone to light the way.

This is Darla's favorite row. It has some of the oldest graves in the cemetery, dating back to before the earthquake. The intricate stonework is weathered and amazing, and when she was teaching herself photography, Darla made oversize prints from some of the more haunting inscriptions. One of her favorites still hangs on the wall over her computer desk. It features an epitaph that reads:

REMEMBER ME AS YOU PASS BY
AS YOU ARE NOW, SO ONCE WAS I
AS I AM NOW, SO MUST YOU BE
PREPARE FOR DEATH AND FOLLOW ME

I show this one to Mia, leaning in close so that she can read the words under the light from my phone. I also show her my personal favorite:

HERE LIES AN ATHEIST
ALL DRESSED UP
AND NO PLACE TO GO

Mia's laugh is low and smooth and sweet as honey.

"How was your first day at Mission Hills?" I ask.

"Well, I managed not to get expelled for cutting class and smoking up on the roof, so that's a plus, I guess." Then she's silent for a moment. "The private school I went to in the city was super intense. Not that I'm putting Mission Hills down or anything, but it just seems more … mellow, I guess, a lot less frantic. Which is a nice change of pace."

"You went to a private school?"

She nods. "Crazy competitive. Ivy League fast-tracking, that type of thing. And everyone was so full of themselves, so completely self-obsessed. It's nice to be with more normal people."

I laugh. "You might be the first person to call Colma kids normal. When we play team sports against other schools, they call us the Grim Reapers."

"That's better than being called the Bay Area Stick-up-the-Ass Snobs. But that might have just been me leading that chant. Last year, I saw two girls get into a fight over their parents' net worth."

I shake my head as we make our way up A5, where, for some reason, a lot of Latino families ended up. There are, like, six different groupings of Ramirez plots, and as far as I can tell, none of them are actually related. A5 is also where all of the raccoons like to hang out, so I stay alert for eyes glowing in the dark.

"I've heard that some of those Bay Area billionaires are sniffing around Colma, trying to buy up our land," I say.

"I bet Google will try to rent out ad space on the gravestones soon."

"And I'm sure Amazon is looking into one-hour graveside flower delivery—"

"By drones!" Mia adds.

"But of course! Anything else would be so old-fashioned." I smile, and I can just make out that she's smiling back at me in the dark. "That's not why you're here, is it? You aren't an advance scout for Facebook or Apple or something, trying to get private tours of the cemeteries so you can figure out the optimal placement for your next data center?"

"Do I look like a billionaire to you?"

You look like at least a billion bucks to me. It's the perfect line, but I'm too chicken to say it out loud. Instead I go with, "Billionaires don't always look like billionaires."

"Be that as it may, I'm not even close. I was on scholarship at my last school."

We pass under one of the few lights in A5, and I watch as she waves her arms and makes her shadow dance across the stone pathway.

"You said your mom lives here?"

Mia nods. "She grew up here, and I was actually born here. My parents got divorced when I was three, and my dad and I moved up to San Francisco. My mom and aunt stayed here." She pauses for a moment. "I've visited a few times, but only briefly. My relationship with my mother's always been kind of strained. It's only recently that I've been trying to make things work between us."

I nod. Then I raise a questioning eyebrow. "I thought I knew everyone who lived in Colma. I've never heard the name Chevalier before."

"After the divorce, my mom went back to her maiden name." Mia pauses for a moment, and her voice drops a little bit lower. "It's Iverson," she says.

I stop short in front of the Vasquez family mausoleum—it's an imposing, double-decker piece of travertine stone, and a bit gaudy. "Iverson, as in Melinda Iverson?"

"Bingo," Mia says. "You got it in one."

"Oh," I say, and we start walking again, suddenly caught in an awkward silence. Melinda Iverson is ... well, to put it politely, the town kook. I haven't seen her in a while, so I don't know if she's still wearing Romany-style headscarves and bracelets, but I know for a fact that she still runs Other Worlds, a little psychic shop over on Junipero Serra Boulevard. It's a total scam, my dad assured me. Crystal balls, auras, astrology, and her premium service: channeling the wisdom of the dearly departed. As you can imagine, Colma sees a lot of people desperate to commune with the dead.

Years ago, not long after my mom died, my dad had gone over to Other Worlds to check it out. He'd probably had a tiny bit of hope in him—you can't have the gift that he had without also being open to the possibility that there are other "anomalies" out there. I imagine that he was thinking that maybe, just maybe, he'd be able to reach out and find my mom. But when he stepped inside that store and saw the dangling crystals and dream catchers, the ankhs and tarot cards, and the collection of hopeful suckers waiting in the lobby, my dad turned right back around. "Disgusting," he'd told me. "It's all just stage dressing, just a way of exploiting people's desires and grief."

"That's cool about your mom being from Colma," I say, breaking the silence.

Mia scoffs. "No, it's not. I know what people think."

We continue walking, again trapped in that awkward silence.

We're in row A6 now, and the path takes us past the Zimmerman mausoleum—the big, gated one that got tagged with graffiti sometime over the weekend. Someone has spray-painted a pot leaf and an intricate "420" across the polished white marble, and despite my best intentions, I still haven't gotten around to scrubbing them away. At least there are no swastikas visible from where we're standing.

"Nice," Mia says. "Who did this?"

"Kids, probably. There are people who like to come out here to drink and smoke and screw. It's a pain in the ass."

"What? You're not a fan of drinking and smoking and screwing?"

My throat closes up for a moment. "Uh … sure I am. It's just … not when I have to do the cleaning up afterward, you know?"

Mia laughs and runs her hand across a flower etched into the white marble. She peers down the dark path in front of us, and then up at the cloud-dotted sky. "It must be weird," she says, "being around this stuff all of the time."

"What do you mean?"

"You know," she says, "all of this death, all of this despair. It seems like, every day, the world is trying to help us forget about this kind of thing. There's school, TV shows, Twitter posts, selfies on Instagram. All putting space between us and places like this."

I smile. "Is this tour freaking you out?" I ask.

She smiles back. "Nah. I'm not a wilting flower. Besides, this is far less freaky than the stuff you'd see hanging around with my family."

No doubt, I'm tempted to say, but I don't.

We keep walking. We're in the quiet, respectable B rows now, with all of the modest, classy headstones. There's another long silence between us, but it's more comfortable this time.

"So, you like Florence and the Machine?" I finally ask.

"Yeah, they're one of my favorite bands. Florence Welch is amazing. They're headlining a one-day event in San Francisco next week. I wanted to go, but couldn't afford a ticket, and now they're sold out. I even entered to win one on Instagram. I had to write why I deserved to go. I said, 'I deserve to go because I just moved to a small, backward-ass suburb and have nothing else to live for.' Needless to say, I didn't win. Think they were looking for something a little more upbeat and inspiring."

"Maybe," I say.

"Besides, maybe I judged too soon. Maybe I *do* have things to live for here in Colma."

She flashes me a sly smile, and my heart starts pounding in my ears. Her smile is radiant in the moonlight, a warm flash chasing away the cold night. I feel downright giddy.

She steps toward me, so I close my eyes and lean in to kiss her—

"Whoa!" And I feel her hand on my chest, pushing me back. I open my eyes and see her embarrassed face turning away from me. "I didn't mean …" She trails off into silence.

"I … I thought …"

"Listen," she says, "I better go home now. It's late, and my mom's expecting me."

Oh God, how could I be so stupid? How could I read everything so wrong?

I mean, I'm no Casanova, okay—no serious girlfriends—but I've made out with my share of girls, and I always thought I was pretty good at picking up signals.

But not tonight, apparently.

"I'm so sorry, Mia. I thought …"

"It's okay." And she turns and starts heading back toward the house. "Forget about it. It didn't happen."

———

When we reach her truck, I try to meet her eyes, but she keeps looking away. "Um, well, thanks for dropping off my phone. I—"

"No problem," she says, cutting me off.

She slips into the truck and drives away, not even bothering to give me a half-hearted wave. I watch her taillights disappear into the distance.

Stupid. So stupid.

I reach into my pocket and grip my phone, ready to hurl it out into the sea of headstones. *Talk about making a bad situation worse.* Then I take a deep breath and manage to regain a little bit of self-control.

I head back up A5, not quite ready to go back inside the house yet.

The dead don't have to worry about shit like this—embarrassment and failure, heartache and confusion.

I leave the main path and duck behind a grove of trees, finding the protected little clearing where my mom's and dad's angels stand guard over their graves. I sit down in front of them and stare up at their outlines. Moonlight cuts through the trees, lighting up just a section of cheek here, part of a wing there, and a pair of outstretched hands.

I dig into my pocket and come up with three coins, a Coke bottle lid, a folded-up receipt, and a ballpoint pen. Not exactly the offerings I'd intended to leave when I wrote the reminder on my arm earlier this morning, but better than nothing, I guess.

I balance my tributes on the angels' bare feet. Then I touch one of their empty hands and trudge back to the house alone.

4   Mia's not in the senior locker bay before first period, she's not in the cafeteria at lunch, and she's not smoking up on the roof any of the three times I check. All I want to do is say I'm sorry, but she's absolutely nowhere to be found.

Maybe she's skipping school. Maybe she transferred back to San Francisco just so she'd never have to see me again.

English lit is my last class of the day, and I have a hard time paying attention. I stare out the window, watching the clouds blow across the sky. I don't think I've heard a single word that Mrs. Trudeau has said all class.

Mia's like no one I've ever known, and I *knew* I needed to take it slow. So why couldn't I just hang back? Why did I have to try to kiss her?

After the bell, I wait for nearly everyone else to leave before I finally get out of my chair, trying to avoid jostling and accidentally touching someone. The last thing I need right now is courtside seats to someone's horrible death. I reach the hall just as Erin and Amy are coming out of Spanish class. They give me a wave.

"*Hola, Señor Luke,*" Amy says as I walk over to them. "*¿Qué pasa?*"

I haven't touched her in years, but hearing Amy speak a third language reminds me of my vision of her death. Right before she dies, she'll be lying inside some type of futuristic oxygen tent. She takes her last breath, struggles up, opens the tent, and steps out onto the marble floor of a beautiful bathroom that's nearly the size of a house. It's obvious that she's ridiculously rich at this point. From the art on the walls, and the open sketch pad next to the oxygen tent, I can tell that she's become some type of famous artist. Anyway, when she falls to the ground, a robotic voice alerts the house that there's been an accident. It says this once in English and then in a language I've never heard before. It sounds like some kind of advanced future language, something that hasn't been invented yet.

As she's standing there by the water fountain, speaking Spanish, I can imagine that other language coming out of Amy's mouth. Hell, maybe she invents it; maybe it's a piece of art.

"Earth to Portland." Erin waves a hand in front of my face and turns toward Amy. "Yeah, *that's* a familiar look. Luke's our very own space cadet."

I shrug, then scan the hallway, looking for Mia. "Have you guys met the new girl yet?" I ask. "Her name's Mia?"

The girls glance at each other. "I heard that she's an Iverson," Erin says with a sneer. "Maybe she's a psychic, too."

"If so, do you think she knew that her mom was going to get arrested before it happened?" Amy asks Erin.

"Her mom got arrested?" I say. "For what?"

"I heard that one of her 'clients' found her stealing mail, trying to get private information. That's how she does her 'readings.'"

"That's not the whole story," Erin says, her eyes wide. "My aunt went to Other Worlds after my uncle died. He was getting a bit loony toward the end—brain cancer, dementia, that type of thing—and he kept hiding all of their money. And when he finally passed away, my aunt couldn't find any of their important documents and a large portion of their personal savings. Anyway, during a reading, the Iversons were able to contact him, and he told them right where he'd buried it all." She looks from Amy to me and gives us a wide-eyed nod. "It was buried at the base of a tree, half a mile from their house. There's no way anybody could have known that. Nobody but my uncle, that is."

Amy lets out a skeptical chuffing noise. "That's not too freakin' likely," she says. "There are ways to lead people on, you know, to get them to clue you in on what you want to know. It's a whole branch of psychology. I'm betting that your aunt gave them enough clues to make an educated guess."

"I don't know about that," Erin says. "The way my aunt describes it, it sounds pretty real. And totally creepy."

I grunt. Could it be possible? Maybe my dad dismissed it too quickly.

"Well, I heard that the business isn't doing too well, and that they're on the verge of shutting down," Amy says, flashing us a wicked smile. "You'd think, if they had *real* powers, they would have been able to see that coming, right?"

"Whatever. The whole thing just gives me the creeps." And Erin mimes an exaggerated shiver. "Anyway, the girl seems just as loopy as her mom. I saw her up on the roof between second and third period. She was standing right near the edge. For a moment, I thought she was going to jump."

"Nah," I say. "She just goes up there to smoke."

"I saw her, too," Amy chimes in. "We have fifth period together, and she was telling a couple of us a weird story about some homeless guy who used to follow her home from school trying to throw soup on her."

"Yeah, that's not surprising," Erin says. "I don't know why, but she just seems like the kind of girl who would get soup thrown on her."

"You should give her a chance," I say. "She helped me out. I almost fell down the stairs, and she stopped to make sure I was okay. Anyway, she seems pretty smart to me. And funny."

"I *knew* it!" Erin says. "You *like* her!" She's smiling, but I can hear something cold in her voice. Jealousy, maybe? Gael says that Erin's had a crush on me since middle school.

"No, no," I say, way too defensively. "I just said that she's smart and funny. Heroji's smart and funny, too, but that doesn't mean I'm looking to hook up with him."

"That's probably for the best," Amy says. "I'm sorry to have to be the one to tell you this, Luke, but Heroji's *way* out of your league." And both of the girls break down laughing.

After they're done making fun of me, Amy hoists her bag into her arms and starts digging through it, her movements getting increasingly frantic.

"What's wrong?" I ask.

"My sketchbook," she says. "I always have it with me, but now it's gone."

"Did you leave it in your locker?" Erin asks.

"Maybe." But the worried look stays on her face.

Erin and I walk her to her locker, and as Amy digs inside, I look around the hallway, hoping to spot Mia. Unfortunately, she's nowhere to be found.

She's got to be avoiding me. Is she peeking around every corner, spotting me and running away?

"Goddamnit!" Amy growls, slamming her locker shut. "It's not here. I've got to go back and check everywhere. Jesus, I spent so much time working on those studies. And that sketchbook was expensive, too! It was imported from France!"

She hurries off, too rushed to say goodbye.

"I've got to go, too," I tell Erin as Amy disappears around a corner. "I'm supposed to walk home with Darla. She's probably pissed off at me for making her wait."

"How's Darla doing, anyway?" Erin asks.

"She's okay, I guess."

"I saw her in the hall yesterday and tried to say hi, but she just took off, didn't even want to acknowledge my existence. It was kind of rude, actually."

"Yeah, that's Darla," I say with a sigh. "She's getting quieter, playing more video games. She's still pretty upset about my dad, I think. She doesn't even want to talk to me about it."

Erin flinches, suddenly mortified. "Yeah, yeah, of course. I didn't mean anything *bad* by what I said, you know?"

I nod, trying to tell her it's okay.

It's not that I don't like Erin—I actually do. Quite a bit, in fact. She's beautiful, and funny, and sometimes I can see a good heart beneath her too-cool attitude. But … well, I get uncomfortable around her, knowing that she will be dying early, that she won't be making it out of her thirties. It gives me a supremely weird feeling. If she only has twenty years left, should I be telling her not to make any long-term plans? Should I be encouraging her to visit Europe? Saying, *Maybe you shouldn't worry too much about making that trust fund last?*

In the end, it's just easier for me to withdraw. Twenty years is a long time, yeah, but—

Don't get too attached, Luke. Don't get involved.

And these thoughts make me feel like a total shit.

"How's it going, kiddos?"

Erin and I turn. Gael's got a big smile on his face. His hair is slicked back, and he's wearing a brown corduroy jacket over jeans tucked into big black boots.

"Are you two coming to Deacon's party?" Gael asks, as we all head down the hallway. I can see Darla standing just outside the front door, her arms crossed, looking bored and angry.

I've known Jim Deacon since I was little; like Gael's and mine, Jim's family was one of Colma's founding clans. He's having a big back-to-school bash tonight, and everyone's been talking about it. It's going to be *huge*. Unfortunately, crowded parties aren't really my thing—too much standing around, chugging beers, trying to flirt and dance, all while under the constant threat of unwanted death visions. Not exactly my idea of fun.

"I'll think about it," I say, trying to sound noncommittal.

"You should come," Erin says, offering me a sly smile. "You won't regret it." She's not exactly subtle about her intentions here, and Gael gives me a wide-eyed, conspiratorial nod.

"I'll think about it," I repeat.

Then I give them a weak smile and head to the door.

———

There's a path a quarter mile up the road from the school. It cuts through a field toward our house, while the road continues east into town.

I think about asking Darla to go with me to Other Worlds and keep me company while I look for Mia, but I decide against it. She'd probably just make fun of me. Or worse, she'd scoff and look back down at her phone, completely ignoring me.

"Tell Roy I'll be home soon," I say, continuing past the trail-head. "And I'll actually get around to cleaning up the Zimmermans' mausoleum tonight."

"Where are you going?" she asks, looking up, confused.

"There's … there's just something I need to do."

"This is about that girl, isn't it? Mia?" She smiles briefly, then glances back down. "Don't blow it," she says sarcastically. Then she turns and continues out into the field.

I speed up into a jog, anxious to find Mia and try to set things right.

This whole day, my romantic fail has been hanging over my head like a storm cloud. Leaning in for that kiss—how could I have been so stupid? The sooner I can put that behind me, the better—even if I am horrified at what she's going to say. Probably a brush-off, another *forget about it … it didn't happen*, before she freezes me out of her life for good.

Why didn't I at least get her phone number? This type of thing would be so much easier over text.

In Colma, the shortest path between two points is almost always through a cemetery. Right now, it's the Serbian cemetery. I jump across a ditch, cut through a hedge, and head into its depths.

A lot of the kids think that this is the most beautiful cemetery in Colma, perfect for illicit nighttime wandering and drinking and hooking up. In daylight, however, it's hard to see why. The cross-shaped headstones are far too ornate, and the mausoleums look downright ugly. I prefer my family's cemetery. The pathways are wider, the headstones are well spaced, and at nighttime everything looms in all the right ways.

Being there with Mia last night had been downright magical.

Right up until those final moments, of course.

The Serbian cemetery's back gate is surrounded by trees, and it drops me right into the Target parking lot. The main street, Junipero Serra Boulevard, is Colma's fast-food/supermarket/big-box-store district. We have a Target, a Safeway, the Silva family's Home Warehouse, a McDonald's, a Starbucks, and an always-packed Tacos Por Favor, among other less notable stores and restaurants.

Other Worlds is right on the edge of the three-block district, on the bottom floor of a two-story building. It looks like a converted house—painted a pale pink and surrounded by a small garden. Hidden among the overgrown flowers and shrubbery out front is a hand-painted sign:

OTHER WORLDS
A VIEW INTO THE GREAT BEYOND

I'm pretty sure that Mia's family lives in an apartment up on the second floor.

I'm surprised at the number of cars parked out front. Amy had said that the store was struggling, but it definitely doesn't look that way to me. As I walk closer, three women trickle out the front door, and a man and a woman make their way inside.

There's a laminated sign posted next to the front door: "Our loved ones, passed over, surround us still. They speak, if we're willing to hear their words.... Hear their words!"

Can this be real? I stare at the front door for a while, thinking about my dad and remembering the pain of his loss, and I start to get angry. If it's *not* real, if Mia's mom is just faking all of this psychic bullshit, then she's taking advantage of gullible people's grief, and that's a horrible thing to do.

Suddenly, there's a voice behind me. "Darkness drowns a hopeful light, and it's getting darker around here, isn't it?" I turn around. There's a woman holding a shopping bag a couple of feet away. She's maybe in her fifties. Her hair is gray and messy, sticking out from beneath a wide-brimmed hat, and a rumpled light-blue dress hangs on her body. "Will you come inside, young man? Will you listen to your elders? Will you heed their words?"

I take a step back, startled to find the woman standing right there at my elbow. I watch her eyes dart back and forth, refusing to rest in any one place.

I open my mouth, but I really don't know what to say.

Thankfully, the door swings open right then. "Lena!" Melinda Iverson says with a growl. "Where have you been? We have appointments all afternoon. Mrs. Halverson—" Mia's mom lifts a no-nonsense appointment book, consults an entry, and lets out an annoyed grunt. "Yes, Mrs. Halverson has been waiting for you for twenty minutes now!"

"I was just consulting with the scion here," the gray-haired woman says. "We were just talking about light and hope, and the presence and absence, therefore, of … and … and …" She looks at me for a moment, and then her brow crinkles in confusion. "What was I saying?"

"There's no time for this," Mia's mom says. She grabs the gray-haired woman's arm and pulls her inside. "Get to the consultation room. I'll send your client back in a couple of minutes."

Lena hurries back through the crowded lobby, her eyes focused on the floor. She disappears through a beaded door hanging at the back of the room.

As soon as she's gone, Mia's mom turns back my way. "I'm sorry about that. My sister gets confused sometimes. Won't you please come in?"

She's wearing a black pantsuit belted with a wide pink-and-yellow scarf. She is pale, and her dark hair is long and pulled back tight. *Mia must take after her dad*, I think. But then I notice Melinda Iverson's pale eyes. They are a super-light hazel, the exact same shade as Mia's.

I take one step into the lobby. There are lit candles in all four corners of the room, and the walls are layered with bolts of thick fabric. There are dream catchers scattered across one side, and hanging crystals on the other. This is what my dad was talking about. So new age-y. So ridiculous.

"I … I'm just looking for Mia," I stammer. "Is she here? Did she come home after school?"

Melinda Iverson gives me a skeptical look. She stands up straighter and crosses her arms, transforming from businesswoman into concerned mother. "She's not here yet," she says. "Why? What do you want with her?"

"I just … she found my phone, and I wanted to thank her for that." I take my phone out of my pocket and show it to her.

"That's very nice of you. Unfortunately, I don't know when she's going to be getting home. She's supposed to be here helping out, but …" And Ms. Iverson shrugs.

"Okay," I say. "Just tell her—"

"You're welcome to wait." She gestures around the lobby. There are a couple of empty chairs on the far side of the room, but the rest are all occupied, and suddenly I'm aware that there are at least a dozen pairs of eyes watching our exchange. "I could give you a tarot card reading in the meantime," Ms. Iverson offers. "I'll have an opening in about ten minutes. It's thirty dollars for a full reading, and fifteen for a three-card flip. All one hundred percent accurate, of course—if you have an open mind about that type of thing." And she flashes me a smile.

"No, that's okay. Just tell her that Luke stopped by, okay? And … and I'll talk to her later."

Ms. Iverson smiles and nods. "I'll do that."

I mumble my thanks and step back out the door.

Could she really be psychic? Could any of her "services" be real? No, of course not.

But …

Darkness drowns a hopeful light.

I shiver, thinking about Mia's aunt's words.

Walking through the parking lot, I notice a biker parked in a dirt rut on the other side of Junipero Serra Boulevard. The big guy's sitting still, straddling his bike with his hands tucked into his pockets. Even though he's wearing dark sunglasses above a bushy beard, I can tell that he's watching me intently as I leave Other Worlds and make my way up the front path. It totally creeps me out.

When I get to the other end of the parking lot, I glance back over and see that the biker's still there, still sitting motionless, watching Melinda Iverson's front door.

5

I'm just finishing up with the Zimmermans' mausoleum when I get a text from a number with a 415 area code.

Are you coming to the party tonight? ~*Mia*~

How did she get my number? Not that that would be a difficult thing, of course—she could have just asked anyone in our class—but it still makes me smile. She hunted me down!

I haul my empty bucket and bag of cleaning supplies back to the house. It's almost dark out, and the party should be getting started right about now. Should I go? Should I risk the crowds and potential embarrassment just for a chance to see Mia again? The fact that she's texting me has to be a good sign, though, right?

As I'm thinking about it, she texts me again.

You should come. All dressed up and no place to go, amiright?

I smile.

———

Uncle Roy isn't too happy about me going to a party on a school night. He grunts and says, "Thursdays should be for work and studying." When I tell him that I don't have anything to study yet, he just shakes his head and turns back to an old episode of *Parks and Recreation.* "Just be back before … midnight," he says, pausing to figure out what an appropriate curfew should be. He's still getting used to this whole parenting thing, trying to feel his way through.

I agree to his terms and grab a couple of slices of pizza before I head out the door.

I take my dad's old car, a five-year-old forest-green Ford Focus. It's actually my car now—Roy gave me the keys about a month after my dad's funeral—but I still think of it as my dad's. Hell, the radio stations are still set to his favorites: NPR, sports radio, and classic rock.

The Deacons live in a big, Tudor-style house in the hills over Colma Valley. By the time I get there, cars are parked up and down the street. I find a spot not that far away from the entrance to Hills of Eternity Memorial Park.

Music greets me as I walk up the driveway: EDM with a fast bass beat. There are kids on the Deacons' lawn, laughing and drinking beer from red Solo cups, and I can smell cigarettes and pot blowing from the porch. It doesn't look like anyone's too worried about getting caught.

Jim's parents must be very, very far away.

Across the street, I see Gael and Cole Rose getting out of Gael's Jeep Cherokee. They notice me and wave. Then, laughing, they head my way.

Cole is Gael's boyfriend. When Gael came out to me in the middle of sophomore year, I couldn't quite figure it out at first. I asked all of the stupid questions—*Are you* sure *you're gay? Couldn't it just be a phase?*—but I got over that pretty quickly, and

I tried to give him as much support as I could. I was actually pretty flattered when he told me I was the first person he'd ever come out to.

He finally managed to tell his parents last spring, but he's been dating Cole on the sly for nearly a year now. Cole is a junior. They met in jazz band, bonding over how much they both hated sheet music.

Cole gives me a nod and a smile. He is tall, with cropped blond hair. He's wearing a shiny leather jacket with "Super Lovers" stitched on the back. "Welcome back, Luke," he mumbles. He tends to mumble.

"You made it!" Gael says. "I didn't think we'd see you. I thought you'd go full hermit mode on us, like this one here tends to do." He wraps an arm around Cole and plants a big kiss on his cheek.

"You only live once," I say with a shrug, but I'm already scanning the crowd, looking around for Mia. "Since when did Jim's house become the party house?" I ask.

"Since Jim's parents got divorced," Gael says. "Jim's dad lives in the city now, and his mom goes out of town a couple of nights a week."

"Leaving the house in his incredibly responsible hands," I finish. Gael and Cole laugh.

"Why aren't the cops swarming this place?" I ask.

"Give it an hour," Gael says. "And seeing as we're short on time here …" He grabs Cole's hand and starts dragging him toward the front door.

"Oh, I see," I say, amused. "No time to socialize. This is all just an excuse for private Gael-Cole hookup time, right?"

"Well, you can tag along if you want," Gael says as they start walking toward the house, a wide smile on his face. "But I didn't think you were into that type of thing. Plus, I wouldn't want to make Erin jealous."

I dismiss this with a laugh and follow them into the house. They quickly disappear up the stairs.

The inside of the house smells of sweat, pot, and noxious body spray. I pull my sleeves down and the hood of my hoodie up, trying to cover my skin. Then I grab a beer from a cooler by the front door.

I already feel awkward, not quite sure what I should be doing.

The bass beat morphs into a hardcore Skrillex remix, and I wonder if Mia would like this type of music, or if she's solely into dark, melodic alternative rock. Would she prefer some Broods, Metric, and Lana Del Rey? Maybe some FKA Twigs and some Lorde? Or maybe Mia's into her namesake, M.I.A.

I lift myself up onto my tiptoes and try to peer out over the sea of people in the entryway and living room. Still no sign of Mia.

Elbows, knees, legs, and feet all knock into me as I make my way through the crowd, but I manage to avoid any skin-to-skin contact. The crowd shifts, and I'm pushed sideways into the kitchen, where I find Jim Deacon pouring drinks for a gaggle of sophomore girls. Someone runs into me, and I stumble into Jim's side, my shoulder slamming into his face.

"Jesus Christ, man!" he barks, clasping his hand over his left eye. The sophomore girls are now covered in spilled drinks. They make annoyed sounds and move away.

"Oh man, Jim, I'm so sorry," I say as I grab for an overturned bottle of vodka that's rolling toward the edge of the kitchen counter. I manage to snag it before it can go crashing to the floor.

"Shit," Jim says. Then he lets out an out-of-place laugh. "What the hell, man?"

"I was pushed," I say, lamely.

"Luke?" he says finally recognizing me. The left side of his face is bright red, and his eye will probably be swollen shut tomorrow morning. "Luke, man, it's good to see you!" he says, and he lets out another drunken laugh.

I grab a dishcloth from the kitchen counter and wrap up a handful of ice for his eye.

"I can't believe it," Jim says when I return. He tilts his head back and presses the ice to his face. He's shorter than I remember, which might explain how my shoulder ended up in his eye socket. He's laughing again. "I heard that you were back, and I've been meaning to look for you. But here you are, barging into my house and smacking me around."

"Hey, I said I was sorry. Besides, it's your fault for being so damned popular." I gesture around the crowded kitchen, and he nods. "But what were you saying?" I ask. "You were looking for me?"

We actually don't know each other all that well, so this is a bit of a surprise. I mean, we've grown up together, gone to all of the same schools, but he's been nonstop focused on sports and being popular, whereas I've just been trying to avoid running into bodies.

"Yeah," he says. "I've got something to show you. It's pretty cool, actually."

There are a handful of freshmen standing next to us, talking loudly and pouring shots of whiskey. Jim leans in close to me.

"C'mon," he says, "it's in my dad's old office"—then he raises his voice so that the freshmen can hear him—"away from these little snots, and the stink of their unbearable lameness!"

———

Jim's dad's office is on the second floor, and I don't see Mia on my way upstairs.

There's a chair set in front of the door, with a sloppily hand-written sign taped to it, reading, "Off-limits! No screwing in here!" Jim pushes the chair out of the way and we go inside.

The office is a wood-paneled room with bookcases on three sides and a desk facing a large window. There's a low coffee table in the middle of the room with three plush chairs arranged around it. The room looks like it's being taken apart. There are boxes scattered across the floor, and the bookcases are half-empty.

"My parents just got divorced, right?" Jim explains. "So I've been packing stuff up for my dad. My mom didn't even want to look in here, so she's having me do it."

He plops down in one of the leather chairs and leans his head back. He's still got the dishcloth pressed against his face, but most of the ice has already melted, wetting his shirt collar. After a moment, he sets the dishcloth on the floor.

"Anyway," he continues, "while I was going through his old stuff, I found all of these books of news clippings." He picks up a stack of three thick binders and sets them on the table. "My grandmother was a historian, right? She used to work in the University of California system, moving from campus to campus, overseeing a lot of projects. Her focus was on California history, and she had a special interest in Colma—she was absolutely nuts about the subject. She spent decades researching the town, and this is some of her work."

I make my way to the table and flip back the cover of the first binder. The book is thick with photocopies of news clippings, and I crouch down and start flipping through its pages.

"It goes all the way back to the start of Colma," Jim says. "There's a lot about the six founding families in there, including the Cressmans."

"My family?" I say. I continue flipping through the book.

Jim gets out of his chair and settles down at my side. "Yeah. My grandmother died a couple of months back," he says. "On her deathbed, she made us promise to give all of her research to the library—over twenty boxes, locked up in her house! I'm going to have to cart it over soon. Apparently, they're planning on featuring it in a town history display."

I flip back to the first page of the first book. The news clippings here are from March 1900, when San Francisco first outlawed building any new cemeteries within city limits and people in the death industry started looking elsewhere. The north end of the San Francisco peninsula, the area that would later be incorporated as Colma, was mentioned as a possible destination.

I flip to the second page, then the third. Mrs. Deacon's book skips to 1912, when the law that shut down all of the existing cemeteries in San Francisco finally went into effect. This is when all of the dead were exhumed and moved out of the city.

"That's Ordinance 49B," Jim says, looking over my shoulder. Then he taps his finger on the next page. "Check it out."

He's pointing to an article reporting that Colma is opening its gates to more cemeteries, and that the small town government has ratified its *own* Ordinance 49B, which assures that if San Francisco does indeed move their dead to Colma, the land will remain untouched, in perpetuity. Families will never again have to worry about cities or towns messing around with the remains of their dearly departed. *Colma will be their final resting place,* an official spokesman proclaims. *Forever and ever. Encoded in law.*

Suddenly, as we're reading, the door starts to rattle behind us. "God, you're so damn hot," a voice murmurs out in the hallway, and the door swings open.

Two juniors start backing their way into the room. They're pawing at each other drunkenly. The girl has long red hair and alabaster skin and is much more attractive than her pimple-faced basketball player companion. But he's varsity, and a starter, so maybe it all balances out.

"Jesus, can't you guys read the sign?" Jim barks, and the couple pulls apart, still sober enough to be a little bit embarrassed.

"Try the pool house," he continues, shaking his head. "But don't stain the upholstery. And for God's sake, use a condom!"

The girl giggles and the basketball player grabs her hand and leads her back out into the hallway. She flips us an embarrassed wave as the door closes behind them.

Jim grunts, then turns his attention back to the book. "Let me see it," he says, and he flips the pages almost all the way to the center of the binder.

"Ah, here it is," he says, and he points to a name circled in yellow highlighter. "Look familiar?"

The name reads *Aaron Louis Cressman*.

My great-great-grandfather.

The article is from October 1917. Just over a hundred years ago. The headline reads, "Heroic Colma Councilman Saves Trolley Passengers."

> More than a dozen people, including six women and children, were saved from sure disaster by the daring, heroic efforts of Colma Councilman Aaron Louis Cressman. Mr. Cressman was walking down Lawndale Boulevard when he spotted a trolley car in danger of hitting a horse-drawn Fresno scraper stopped in its path. Jules McNulty, conductor, noticed the equipment too late, and would have been unable to bring the trolley to a halt in time to avoid the imminent collision. Cressman "came out of nowhere," the conductor reports, and managed to move the construction machinery off the trolley tracks before disaster could strike. According to Mr. McNulty, the trolley would have likely been laid on its side if the collision had occurred, and all of the passengers might well have perished. Councilman Cressman dismissed his actions as simply what any reasonable man would have done if faced with a similar situation, but he is actually no stranger to averted tragedy. Less than one year ago, he happened upon the struggles of a boy drowning in Colma Creek and managed to pull him from the clutches of death. In the view of our editorial department, it would seem that the people of Colma are indeed lucky to have such a man in their ranks.

As I'm reading, my heart starts to race, and the room starts to spin around me.

"Have you heard about this?" Jim asks.

I read the article through one more time before I respond. "No," I say, shaking my head.

"I have," Jim says. "No one knows for sure, but my dad thinks that my great-great-grandfather and his wife were on that trolley. Which means"—Jim gives me a curious smile—"if your great-great-grandfather hadn't been there, in just the right place, at just the right time, and done that, I never would have been born. My whole family would never have even, you know, *happened.*" He lets out a carefree laugh. "That's crazy, right?"

"Yeah, crazy," I agree, but I'm barely aware of what I'm saying. My mind is racing, full of questions.

Did my great-great-grandfather know that the trolley disaster was coming before it happened? Did he know that that boy would be drowning in the creek?

It seems likely.

My dad had told me over and over again that we couldn't intervene, that toying with the universe would have disastrous consequences. He said that no Cressman was supposed to change fate, that it would be incredibly dangerous if we ever did.

Was that all just a lie?

I look up from the photocopied article into Jim's smiling face.

Jim sitting here, smiling at me—this is proof! Proof that my great-great-grandfather *had* intervened. At least once. And Jim's entire family is here today because of his actions.

"I guess my family owes yours big-time," Jim says.

By the time I make it back downstairs, the Skrillex has been replaced with a less intense house mix.

Standing against the wall in the kitchen, I close my eyes and try to slow my heart to the beat of the music. I can still hear the sound of my dad's voice on the last night of his life—chastising me, resigned to his fate—and my chest tightens with intense anger. He had believed, unquestioningly. He had taken his father's and grandfather's rules as gospel, but maybe I could have saved him, if he'd let me. If I hadn't let him stop me.

Then he'd be alive today, and Darla and I wouldn't be orphans.

I could have—

A hand touches my cheek. I open my eyes and see Erin's flushed face smiling at me. "Where were you, space cadet Luke?" she asks with a sly smile. "You were totally zoned out just now."

Before I can answer, she finishes off her beer and digs a new one from a cooler against the wall. Her face is red and her eyes are swimming. She's already tipsy, if not totally drunk.

She touches my cheek again, and suddenly I see her death. This isn't the first time I've seen it, so the experience isn't all that intense. She's behind the wheel of a self-driving car. She's reading something on a futuristic, paper-thin iPad, not paying attention, when the car spins out of control. Her death is quick at least. Crushed against the steering wheel, she doesn't linger.

"I think she's a lesbian," Erin says.

"What?" This jerks me back into the present.

"Your new friend? That Iverson chick? She's in the living room, dancing with Sonja Thompson. They seem pretty chummy at the moment." Then she grabs my hand and smiles up at me—a sweet, pretty little smile. "Why don't you come outside with—"

I don't hear the rest of her question because I'm already moving toward the living room, where kids are dancing in the low-lit space.

I see Mia in the middle of the room. She's dancing super close with Sonja, a pale-skinned brunette from our class. Sonja has long hair and freckles, and she's openly bisexual. Mia's wearing a leather jacket over a long T-shirt dress and a tight pair of leggings. Her boots are the same clunky ones that she had on yesterday.

Mia's face is flushed from dancing, and her eyes are closed. She seems lost in the moment. I watch as her hips grind against Sonja for a long minute. I'm both turned on and incredibly jealous.

I'm also pretty damned embarrassed.

It's not like I care if Mia's bisexual—people like who they like—but if Erin's right, if she actually is a lesbian, with absolutely no interest in guys, then I *totally* misread the situation the other night and I never had a chance. Maybe that's why she texted me tonight, why she wanted me to come to the party: to tell me, to let me down easy.

Mia reaches for Sonja's ass, and I'm just about to turn away—I should go home, get away from all of these people so I can mope in peace and quiet—when I notice Mia's fingers slipping into Sonja's back pocket. She slides Sonja's phone into the palm of her hand and quickly transfers it to the inner pocket of her leather jacket in one smooth motion. She integrates this move into her grinding, so Sonja doesn't even notice that it's gone.

I'm in disbelief for nearly half a song, not quite sure if I actually saw what I think I saw: Mia stealing Sonja's phone. Did that just happen?

It did. And she did it with such ease. Like a professional pickpocket.

She must have stolen my phone, too. *But then why did she give it back?* And just to make sure, I touch my pocket to confirm that my phone's actually still there. It is.

Is this how she makes spending money—stealing people's stuff and pawning it on the side? Then I remember Amy's sketchbook. Amy said that she'd had a class with Mia and then suddenly her sketchbook was gone. But what the hell would Mia want with a used sketchbook? Not a lot of resale value there. It's all just personal stuff.

Unless … unless she's stealing it for her mom, to help her with those phony psychic readings.

A coal of anger starts to burn in the pit of my stomach.

Mia leans in and kisses Sonja on the cheek. She whispers something into her ear, then slips off the dance floor, leaving Sonja looking confused and frustrated. I follow Mia through the crowded kitchen and out into the backyard.

It's quieter out here. There are only a handful of kids—some making out, others lost in intense conversation.

"Mia," I say, and she turns, pausing with her lighter raised halfway to an unlit cigarette.

She smiles. "Luke! You made it!" She finishes lighting up. "I'm glad you came."

I want to confront her, but her smile freezes me before I can even begin. I look down. "I saw you," I finally manage. "I saw you—"

But before I can get the words out, the sliding door crashes open behind us, and at least a dozen sophomores come streaming out onto the lawn, laughing and talking loudly.

I can hear Jim Deacon yelling behind them: "If you're going to be puking, do it out there, not in my mom's fucking china hutch!"

One of the sophomore boys tackles another, and they both crash down onto the lawn, laughing loudly.

Mia catches my eye and smirks.

"C'mon," I say, and before she can say no, I grab her hand and start pulling her up toward the street.

Mia comes along willingly.

———

There's been a gap in the fence around Hills of Eternity for years now. I lead Mia to the opening. She slides through without a problem, but I have to suck in my breath and wriggle back and forth in order to get inside. It's a much tighter fit than when I was twelve, that's for sure.

We trot down a grassy hill and into the main part of the cemetery. This area is enveloped in fog, and it feels like we're stepping into the heart of a cloud.

Hills of Eternity is beautiful. The grass is always green, and the gravestones are always well maintained. Families of those buried here pay a *lot* for this pristine beauty. If my family wanted to provide this type of care, we'd have to hire at least three more full-time workers, and that thought depresses me.

"Where are we going?" Mia asks.

"It's just up here." I figure that out here, we'll be able to talk—

if I can figure out a way to bring up what I saw without offending her, that is.

The cemetery lights are haloed in fog, and the trees cast sharp shadows. I turn and lead Mia into a small clearing, where I point her toward a specific grave.

"Wyatt Earp," she says, reading aloud. "No freaking way!"

"Yep. The legendary Wyatt Earp himself—cowboy, gunfighter, sheriff—right here, in the decayed flesh and bones." He's buried next to his wife, under a classy-looking tombstone and monument.

"That's pretty cool. History come to life." Then she pauses. "Or come to death, really. Who else is buried here?"

"At Hills of Eternity?"

"In Colma."

"Well, there's Joe DiMaggio, there's the guy who started Levi Strauss, there's William Randolph Hearst."

"You'll have to take me on a tour sometime. You can show me all of the local celebrities."

I nod. "So …," I begin, trying to gather up my courage. "I saw you take Sonja's phone."

"What?" She acts surprised.

"I *saw* you do it. While you were dancing. It's in your pocket right now."

She doesn't respond. She just bends down and touches Wyatt Earp's headstone, her face turned away from me.

"I think you took my phone, too," I continue. "And maybe Amy's sketchbook. I don't know why. And I don't know why you gave me my phone back."

She stands up, angry. "Fuck you, that's why." And she starts to stride away.

"Wait, Mia, it's not like that," I call after her, pleading. "I'm not going to tell anyone. I just want to know why. Is it a money thing? Or, like, a compulsion? Are you doing it for your mom?"

She stops and turns her pale eyes back toward me.

"Fine," she says. "I'll tell you. But you have to promise to keep everything to yourself. I don't want to hear any rumors about the new klepto freak that just moved into town. That's about the *last* thing I need."

"Your secret's safe with me," I promise. "So, why do you steal people's stuff?"

"It's just that … I want to know people, really *know* them." She takes a deep breath, gathers her strength, and plunges on. "Everyone has all of these walls built up around them. They tell lies and create fabulous stories about themselves, but in the end it's all meaningless. I want to see the actual person behind all of that, the naked, broken soul hiding behind all of that fluff." She pauses for a moment, looking for the right words. I can tell that she's trying to say something that's truly important to her.

"We all like to act like we have everything under control," she explains, "but we really don't. We tell lies on Instagram and Snapchat, sharing photos of us smiling at parties and laughing with friends, but it's all fake. Real life just isn't like that. It isn't an endless string of happy, smiling people; it's actually a weird, complicated, *beautiful* mess. And that's what I'm looking for; that's what you can find in people's phones: the pictures they'd never post, the heartbreaking texts, the late-night browsing histories. And you should see some of the shit in Amy's notebook! Horrible things and stunning things, sketched out in charcoal and ink. That's the kind of thing I'm looking for, the kind of thing I'm trying to steal: the truth. The raw, magical truth."

I'm left totally speechless. She's given me such an honest answer that I don't know how to respond.

She stares at me for a while, searching my face. Then, seeing a change in my expression, she nods. "Okay. Now it's your turn," she says.

"My turn for what?"

"To answer one of my questions."

"Okay," I say, trying not to sound too anxious. "I'll try."

"Why were you and your dad so close?" she asks.

"What?"

"I know he's dead, but while he was alive you texted him all the time. I've never seen anything like it. Most of the time, if I get someone's phone, I'll see an occasional text to their parents. It's mostly stuff like checking in, and saying why they're going to be home late. That's how I am with my mom. But you guys had actual conversations, almost every single day. I could barely understand any of it. It's like you guys had your own secret language."

My stomach drops. "So you were able to break into my phone."

She hesitates for a second, then nods. But she doesn't look ashamed or embarrassed. "I use a hacking program to guess passwords. You put in as much information about the person as you can—name, birthday, birth city, favorite band and sports team, that kind of thing—and it runs through all of the variations of that info. You used the address of your father's cemetery."

"I'll have to change that."

She nods but doesn't say anything. She's still waiting for my answer.

"I don't know why we were so close," I finally say. "My mom died when I was born, and my dad had to raise me on his own. Maybe he treated me more like a friend than a son." I can't tell her the real truth: that we bonded over our superpowers.

"Well, it makes you seem much more *real*," Mia says. "You're perhaps the realest person in Colma. With your dad, you didn't do any of that fake shit. You just treated each other like human beings. And that's pretty amazing."

I blush.

"I'm sorry he's dead," Mia adds.

"Yeah." *I'm sorry I didn't save him.*

She sees me getting sad and steps up close, putting her palm against my chest. "And I'm sorry I stopped you from kissing me yesterday," she continues. "I … I just couldn't. I was feeling guilty for taking your phone. But still, I was glad that I *had* stolen it, you know? And that made me feel even guiltier … if that makes sense."

"You have way too many feelings," I say.

And this time, she's the one who leans in to kiss me.

For a moment, I consider pushing her away and darting off, just like she did to me, and the ridiculousness of this thought almost makes me laugh. But then I catch her scent—rose perfume over sweat and leather—and suddenly I'm not thinking about *anything* anymore.

Her hand moves to the side of my face and her lips touch mine. I hold her shoulders and pull her in close, wanting to feel her entire body pressed up against mine, wanting to feel her heat. My heart racing, I—

The darkness is sudden.

No! Not now. Not her!

And a small pinprick of light grows larger in my mind's eye. I'm looking into a small space that's lit only by a single flickering flame. Mia's hand moves suddenly and her lighter gutters out, plunging everything into darkness. There's the scraping sound of her lighter's flint wheel spinning, and the flame returns.

In my vision, Mia's hand is shaking. Her breath is quick and shallow. She lets out a low keening sound, somewhere between a whisper and a sob.

There are satin-covered surfaces on every side of her body, just inches away from her shoulders, her chest, and her feet. She is in some kind of box—a coffin!

The satin in front of her face is torn, revealing the hard wood hidden underneath. She starts scratching at it and pounding. The sound is solid. There is no echo.

She's underground, buried alive.

The flame drifts closer to her face, and I can see that she still looks young. She can't be much older than she is right now.

"Don't do this!" she calls out, her voice hoarse. I'm not sure, but it sounds like she's been yelling for a long time. "Let me out! Let me out! Please, for the love of God, let … me … out.…"

Then her voice fails, and her breath hitches. I watch as her eyelids flutter shut.

The last thing I see is her hand falling, suddenly weak, down to her side.

Then the lighter flickers out, and there's nothing but darkness. And silence.

"Luke?"

Mia is staring at me, looking concerned and confused. I realize that I've stumbled back, away from her kiss, away from my vision of her death.

I'm back in Hills of Eternity.

"What is it? What's wrong?" she asks.

You're going to die. Soon. Horribly. Buried alive. But of course, I don't say any of this.

You can't *say any of this,* I hear my dad's voice say, echoing in the back of my skull. *We can't go messing around with other people's fates.*

"Luke?"

"I … I'm sorry," I say. "I got dizzy. I think the beer's finally hitting me, and I haven't had much to eat today."

She laughs. "You say that, but I think you're lying. I'm just an incredible kisser. I damn well took your breath away."

I force a smile. "That might be the case," I manage, taking a deep breath. "You're very talented."

Before she can respond, a loud, mechanical roar fills the night. I hear laughter toward the cemetery's front gate. Then there's a drunken holler and a loud crash.

"What's going on?" Mia asks.

"I think that was the front gate falling over," I say. "C'mon!" I grab Mia's hand and pull her away from Wyatt Earp's burial plot.

We duck behind a row of trees and peer out across the cemetery's main thoroughfare. Clumps of motorcycles roar past, braking erratically and fishtailing through the well-manicured grass, leaving behind giant clumps of torn-up dirt. I watch a motorcycle skid sideways toward a headstone. The rider lifts his foot and knocks the stone over, leaving a trench of upturned dirt in its wake. Other riders try to do the same thing, and pretty soon there are at least a dozen uprooted gravestones and three or four banged-up bikes.

Several of the bikers are on the ground laughing. They remind me of the drunk and stupid sophomore boys Mia and I had left behind at the party.

"Let's get out of here," Mia whispers. She sounds concerned but also a little excited. I nod and lead her back toward the gap in the fence. Luckily, the bikers are still on Hills of Eternity's main path, and we make it back out to the road without being spotted.

As soon as we're outside, I hear a loud female voice echoing through the fog behind us. Whoever this woman is, she sounds joyful. "Gear up, boys! We've got places to go, more dead people to meet!"

We jog back to Jim Deacon's house. The motorcycles in the cemetery are starting to rev up just as we turn into the driveway and slow down.

There are a lot of kids out on Jim's porch, and a lot more on his front lawn. They are staring out toward the sound, all looking confused.

"What's going on?" somebody asks.

"It's the bikers," someone else answers. "They're ruining this town."

There's another rattle and crash—it sounds like more of the fence coming down. Then the motorcycles start to stream past the driveway, one by one. I count sixteen of them in all. The last one veers onto Jim's lawn, and the driver lets out a savage war cry. Kids dive out of the way as the biker sends a beer bottle crashing through Jim's front window. I can hear the driver laughing as he speeds away, the lights on his motorcycle disappearing into the fog.

There's an extended moment of silence, and then a loud "Are you shitting me?" as Jim Deacon sticks his head out of the shattered window. "What the fuck happened here?"

A couple of the kids on the lawn laugh, but everyone else stays silent, too stunned to say a word.

Then a phone rings behind me.

"Slow down, Dad. Tell me what happened."

I turn around and find Amy on her phone. Erin and Heroji are at her side. Erin gives me a cold look, then turns away, grabbing Heroji's hand and pulling him toward the house. I guess I deserve that. She was being affectionate with me and I ran away to check on Mia. She probably hates me now.

"What? Yeah," Amy continues, a serious look on her face. "They got Hills of Eternity, too. I'll come home. I'll be there in fifteen minutes."

"What happened?" I ask.

Amy glances up from her phone. "The bikers tore up the lawn of our cemetery. And my dad drove down to Holy Cross—their beautiful wrought iron fence is leveled flat."

"Damn," I say. "If they're hitting cemeteries ..." Mia's now standing at my side, her forehead scrunched up with concern. When I look over at her, I can't help but remember the fear that

I saw on her face in my vision, the fear of suffocating underground, dying in a far-too-early grave.

I turn away. I can't look at her. I don't have time to face this yet.

"What's going on?" she asks.

"I have to go," I say. "I have to check up on our place. If the bikers are trashing cemeteries ..."

"Do you want me to come along?" she asks.

"No. I should go alone. I don't know what it's going to be like when I get there."

I start to walk away and Mia grabs my hand. I pull back, suddenly terrified to be touching her.

"I'll see you later," I say. Then I start to run, heading blindly toward my dad's car.

———

Uncle Roy is standing in the driveway when I get home. He's on his phone.

"Yes, I know," he says, sounding frustrated. "Fine. Fine. I'll be here." And he hangs up.

"The bikers?" I ask.

"Yeah. They spun donuts up and down A5. They took off as soon as I got outside." Then he gives me a curious look. "How did you know?"

"They hit Hills of Eternity, too—we could hear them from the party. They messed up some of the other cemeteries as well."

"Great," Uncle Roy says, steaming with frustration. "I guess that's why the cops are so busy. They say they won't be able to stop by until tomorrow." He looks angrily at his phone. "The local police here are worthless," he says, "absolutely worthless."

Darla emerges from the grounds, a flashlight swinging from her hand. "It doesn't look too bad, actually," she says. There is no hint of surly teenager in her voice, just calm, kind Darla.

Roy grabs the flashlight out of her hand and speeds off toward A5. Darla and I follow.

There are twirls of dirt cut through the grass lane, stretching almost all of the way from one end of the cemetery to the other. I survey the damage, then turn toward Roy. "Darla's right. It's not that bad," I say. "They crashed through the gate at Hills of Eternity and managed to knock over a bunch of tombstones. It could have been a *lot* worse."

"Yeah, I guess so," Roy says, starting to sound a little bit calmer now. "We'll have to buy some new sod, spend some time tearing up the old grass and replacing it. You kids will help, right? You'll come home right after school tomorrow? We should be able to do it ourselves."

"Of course," I say, and Darla nods in agreement. It seems like she's placed her whole "teen angst" thing on pause for the time being.

"This is just about the last thing we needed," Roy says. "A great 'how do you do?' on your first week back to school." He offers us a tiny smile. "Hell, why don't we go back to the house and get some ice cream. This crap practically demands a boatload of sugar."

Darla and I both nod, and we all head back toward the house.

Just as we're about to reach the driveway, Darla pauses and takes the flashlight from Roy's hand. "There's one more thing," she says.

"It's pretty minor, though. A bit of scrubbing should clean it right off."

She lifts the beam and lights up the front of one of our biggest mausoleums. There's fresh graffiti scrawled across the gray granite, red lines forming surprisingly graceful capital letters: FROM BAD 2 WORSE.

What does this mean? Is it a threat? Are the bikers saying that things are going to get worse for us?

And then my heart drops, as I suddenly remember my vision of Mia's death.

The adrenaline of the bikers' interruption had pushed it out of my mind, but now that it's calmer, the horrible vision comes flooding back in. I can see it and hear it: the panic in Mia's voice as she fights for air. "Don't do this," she pleads. "For the love of God." Then everything falling dark.

From bad to worse?

How could things get any worse than that?

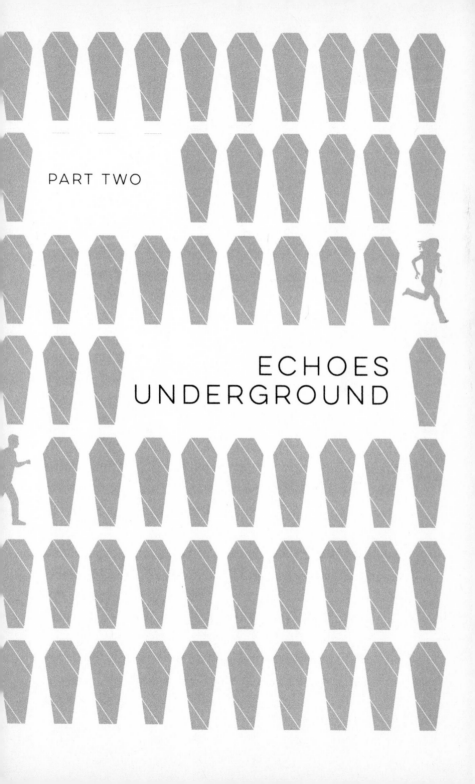

PART TWO

ECHOES
UNDERGROUND

6 I avoid Mia all of Friday.

I *want* to see her, I can't stop thinking about her, but it's no longer giddy thoughts filled with wonder. Instead they are dark and horrifying.

She texted me on Thursday night, right after she got home from the party, and asked me if everything was okay. I filled her in on the damage to the cemetery, but I kept it brief. I just didn't know what to say to her.

How do you flirt and joke and talk about schoolwork when you know that you're talking to somebody without a future? You might as well be whispering into a bottomless pit.

That's why I transferred to the school in Portland last year. Because I couldn't bear interacting with my dad when all I could see was that one horrible vision.

My dad falling off a ladder.

Mia suffocating in a coffin.

I should just run away again—just turn around, apologize to Roy and Darla, and head right back up to Portland. But that hadn't turned out so well for me the first time around. After my dad's death, I regretted all of that missed time, all of the months of bonding that I'd thrown away—all because I was scared.

But that's not my greatest regret. My greatest regret is not saving him.

And *that* is my big problem. A new choice, but painfully familiar.

Do I try to save Mia, or do I let her die? Do I follow my dad's teachings, or do I venture out into the unknown?

I have no idea.

———

Uncle Roy has Darla and me stop by Gael's dad's store after school.

He's already called in a special order of sod, and we fill the trunk of my dad's car with as many rolls as we can fit. Then bags of fertilizer, a pair of shovels, and a bin of extra-large zip ties go into the backseat.

When we get back to the house, Roy is waiting for us in the driveway. He's got on his wool cap, his thick pants, and his long-sleeved jacket, and all of it is already drenched in sweat.

"What took you guys so long?" he says, smiling from beneath the bill of his cap. "C'mon, c'mon, c'mon! We're losing daylight here."

Darla flashes me an already exhausted eye-roll, and I stifle a laugh. It looks like surly Darla has resurfaced. It's just good to know that helpful Darla is still hidden away somewhere inside that eye-rolling skull of hers.

I grab a wheelbarrow and help Roy drag the first roll of sod out to A5. He's already cleared out rectangular patches of damaged grass, leaving muddy beds for the new turf. When we get the sod down, he widens the space to a better fit. Then Darla shovels out a coat of fertilizer, and Roy and I finish rolling out the new grass.

Once we're done with the first roll, Roy takes a step back. He puts his hands on his hips and admires our work for a handful of seconds, satisfied.

"Just forty more to go," he says.

Both Darla and I let out loud groans. It's going to be an exhausting afternoon and evening.

———

My arms are already sore by the time I wrestle the fifth roll of sod from the wheelbarrow. Darla's gone back to the store to get the second load of sod, and I collapse to the lawn while Roy works on resizing the most recent bed of soil.

"Oh," Roy says, suddenly lowering his trowel and sitting up straighter. "I forgot to tell you, but Mrs. Rosen passed away yesterday. It sounds like she went peacefully, in her sleep."

Not really. The way I saw it, her death had looked pretty horrific.

"That's too bad," I say. "I just talked to her."

"Yeah. I didn't know her all that well, but she seemed like a very nice lady."

"She was," I say with a nod. Then, trying to sound nonchalant: "Where are they going to bury her?"

"It sounds like her family's going to go with Olivet."

"What?" I ask, surprised. "You called them, right? Invited them over? Why didn't they go with us?"

"Yeah, I called, but ..." Roy pauses for a moment, giving me an odd look. "We shouldn't be doing that, Luke," he says, his voice turning a bit cold. "We shouldn't be taking advantage of what we see coming."

"What do you mean?"

What we see coming? What exactly does Roy know?

"You had me invite the Rosens over," Roy says. "I assume that when you ran into her at the store, you saw that Mrs. Rosen was frail, that she was sick, and you wanted to take advantage of that. You were hoping to drum up business, right?" He shakes his head and looks away from me, a hint of disappointment in his eyes. "That's not right, Luke. We're in the death business, yes, but death shouldn't be about business. It's bigger than that—I learned that in Iraq. Death is something ... *profound*." It takes him a moment to find this final word, but when he does, he seems satisfied.

"Yeah," I say. "You're right."

And he *is* right. My dad used to do something like what I tried to do, but he'd always been much more subtle about it, and much more humane. When he saw that someone's time was almost up, it was more like he was offering comfort to the soon-to-be-grieving rather than just grabbing for their cash. He let families know, subtly, that we were here for them, that it was our job to help people get through horrible times. And he'd do it with compassion and an understanding of what loss was like.

Hell, maybe it was never about business for him. Maybe it was all about doing something good.

If I'm going to use my abilities to help out the cemetery, I decide, I'm going to have to learn from his example.

We hear the distinctive sound of a car turning from the country road onto our driveway, and from the low purr of the engine, it's pretty obvious that it's not Darla driving Roy's truck. We both stand up, and Roy shucks his work gloves off his hands. I look him up and down: he's a sweaty, dirty mess.

"If it's customers, maybe I should take the lead," I offer. I'm not exactly in great shape myself, but at least I don't look like a dirt-encrusted hobo.

We make our way back toward the driveway and watch as a sporty light-blue Tesla pulls to a stop at the edge of the turn-around. A tall woman in an immaculate gray suit gets out of the driver's seat. She's wearing dark sunglasses and has short blonde hair. When she sees us, the woman takes off her glasses, smiles, and heads our way.

"Shit," Roy mumbles beneath his breath. "She buried her teen-age daughter here last March, while you were still up in Portland, but I'm totally blanking on her name right now."

"I've got this," I whisper. Then I step forward and introduce myself. "I'd shake your hand, but …" And I hold up my dirty palms. At least I won't have to risk any new death visions today.

The woman gives me a warm smile. "It's nice to meet you, Mr. Cressman. My name's Cora Bell."

"Ms. Bell!" Roy exclaims, happy for the reminder. "I should warn you that we suffered a little bit of vandalism last night. But I believe your daughter's part of the cemetery was completely untouched."

"Vandalism. That's horrible." Then she shakes her head. "I'm planning on visiting with my daughter, but that's not the sole reason for my visit."

She goes back to her car, grabs a thin folder from the passenger seat, and returns. "Usually, I'd have my business people deliver something like this, but your family's been so good to me this last year. Your brother, *your father*—" She turns from Roy to me, her voice cracking. "Anyway, I felt like I should give this to you in person. It's an offer. From my company, Coriolis Solutions. We're looking for land in the Colma area, and your property fits all of our needs." She hands the folder to Roy, and I can see that it has CRESSMAN printed in all capitals on its cover.

"We're not interested in selling the cemetery," I say, not even stopping to think about it.

"I understand your reluctance," she says. "Your family's had this business—and this property—for generations now, and I can appreciate how meaningful that is." Then she turns to Uncle Roy and fixes him with soulful eyes. "But lord knows times are tough right now, and my offer—right there, on the first page of that document—is good, better than market value, I believe."

Roy turns the folder over in his hands. He opens it briefly, looks at the first page, and his eyes go wide. "Ms. Bell, I appreciate you coming out here to hand-deliver this offer, but this … this is a big decision for us. It's something we're going to have to sit with for a while and talk about." He shoots a questioning look my way.

I shake my head, feeling sick at the thought.

"I understand," she says. "Read it, hold on to it, and think about it for a while. It's a standing offer." She smiles and gives Uncle Roy a conspiratorial look. "And if you think those terms are unfair—too low, maybe—feel free to make me a counteroffer. I have a reputation for being generous. My business card is in the folder."

Uncle Roy gives her a serious nod.

Then Cora Bell goes back to her car, leans inside, and picks up a bundle of beautiful, freshly cut lilies.

"And if it helps, I'd never do anything bad to your family's graves—I'd keep the main yard open." She lifts the bundle of flowers and gives us a melancholy smile. "After all, I've got my daughter to think about, too."

Then she turns and heads out into the grounds.

———

Roy refuses to talk about the offer until we finish working.

We make it through seventeen rolls of turf before we finally call it a day, and at this point, the sun is down and we can barely see what we're doing. Darla and I agree to get up early tomorrow morning so we can finish fixing up the rest of the damage. It's going to be a *loooooong* Saturday.

By the time we get back to the house, Darla and I are exhausted, but Roy seems as energetic as ever. The physical work of running the cemetery has never been a problem for him. It's the business side, and dealing with people, that seems to wear him down.

Darla and I stand behind him as he sits down at the dining room table and flips back the cover of Ms. Bell's offer. He points to a highlighted number, and I can see that his finger is shaking. He's tempted.

And really, who could blame him? Seeing those numbers, even *I'm* tempted.

"Maybe we should do it," Darla says, in a low voice.

"No, no," I plead. "This is our family, Roy. It's what our dad worked for. It's what *your* dad worked for. And his dad. And *his* dad. Do you really want to trade that in for a check, just so these strangers can do whatever it is they're planning on doing—fencing in a little part of the grounds, bulldozing the rest, and putting up … what? An office building? Luxury condominiums?"

"We're not doing well, kids," Roy says plainly. "I just don't have your dad's business sense." He shrugs. "And if things don't pick up soon, we might go out of business anyway, and if that happens, we won't get anything close to what she's offering. We might get nothing at all!"

"I'll step up," I say. "Darla and I will help. We can make this work." Darla gives me a skeptical look.

Roy stares at me for a time, then looks back down at the big numbers on the offer sheet.

"Death shouldn't be about business, Uncle Roy! Remember? It's more *profound* than that?"

He chuckles, shakes his head, and runs a dirty palm down the length of his face. "God, I did say that, didn't I? Damn it, Luke," he grumbles. "Damn it all to hell."

I'm overcome with relief.

Roy smiles at me gently. "Easy come, easy go, right?" Then he stands up and shrugs. "I'll order a couple of pizzas, and we can watch a movie. Maybe one of the new James Bond flicks." For Roy, anything that came out after 2000 counts as new.

Darla lets out a sullen sigh. "I'm tired, Uncle Roy. I'm going to go crash in my room for a little while. I'll come down for pizza later."

Roy and I both know that *crash in my room* is Darla code for "log in to *World of Warcraft*."

"What about you, Luke? Are you going to keep me company?"

I nod. What else am I going to do? Talk to Mia? Warn her about her imminent death? Or maybe pack up my bags and run away?

Roy picks *Quantum of Solace*, and I don't object. Daniel Craig, so stoic and powerful. He'd know what to do in my situation, I'm sure. He'd save Mia, and damn the consequences, whatever they might be!

My whole body is tired, and my eyes drift shut not long after the movie's opening sequence.

Then there is the smell of freshly cut grass in the air.

And I open my eyes.

I'm in the cemetery, standing by A5. There are motorcycles sliding past, and smiling, bearded faces. But I can't hear them, just the whooshing sound of wind blowing through the trees.

Adrenaline courses through me, and I trip and fall over, landing at the feet of my parents' angels. Staring up, I see that the statues' hands are no longer held out in offering. Instead, they're covering up the angels' eyes, shielding them from the world.

My dad is here, dressed in his standard flannel shirt and dirty jeans, crouched down in front of my mom's grave.

"You saw it coming," he says. He's looking at my mom's gravestone, and for a moment I can't tell if he's talking to me, or her, or himself. "You saw it coming, didn't you?"

"I saw it coming," I say, remembering my vision of his death—the way that he hit the ground, the sound of his neck breaking. It was like a thick, wet branch snapping under pressure.

"Not all of it," he says. "We see so little, Luke. Our visions are just the first part. But death is bigger than that. It's so *profound*." I can't see his face, but I think I can hear a wicked smile in that final word. I try to imagine my dad's smile, but I can't. I haven't seen that face in so long.

Is that even possible? I've heard his voice in my head so many times, but his face? Is his face totally gone? Have I erased it from my memory?

"Should I tell you what I saw, Luke, when I first touched you, when I held you as a baby? Should I tell you how you're going to die?"

"No," I say, without hesitation. "I don't want to know."

He turns slightly toward me, and now I can see the side of his face. Just the side—no eyes, just the twitching of his lips as he smiles and starts to tell me that—

"No!" I try to yell again, but I can't find the words.

And then I'm gasping, suddenly awake.

I'm back on the living room sofa, in front of the blaring TV. There's an open pizza box on the coffee table in front of me.

"You should eat your pizza before it gets cold," Uncle Roy says, watching me from his armchair and smiling sympathetically.

He has bad dreams, too, I know. He's haunted by his own ghosts, his own demons.

I wonder if any of them look like my dad.

7

We finally finish fixing the bikers' damage early Saturday night.

"As good as new," Roy says, his hands on his hips, surveying our work.

Not quite. The new turf is greener than the rest of the grass, giving the lawn a checkerboard look. But it'll grow out soon. In a week or two, it'll all be a uniform color.

"I just hope the bikers don't come back," Darla says. "I don't want this to become a regular chore."

Roy frowns at the thought. "Maybe I'll look into better fencing," he says.

"Something with deadly, foot-long spikes," Darla suggests. "*Poisoned* spikes."

"And electricity," I add. "A *lot* of electricity."

"And feral wombats," Darla continues.

I think about it for a moment, but I'm too tired to come up with anything to top her wombats. So wombats it is.

Tonight, Roy's queuing up *Skyfall*, continuing on his James Bond marathon. I take a pass, grabbing some leftover pizza and heading up to my room. The day's work has helped keep me distracted, but as soon as I'm alone, an overwhelming wave of thoughts and images comes rushing in: Mia gasping to death in her coffin; my great-great-grandfather stopping a trolley car accident, fishing a drowning kid out of Colma Creek; Cora Bell in her fancy Tesla, smiling sympathetically and trying to buy up our land.

I collapse back into my bed and stare up at the ceiling.

Where do I start? What do I do?

According to the articles that Jim had showed me, my great-great-grandfather had used his visions to save lives. Obviously, the planet didn't spin off its axis, and the universe wasn't destroyed, but maybe there were other consequences. Maybe he paid a price of some kind—even if it was nothing as serious as what my dad had led me to expect.

My phone vibrates. It's Mia, texting me. Her profile picture shows her sticking her tongue out, with her right hand raised in a pair of old-school death-metal devil horns.

Even pulling that face, she looks gorgeous.

R u avoiding me??? didn't see you at all yesterday … been wondering.

No, I lie. It's so much easier to lie in a text. *Just working hard to help fix up the cemetery. tired. sorry I haven't been around.*

Thought I scared you off.

No, I reply. Then I lie there staring at my phone for a while, wondering how I can let her know that I'm still interested in her, despite how I've been acting. *You just … make me nervous, that's all. you're far too cool for me. I'm waiting for you to realize.*

Perfect, I think, smiling.

Bullshit, she types. *I'm not falling for any freakish modesty. I'm only cooler than you by, like, 10%. Maybe 20%. okay, maybe 30.*

Talk about freakish modesty, I send.

And she responds with a smiley face.

I want to see you. tomorrow, she types.

I don't respond immediately; I'm not quite sure what I should do. I want to see her again, of course, but there's that whole short-timers thing to think about: the fear that she's dying soon, and that all of this is pointless, just me whispering into a bottomless pit.

I'm asking you out on a date, asshole, she texts. *This shouldn't be taking you so long.*

Yes, of course. I just … fainted there for a moment. happiness, you know … all of that shit. Butterflies and rainbows exploding in my head.

OK, maybe I'm cooler than you by at least 40% now. Maybe 50.

Just round it up, I say. *Make it an even 100.*

———

I'm still staring at my phone when Darla knocks on my door.

Mia wants me to meet her outside her family's shop at four tomorrow. When I ask her what she's got planned, I get nothing back but a smiley face and then radio silence.

I have no idea what to make of any of this.

"Luke?" Darla says. She knocks again, then opens the door.

"What?" I bark, ready to lay into her for invading my personal space. Then I see the look on her face. She looks worried—her arms are crossed in front of her chest and her forehead's scrunched up.

"Can I … can I get you to look at something for me?" Her voice is trembling.

"Sure."

This isn't sullen Darla or helpful Darla. This is worried Darla, and this Darla scares me.

I follow her back to her room. It looks like there's been a tiny, very localized tornado in here. All of her bookcases are empty, and her game guides and fantasy novels are scattered across the floor. Her clothes have been pulled from her closet and heaped on top of her bed. Even her backpack's been turned inside out.

"What happened?" I ask.

"I was looking for something," she says.

She heads to her desk, and I see that her heavy-duty gaming laptop has been knocked out of place. She sits down, adjusts its screen, and pulls up a window. I recognize the bright, cartoony colors almost immediately: *World of Warcraft*.

"This is about your game?" I ask, exasperated.

"Shut up," she says. She clicks on something and the whole screen fills with text. "So, anyway, there's this guy in my class, Tony Balint, who was bugging me in *Warcraft* for a while. He was always tagging along on raids and daily quests, constantly chatting at me, that type of thing. I let him join our guild, but it got to be too much; it was like every time I logged in, I'd get messages from him—just, like, nonstop. Anyway, it got so bad that we had to kick him out of the guild and block him."

"He's bullying you?" I ask.

Darla shakes her head. "No. Nothing like that. I mean, he's just this shrimpy little kid who has a crush on me, but he's too afraid to say anything at school. At first, I just felt sorry for him, but online he's got serious boundary issues. I think he might have Asperger's or something."

I nod. "So what did you want to show me?"

"Well, tonight it got weird. He created a new character and started chatting at me again. But before I could block him this time, he sent me these messages."

I read the highlighted text. Both messages are sent from a character named Vengefallorc.

> **Vengefallorc:** u should be impressed, Darla, you see I'm magic
>
> **Vengefallorc:** I always liked that white sweater on you, but yr wearing it inside out right now

I glance up and see Darla pointing to a label jutting out of the back of the sweater that she is, indeed, wearing inside out.

"The thing is," she says, "I wasn't wearing this today. I put it on after dinner. I haven't worn this sweater in weeks! And *never* inside out. I've been up here, door closed, ever since I put it on!"

"Then how—?"

"Exactly." And she sweeps her arm around the room. Her blinds are shut tight.

"I looked all over for spy gear," she says, "and I'm smart enough to tape over my computer's camera and microphone." *You've gotta be vigilant,* she'd explained, when she first told me about this precaution over a year ago.

How did this kid know what Darla was wearing? It's like a locked-room mystery, one without an immediate solution.

I'm suddenly overwhelmed with anger. "I'll talk to him," I say. "He'll tell us how he's been spying on you, and I'll force him to stop. Okay? I'll deal with this." I look down and see that my hands are clenched into fists.

Darla gives me a surprised look, like she didn't realize I had this much venom in me. Then she smiles. "I don't need you to protect me, Luke," she says. "Like I said, he's just a twerpy little kid. But still, he's so into me, I'm not sure if he's going to be able to take me seriously, so I was thinking you could be there as my backup when I confront him on Monday. You can hold me back if I end up trying to go all Leeroy Jenkins on his skinny little ass—like, if I just totally rage out on him, all berserker-style?"

"Okay," I say, relaxing my fists. "I can do that."

She nods and stares at me for a couple seconds, like she's picking me apart with her eyes. "And how about you try to wear something scary, okay? No sweater vests or floral prints. Maybe something leather, if you've got it. With studs. And chains."

"And feral wombats?" I finish.

She laughs, and I join in, happy to see my little sister relaxed and smiling again.

8

I know my uncle Roy is going to die of a stroke. He looks old in my vision—at least seventy-five—and I think he's in an assisted care facility when it happens.

I can't tell if he's a happy old man, or a sad old man.

There are photos of our family on the wall, but he's all alone, sitting on a sofa and watching TV, when it starts to hit. He grabs the back of his head, the left side of his face droops, and he sways back and forth for nearly a minute. Then he collapses to the floor.

And that's it. RIP Uncle Roy.

Cary Grant died of a stroke. So did Winston Churchill, Joseph Stalin, Richard Nixon, and L. Ron Hubbard. During an untreated stroke, the blood stops flowing properly inside the brain, cells die, and autonomic functions stop. It can happen quickly, or it can happen slowly.

I have no idea where I am when it happens to Uncle Roy. Am I still in Colma? Am I working at our family cemetery, growing old myself?

Am I a happy old man, or a sad old man?

And is Mia still dead in her coffin? Or have I somehow managed to save her?

I get to Other Worlds fifteen minutes early. I sit in the parking lot and watch customers going in and out through the shop's frosted glass doors. They look like regular people—some still in their Sunday morning church clothes. I wonder if Mia's mom's tarot card readings give them hope, maybe a sense of peace that their churches just can't provide.

At exactly four o'clock, Mia emerges from the store. She's wearing tight jeans, a long jacket, and bright red Converse. In place of a purse, she's got an army-green messenger bag slung across her back. She sees me get out of the car and a wide, infectious smile appears on her face.

She jogs toward me, and for a moment I think she's going to run into my arms. Then she stops short and gives me an awkward nod. I start to blush.

"You're on time," Mia says. "That's good. I like a punctual guy."

"I didn't want to keep you waiting," I say.

And she smiles again.

"So," she says, "since I'm still pretty new here, I was thinking you could show me the town—you know, from an insider's point of view?"

"There really isn't much to see."

"I'm sure you can think of something." She shrugs as if it's not a big deal. "It's like what I saw on your phone, right? I don't need anything super impressive, just something genuine. A glimpse into the *real* Colma, through the eyes of the *real* Luke Cressman."

I nod. After a second, I smile, coming up with an idea. "Okay," I say confidently.

We get into the car and I head north. Mia fools around with the car stereo, scrolling through radio stations. When she doesn't find anything that interests her, she connects her phone via Bluetooth and starts playing music. She pulls up an electronic dream-pop track, a slow jam featuring female vocals floating over a sea of synth. The name on the display reads *Elohim*.

"I saw her perform in San Francisco once," Mia says, a distant look in her eyes. "When I was on the floor in front of the stage, it was like I was moving through a dream. I imagine that's what heaven's like."

A *wave* of nausea rolls through my stomach. *You might find out if that's true soon enough.*

"Where are we going?" she asks as I turn onto Hoffman Street, just past Olivet Memorial Park. Something catches my eye, and I see Cora Bell's Tesla driving our way. She must be doing the rounds, making offers all over Colma.

"It's not far now. It's just … someplace I remember. From when I was a kid."

I head east, until all of the cookie-cutter suburban neighborhoods fall away and there's nothing but green bushes, scrub grass, and sunburnt land ahead. I park at the end of a narrow cul-de-sac.

"This is San Bruno Mountain," I say. "It's not much of a mountain, but it's one of the closest things Colma has to nature. The real trailheads, and the whole touristy park area, are on the San Francisco side. But anyway, c'mon." I get out of the car and gesture for her to follow.

When I was twelve, I knew this area like the back of my hand, but now everything seems strange and out of place. It takes a while, but I finally spot the trail I'm looking for—just a tiny cut in the hillside, zigzagging up toward San Bruno's hidden peak.

I flash Mia a smile and start running up the path.

"Hey, wait!" she calls. "I wasn't expecting mountain climbing today. I'm not exactly dressed for this!"

The path leads down one side of a small valley and up the other; then it gains elevation and dead-ends in a tiny stand of trees. There's a flat spot here that people use for picnics. I sit down on the western edge of the tiny plateau and wait for Mia to catch up.

"Me and my friend Gael used to mountain bike up here when we were kids," I say as soon as she appears. "There are at least a half dozen goldfish coffins buried under that tree over there." I point toward the other side of the clearing.

Mia smiles and hunches over, trying to catch her breath.

"Now, let's see … goldfish names. There was Goldie, Swimmy, Zeus, Neo, Fish Stick, Quakers, and Jeff. May they all rest in peace." I mime the sign of the cross.

Mia sits down at my side and peers out over Colma Valley. "You had a goldfish named Jeff?" she asks.

"Yeah, Jeff… He was a bit of a dick."

She laughs.

The sun is starting to set over Colma Valley, and the land beneath us is glowing in its bright orange light. We can see a golf course directly beneath us, then Olivet Memorial Park, Hills of Eternity Memorial Park, Salem Cemetery, and, just beyond that, downtown Colma. From where we're sitting, we can actually see a grand total of eight cemeteries.

It's a strange patchwork: the land of the dead looks so green and alive, while the land of the living is nothing but gray strip malls, roads, and drab suburban housing.

"They call Colma 'City of the Silent,' and 'City of Souls,'" I say. "Sometimes, when I'm working at the cemetery, I feel like I'm a slave serving my dead masters. There are just so many of them and so few of us."

Mia grunts. Her eyes are a bit wide, and there is a completely unselfconscious smile on her face as she stares out toward the town and the setting sun.

"That's not how I see it," she says. "The way I see it, I'm not a slave living in their world. Instead, it's like I won the freaking lottery. After all, I could be like them: dead, gone, nothing."

I nod, slowly, but she doesn't see it—she's still staring out over the valley.

I can't see much of my family's cemetery from where we are, but I can see a hint of green surrounded by gray, and it's a comforting sight. An office park or an apartment building in that place would be an absolute crime—sacred land turned into something ugly.

After maybe a minute, Mia's fingers brush against mine. She grasps my hand, squeezes it, and holds on tight.

"Thank you for sharing this with me, Luke," she says. "This is exactly what I wanted."

I take the long way back to downtown Colma, skirting east around the perimeter of town. We cross 101 near Oyster Point and head south along the shore of San Francisco Bay.

"C'mon," Mia says. "If you hurry up, I'll buy you dinner. You know, as thanks for showing me around."

She takes me to a Chinese restaurant across the parking lot from Other Worlds. We can see the shop's storefront from our booth in the window.

"Did the bikers do much damage to your cemetery?" she asks after we order our food. "Was it worse than Hills of Eternity?"

"It wasn't quite that bad," I say. "They didn't knock over any headstones, but they did rip up a lot of grass. My sister and I spent the last two days helping my uncle lay out new sod."

"You don't have maintenance people you can call in for that type of work?"

I smile. "You're looking at our 'maintenance people.' We're pretty small, and we could barely afford the materials." Mia nods sympathetically, so I keep going. "It's been pretty slow since my dad died. He was in charge of the business, so we're kinda having to figure things out as we go along."

"That sucks," Mia says, "but I'm sure you'll manage."

Our dumplings and fried rice arrive, followed by chow mein and cashew chicken. We eat in silence for a while.

"I went by your store on Thursday," I finally say as I grab a second helping of rice.

"Yeah. My mom told me." Mia concentrates on a dumpling as she talks, pinching it in her chopsticks and dipping it in soy sauce, all while avoiding my eyes. "What did you think of the place?"

"It's ... it's interesting," I say, not wanting to say anything bad. "And it was crowded."

"Yeah. My mom's actually pretty good at drumming up business. If you wanted some advice for your cemetery, you might want to consult with her." She shakes her head with a slight look of disgust. "For example, you could have a two-corpse-for-one special," she says. "Or maybe a half-depth discount: fifty percent off if your customers are willing to bury their loved ones three feet deep instead of six. Or stacked one on top of another."

I gather Mia's not totally on board with all of her mom's sales techniques.

"Your aunt does readings, too?" I ask, wanting to know more about her family situation.

"Yeah," she says, and smiles. "She does most of the 'premium-level' channeling—when she feels up to it, that is."

"I saw her at your store. She said … she said some interesting things to me." *Darkness drowns a hopeful light*—the words come back to me, floating on the gray-haired woman's voice.

Mia lets out a laugh. "Yeah. She tends to do that, tends to say *interesting* things. She's schizophrenic, and pretty detached from reality most of the time. She's a wonderful person deep down, but she gets … well, she gets confused." Mia glances out the window, back toward her family's storefront. "My mom's been taking care of her for most of her adult life now. She has to tend to her like she's a little child, comforting her when she's scared, holding her hand, making sure she does all of the things she needs to do in order to survive." Mia's eyes turn away from the window as she talks, drifting back down to her plate. "It's horrifying, really, seeing how fragile a person is, how easily everything about who you are can fall apart."

I don't know how to respond to this, so I just nod.

After a few seconds, Mia's face brightens up once again, and she smiles. She spoons a large helping of cashew chicken onto her plate.

"Anyway," she continues, "that's one of the reasons I decided to join my mom here in Colma: so I could help her out with my aunt and the family business. I figure it's about time for me to become a more responsible person, you know? My mom's got me working behind the front desk most afternoons now, scheduling tarot readings and séances, that kind of thing."

It's strange to imagine Mia sitting there behind the front desk of Other Worlds, surrounded by dream catchers and colored crystals. She seems far too cool for any of that stuff.

"Is it real?" I finally ask. "Do you believe in all of those things? Psychic phenomena? Contacting the dead?" *Seeing the future*, I want to add, *like ... oh, I don't know, seeing how people are going to die?*

"I believe ... ," she starts. Then she trails off. "I just ... there's a hell of a lot we don't know, and a hell of a lot we *can't* know." She shrugs. "I realize that that's not a great answer, but that's how I feel. Do with it what you will." And she gives me an apologetic smile.

Obviously, she expects me to disagree with her, but I can't. I know all about the inexplicable mysteries of the universe.

"And now, if you don't mind, I'm going to go use the bathroom." She heads toward an alcove at the back of the restaurant.

While she's gone, I reach for the last dumpling and manage to accidentally knock her messenger bag from the table to the floor. The top is unzipped, and—mixed in with a scatter of makeup, receipts, and other junk—a prescription pill bottle comes rolling out. I glance toward the back of the room to make sure Mia isn't coming back yet, then pick it up.

The prescription label says it's for an Adeline Kutik. Is Mia stealing prescription drugs? I already know that she steals phones and sketchbooks, but she said that that was for a noble purpose: getting to know people. This wouldn't fit her MO.

I don't recognize the drug—clozapine—but the bottle is half-empty.

Is this why she ends up dead in a coffin? Is it an act of retribution for stealing drugs from the wrong person, for going too far to get a fix?

No, no. Don't jump to any conclusions. Maybe this is for her mom. Maybe she's just holding on to it for her, or just picked it up from the pharmacy.

I see Mia emerge from the alcove at the back of the restaurant and scramble to push her things back into her bag.

"Are you ready to go?" she asks as she sits back down at our table. She's smiling, suddenly without a care in the world. "We can get them to split up the leftovers," she says. "And since you've been so very nice to me today, I'll even let you take the last dumpling."

———

I walk Mia across the parking lot to Other Worlds. The store is already closed, but I can see lights on in the upstairs windows. Mia digs through her messenger bag to find her keys, and when she finally gets the door unlocked, she turns toward me.

"Thanks, Luke," she says. "Colma seems real to me now. There are real people who live here, people who stand on mountaintops and think about their childhoods."

I nod, distracted. Maybe she doesn't actually use drugs. Maybe she just steals and resells them. Maybe she's going to get killed thanks to a drug deal gone wrong.

Her hand touches my arm, and I jerk back, startled. Mia laughs, and then leans in. As soon as I realize what she's doing, I lean forward and greet her lips with mine.

Our kiss feels more natural this time, and suddenly all of my thoughts and worries are gone. I feel myself melting against her body.

Kissing her feels so good, so comfortable. …

Then a familiar darkness blooms behind my eyelids, and I can feel my stomach start to drop.

And Mia's death fills my head again, in sharp, high-definition sound and color. The flame of her lighter highlights the horror on her face as she claws at her coffin, at the wood and satin on every side.

I try to keep my shit together and look for clues. I need to find out when and why and where this is happening.

I avoid the terror in Mia's eyes, instead trying to concentrate on all of the peripheral details of my vision. I catalog her clothing and jewelry: jeans, a black T-shirt, her Doc Martens, a pair of crescent moon–shaped earrings.

As I'm scanning the scene, the lighter in her hand trembles, goes out, and she strikes the flame again.

"Don't do this!" she cries, her voice ragged. "Let me out! Let me out! Please, for the love of God, let … me … out.…"

And I know I don't have long. Soon her light will go out, she'll stop breathing, and there'll be nothing but silence.

But wait—what's that?

I notice a spark of color that I hadn't noticed the first time I had this vision: a bright yellow band around Mia's right wrist. It's a stretchy plastic bracelet, the kind some large venues use as concert passes. This one has a design etched in black on one side: a star trapped inside a nest of jagged lines. It looks familiar, but I can't quite place it.

Then the flame flickers out, and I hear Mia breathe her last breath.

"I did it again, didn't I?" Mia says. And she laughs, the sound spiraling in, pushing aside my vision. "I took your breath away."

I'm back, staring down into Mia's pale eyes. She's standing in my arms, smiling up at me.

And I feel so very, very numb.

———

When I get home, I head straight for my computer.

Where do I start?

The first thing I do is look up "clozapine." The Wikipedia entry is very helpful: *an atypical antipsychotic medication ... mainly used for schizophrenia that does not improve following the use of other antipsychotic medications.* So, meds for schizophrenia. And when I'd visited Other Worlds on Thursday, Mia's mom had called her sister Lena. Which could be short for Adeline.

So Mia was just holding medication for her aunt. Or she'd just picked it up from the pharmacy. No big deal. Mystery solved.

Now I lean back in my chair, close my eyes, and try to remember the details of Mia's wristband. After a moment, it comes back to me: simple line art on a yellow background.

I do an image search for "star" and "jagged lines." When this doesn't turn up anything interesting, I add "bracelet," then "concert," then "California," then "San Francisco."

Still nothing but pictures of bird nests and random drawings.

Frustrated, I bring up a calendar of upcoming San Francisco–area events. I can go through the concerts one by one if I have to. But who's to say she's even in California when this happens? She could be anywhere. This could be a long and pointless exercise.

Thankfully, it only takes me five minutes to prove this fear wrong.

There's a listing for Florence and the Machine on the first page. Mia had called them one of her favorite bands, and according to the listing, they're playing an upcoming radio-station benefit at the Fillmore.

I go to the radio station's website, and the logo for the event is right there, center page: the star in the nest of lines.

Now I remember where I've seen this before. There's been advertising for this show all over Mission Hills High; it's in the entryway, taped up over the water fountains, outside every bathroom.

My stomach drops. The concert is this upcoming Friday.

Just five days away.

I scroll down the page. There's a big SOLD OUT banner over the ticket information. Then, farther down, there's a picture of a familiar yellow bracelet. A shiver runs down my spine as I look at it. It feels like I'm staring at a crime scene photo, and I can't help imagining the passage of time in Mia's coffin—this bracelet wrapped around her slender, lifeless wrist, then around decayed flesh, and then, finally, around naked bone.

I click on the picture and find myself at a charity auction site. Apparently, the yellow bracelets are all-access passes that take the wearer backstage to mingle and schmooze with the artists. There were only ten bracelets originally, but the auctions have all finished, and all ten sold for over five hundred dollars each.

How does Mia get one? She mentioned this concert when she stopped by our cemetery on Wednesday night. She'd said that she wanted to go, but that it was just too expensive—and that had been for a $45 general admission ticket, not a $500 super-special VIP pass.

So how does one end up on her wrist? Who gives it to her, and why?

I have absolutely no idea.

———

I have a hard time falling asleep after this.

I do the math in my head as I stare up at the ceiling. Five days is 120 hours. 7,200 minutes. 432,000 seconds.

All in all, that's not a lot of time.

Just the rest of Mia's life.

9

Darla and I walk to school on Monday morning. I'm a little bit groggy after tossing and turning all night long, thinking and dreaming about Mia, but Darla's energized and raring to go.

"The kid, Tony Balint, has a locker in the sophomore bay," she says. "I figure we just storm in like we own the place. We'll scatter everyone, send them flying, and I'll corner him. Balint's kind of short, so I'll lean in … and growl! I'll try to growl."

I nod and grunt.

"And I think I figured out how he was spying on me," she says, barely pausing to take a breath. "He must have been using the camera on my phone, watching me from where I set it down on my desk." She holds up her phone, and I can see that there are two new pieces of electrical tape covering up the cameras on the front and back. "I have no idea how he managed it, but that's the only way he could have seen what I was wearing Saturday night." She's clearly relieved. "Man, I feel so stupid. I never even thought about the cameras on my phone!"

Then she's quiet again as we near the school. We make our way across the street and into the parking lot.

"I wonder what else he saw," she finally says, muttering beneath her breath. I'm furious at the implications.

Gael's near the front door when we enter. He sees us and heads our way.

"Did you get the cemetery fixed up okay?" he asks.

"Yeah," I say. "It was a pain in the ass, but the grounds look good as new again."

"Freaking bikers," he grumbles. "I mean, what the hell are they doing *here*? Do they worship the dead or something?"

"Drugs," Darla answers, distracted. She's stopped next to us, but her eyes are moving from one end of the hallway to the other, looking for Tony Balint. "I hear that they're dealing meth up in San Francisco, and this is just a convenient place between the city and their suppliers."

"Whatever the reason, it's screwing things up," Gael says. "Amy's parents are so pissed off that they're actually thinking about packing things up and leaving. With the money they could get for the cemetery, her parents could probably retire and start living the good life."

"Really?" I say, wondering if Cora Bell has made them an offer, too. Probably.

"Yeah. Apparently, the bikers hit them hard. They lost a few high-value statues."

Darla makes an annoyed sound. I guess I'm not moving fast enough for her. "C'mon, Luke," she says. "I need to get this done with!" Gael shoots her a curious look. "You can come, too, Gael, if you're willing to stay quiet and back me up."

"What?" he asks, confused, but Darla's already moving away, gesturing for us to follow.

I explain the situation to Gael as we go. "We're her muscle, dude. Just try to look intimidating."

"Sweet," Gael says, rubbing his hands together. "I get to be *rough trade*. I'm sure Cole would get a kick out of that."

I groan. "Man, I really did *not* need to hear that," I say, and Gael laughs.

As soon as we turn the corner to the sophomore locker bay, Darla spots her prey and Gael and I have to jog in order to keep up.

"Balint!" she barks. "You asshole!"

Almost everyone in the hallway stops what they're doing and turns her way. Including Tony Balint. She doesn't hit him, but he steps back so fast that he smacks into the locker behind him, making it ring like a bell, and drops his books.

He's no more than five foot three. He's wearing jeans and a plain black T-shirt, and there's an Oakland A's cap pulled low over his eyes. He tries to look away, but Darla reaches forward and flicks the cap off his head, revealing oily blond hair.

He doesn't just look scared now; he looks absolutely terrified.

"Have you been spying on me?" Darla asks, her voice now low and measured. The change in tone is threatening, and I have new respect for my little sister. When she wants to, she can go full-out Hannibal Lecter. I look over and see Gael mouthing a wide-eyed *wow* at me.

"D-D-Darla," the kid manages.

"Did you plant a camera in my room?" she asks. "Or did you hack my phone's camera?" She smiles coldly. "Tell me, Tony, should I be talking to the police right now?"

"I … I'm sorry, Darla," he pleads. "I didn't mean anything by it. It was just a trick, you know, and I got carried away. But I didn't see anything, *I swear*! And there are no cameras in your room. It's nothing like that."

"Then how did you do it?" Darla asks.

"I … I really can't say. I'm sorry, I'm sorry." He looks utterly ashamed. "I'll never bother you again," he says in a low voice. Then he takes off running, leaving his cap and his schoolbooks behind.

I get ready to go after him, but Darla puts her hand on my shoulder. "Don't bother, Luke. He got the message." Then she starts gathering his books from where they've fallen. She piles them into a neat tower in front of his locker and puts his baseball cap on top.

"Are you feeling sorry for him?" I ask, surprised.

She shrugs. "It's just not worth it," she says. "I'll scan my phone for malware, wipe and reinstall everything, but that's it. Drama over, okay?"

I consider this for a moment, then nod.

"Thanks," she says. Then she turns and leaves. There are still a few kids waiting to see if anything else is going to happen, but they hurry out of her way as soon as she gets near.

Gael watches her go, then shakes his head.

"I never realized just how scary your little sister can be." He taps his forehead, giving Darla a salute of respect. "Remind me not to piss her off, okay?"

I agree, and we both head off to class.

What Tony Balint said is troubling, but I have a hard time thinking about it. I have a hard time thinking about anything other than Mia's death, speeding toward us so ridiculously fast.

Friday. It's happening Friday.

I sleepwalk through all of my classes, anxious and miserable, as I try to figure out what to do. The only good part of my day is when I run into Mia between fourth and fifth periods. Suddenly, the whole world changes, the gray school becoming someplace new and magical. She doesn't kiss me in the hall, but I can tell that she's seriously thinking about it, and even that makes me happy.

There's got to be a way. I can't let her die.

Aaron Louis Cressman had saved a trolley car full of people, and that's the kind of magic I need to replicate. *That's* what I need to research!

Were there consequences for his actions, or are my dad's rules nothing but complete bullshit?

From what Jim had said, his grandmother would have been the perfect person to talk to about this—a historian specializing in Colma's past. Too bad she's dead and gone.

But her research isn't, I realize. She left twenty boxes behind!

I have to find Jim and make him help me.

It's time to get some answers.

———

Jim's grandmother's house is on the southern edge of town—a small, cottage-style dwelling, with a once-nice garden that's now wild and overgrown.

"Forty-five minutes," Jim says as he unlocks the door. "Then you help me load up the truck and we go." This is the deal that we made: he gives me access to his grandmother's research, and I help him take boxes to the library. All in all, not a high price to pay, especially considering how important this could be.

Jim turns on the lights, revealing a cluttered entryway. There are boxes on either side of the door, and a mound of clothing waiting to be packed.

"We were just getting started clearing out the house when my parents split up. Since then, everything's just been … kinda on hold." He looks around. "I used to love it here," he finally says warmly. "I'd come over whenever my parents were fighting. My grandma always made the best cookies." He seems genuinely sad.

He leads me into the living room. The air smells musty in here, and there's a thin layer of dust on every surface. Jim pulls open a thick pair of drapes, and afternoon light comes streaming in, illuminating an intimidating stack of boxes set against the far wall.

I let out a low whistle. This might be more of a chore than I imagined.

"Did she ever tell you *why* she was so interested in Colma?" I ask.

Jim smiles. "She said it was a special, magical place, but I always thought that that was kinda stupid. I mean, Colma's just a bland suburb full of dead people, right? And when you get right down to it, death's just not that interesting. It's just … I don't know, an endless nothing?"

Jim lifts a box off the top of the stack and slides it to me across the hardwood floor. "She was planning on writing a book about

Colma at some point. Her notes are in there. Everything else is just binders full of clippings and photographs."

I open up the box and find a stack of spiral-bound notebooks inside.

"And *don't* take anything," Jim says, his voice suddenly stern. "She made us promise to keep this stuff safe for the library, and I don't want to be a liar. Not to her."

I glance up, ready to argue, but I see the look on his face and I just nod. This is a new side of Jim: thoughtful and strong, instead of just goofy.

He nods and leaves the room. After a couple seconds I can hear him in the kitchen, rummaging through his grandmother's refrigerator and throwing things away. I sit down and start flipping through notebooks.

The first notebook has Mrs. Deacon's plans for a prologue. *As a historian,* she writes, *it is my job to look for patterns, for cause and effect, for anomalous trends and events. From the very start, the small township of Colma has been nothing but anomaly, and this book is my attempt to understand how and why.* After these initial sentences, there's nothing but free-form reminders. *Note: talk about census data. When split from SF set, Colma residents seem to have the longest life expectancy in the nation (+5 years for women, 7 for men). Then transition to <u>the 6 founding families</u>.* This is underlined several times.

Then she takes a step back, diving deep into Ordinance 49B's history and Colma's founding. Photocopies of news clippings take up four whole notebooks. I skim past this part, anxious to find something more helpful.

I open the sixth notebook and see *The Mystery of Colma* scrawled across the first page, with a black-and-white photograph taped beneath it. The picture shows a group of four men and two women standing close together, all six of them sporting broad, happy smiles. According to Mrs. Deacon's handwritten caption, these people are Raphael Silva, Joanne Seidel, Ginger Schossler, Aaron Louis Cressman, Daniel Balint, and Able Deacon. I take a moment to study my great-great-grandfather's face. His warm smile is a stark contrast to the deathly serious expression that he's wearing in the family portraits hanging on our entryway wall.

Mrs. Deacon explains that, as representatives of Colma's founding families, these six men and women served as the first town council: *For nearly three years, right up until Aaron Louis Cressman's mysterious drowning death, these six were pretty much inseparable. Their unusual exploits were reported in local papers and gossip sheets, painting a strange, downright supernatural picture of life in Colma after its founding.* Citing a great number of sources, Mrs. Deacon describes a long series of inexplicable events: Joanne Seidel finds the long-missing body of a local sports hero; Able Deacon discovers a cache of honest-to-god prospector gold; Daniel Balint, with the help of Ginger Schossler and Aaron Louis Cressman, delivers a baby in a broken-down car in the middle of nowhere; and Raphael Silva stops a bank robbery cold, somehow managing to knock out three armed gunmen all on his own. And these are just four examples, standouts in a list of dozens.

So many unexplained incidents. But what does it mean?

My great-great-grandfather's abilities couldn't possibly be behind all of this. How would seeing someone's death help Able Deacon find buried treasure? How would it help Gael's great-great-grandfather, Raphael Silva, take out a handful of armed bank robbers?

Could the rest of the council members have had their own mystical abilities?

And what about consequences? Were there any repercussions?

I flip back to the start of the sixth notebook, jumping from the picture of the six smiling council members to the description of my great-great-grandfather's death. Mrs. Deacon had called it a "mysterious drowning death." What exactly does that mean?

I hear Jim back in the kitchen, pulling dishes out of cupboards and putting them in boxes. While he's occupied, I peel the picture of the council members from its backing tape. Then I find an article about Gael's great-great-grandfather's bank robbery heroics. I manage to tear the photocopy nearly in two as I shove it into my backpack.

In Mrs. Deacon's final notebook, there is a single word on the first page: *Conclusions*.

I don't know what any of this means. Her handwriting is loose and messy. *Earlier, I said I look for cause and effect, anomalies and explanations. But what can I say here? Nothing. Nothing definitive. And yet, there is something special about this place—the increased life expectancy is outside any margin of error—but what? Something in the water? No. Something in the land? And there's the rub. This all started with 49B, with the sheer number of bodies moved into the ground. Perhaps the power of the dead is influencing the world, in ways we are just too shortsighted to see.... Giving gifts? Bestowing control?*

There is a bold line scribbled beneath this paragraph, then one final, shaky note: *And this is why I can never publish this book. For fear of tainting a lifetime's worth of hard work, for fear of being laughed out of credibility.*

"Are you ready to go?"

I jump at the sound of Jim's voice, then shove the stack of notebooks back into the box at my side. I nod, refusing to meet his eyes, and we start loading Mrs. Deacon's research into the back of Jim's truck. He seems distracted, still back in his dead grandmother's house, saying an extended goodbye.

"Do you believe in the supernatural?" I ask. After all, his great-great-grandfather had been a founding council member. Maybe Jim has secrets of his own.

"What?" he asks. Then he shakes his head. "I don't think about that shit. It's bad enough that other schools call us the Grim Reapers; we don't need to invite that crap on ourselves." Then he slides a box into the truck and heads back inside for more.

I put a carton on the tailgate and shove it forward. The cardboard catches and several binders come spilling out. I scramble into the back of the truck and start putting them away, but stop suddenly when I notice that the binder I'm holding has my name written across its front—a sharpie-etched *Cressman* on a thick strip of masking tape.

I flip back the cover and see page after page of photocopied news clippings. There isn't any of Mrs. Deacon's commentary, however—just raw source material. I hear Jim coming and impulsively jam the book into my backpack, my heart beating loudly in my ears.

"There are still at least ten boxes left, man," Jim says, annoyed. "You need to start pulling your weight."

"Yeah, yeah, yeah," I say. Then I sling my backpack over my shoulder and get back to work.

———

When I get back home, I stay in my dad's car for a while—*my car, I remind myself; it's my car now*—trying to arrange the scramble of thoughts inside my head.

Maybe it's time I started claiming more things as my own: this car, my powers, my future. Maybe it's time I started living by my *own* set of rules.

I try to imagine the reaction on my dad's face—a disappointed frown, maybe some sun-weathered worry lines—but it's all vague now, his features floating just out of reach.

I'm sorry, Dad, but this is the way it's got to be.

10

My dad's second rule—after *never use your visions to alter someone's fate*—was *never tell anyone about the Cressman family powers*. My heart is beating fast at the thought of breaking this rule. I'm both terrified and excited.

I find Gael before school on Tuesday morning. He's hanging out with Cole in front of his locker. The night before, I'd spent enough time going through the Cressman binder to see that it didn't contain anything too horribly exciting; then I spent the rest of the night coming up with a plan of attack for this encounter with my best friend.

"Do we get to play bodyguard again?" Gael asks as soon as I approach. "I told Cole about what we did for your sister yesterday, and he thinks I might have a future as hired muscle."

"Oh yeah," I say. "You've got a real tough guy here, Cole. So ferocious."

Cole plays along, giving Gael an appreciative look. Then he gives him a peck on the cheek and hurries away.

"He's got a jazz band meeting before class," Gael explains. "He's trying for a solo this quarter."

"That's good," I say. "Convenient, even. I, ah … I need to talk to you. In private."

I drag Gael up to the roof, ignoring his confused questions along the way.

When we get up there, I prop the door open with the cinder block. I half-expect to find Mia standing at the edge, smoking a cigarette, but I check and Gael and I are all alone.

"What's going on?" Gael asks.

"I want to talk to you about your family." I put my bag down and dig into my notebook, coming up with the picture and the newspaper clipping that I stole from Jim's grandmother's house. First, I hand over the article about the foiled robbery attempt. I give him a minute to read it. "That's your great-great-grandfather, isn't it?" I ask. Then I hand over the picture of the six founding council members. I point out Raphael Silva standing at the far left side of the group.

Gael studies the picture for a moment, then looks up, confused. But he also seems a little afraid. "Yeah, that's my great-great-grandfather, Raphael," he says. "What are you getting at, Luke?"

"How did he stop those bank robbers, Gael?" Then, after a moment, "It doesn't actually say in that article, but I think you know what I'm talking about."

Gael opens his mouth. Then he closes it again.

I take a deep breath and ask the question straight out: "Does your family have powers, Gael? Something that's been passed down from generation to generation? From father to son … to you?"

He falters for a moment. "What … what do you mean? I don't

know what you're talking about." But I can tell that this isn't true. He knows exactly what I'm talking about.

"Don't worry, Gael. I get it … because I have powers, too."

His brow crinkles, and he looks conflicted. "My dad and grandfather told me that I'm not supposed to tell *anyone*, Luke. It's a secret. I'm supposed to take it with me to the grave."

I can't help but laugh, and Gael watches on with horror.

"Yeah, I got the same story, too," I tell him. "I'm never supposed to use my powers. I'm never supposed to tell anyone about them. But I think it's complete bullshit. My great-great-grandfather used his powers plenty. As did yours." And I point to the article still in his hand. "Shit! They were working together—all six of the founding families, maybe. They were like the X-Men, or the Justice League, saving lives and stopping bank robberies."

Suddenly, I'm overcome with adrenaline. I jump and spin around, but I stop when I see Gael's face. He looks absolutely drained.

"What can you do?" I ask. "What are your powers?"

Gael sits down on the roof. He studies the documents I've shown him, flipping from the picture to the newspaper clipping, then back to the picture.

"We call it 'deadening,'" he says. "If we concentrate in just the right way, we can 'deaden' people and animals with a touch—just kind of freeze them in place for a while, leaving them totally unconscious, oblivious to the world. It lasts for about five minutes, at the most."

"That explains how your great-great-grandfather stopped those bank robbers."

"But my grandfather told me that right from the start, *his* grandfather—Raphael, the first one with the power"—Gael lifts the article, waving it in the air—"resolved never to use it. He was religious, and he was convinced that the deadening was a curse from the devil, our *burden*; that it was meant to tempt us into evil; and that using it at all would send us straight to hell."

"Obviously, we haven't been getting the whole story," I say. "Our ancestors used to use their powers." I pause for a moment. "Something must have happened to change their minds."

Gael and I stay silent for a while. The first-period bell rings in the school down below, and both of us are now late for class. But neither of us moves. For the moment, we don't care.

"What can you do?" Gael asks. "What's your power?"

I pause for a moment, and the ridiculous surge of energy that I'd felt earlier is suddenly gone. It's different, I guess, hearing about someone else's powers and divulging the long-held secret of your own.

"I can see how people are going to die," I say, sitting down at his side. "When I touch someone, sometimes I get a vision of their last minutes."

He fixes me with a serious stare. "Are you shitting me? That's pretty messed up."

I nod.

Then, in a low voice: "How am I going to die?" he asks.

And I pause for at least half a minute. I could tell him, *You're going to die a happy death, surrounded by love and pictures of a large family,* but why chance it? Especially when it's something I don't want to change?

"I don't think I should tell you," I say. "That was one of my dad's rules—people shouldn't know how they're going to die— and for the time being, I'm gonna stick to that one."

Gael nods.

"Your dad," he says. "Did you know how and when *he* was going to die?"

"Yes."

"That's so messed up," he repeats.

"Yeah," I say. "It was. I should have changed it. If I'd known then what I know now, I would have done everything I could to stop it."

"What do you know now?" he asks.

Gael and I sit on the roof for the rest of the morning, going over what I learned from Jim's grandmother's research. I also tell him about my attempt to stop my dad's death, and the old man's stubborn refusal to listen.

And then, finally, I tell him about Mia.

When I'm done, we sit in silence for a long time. It's almost ten o'clock, and I can see clouds moving in from the west—dark gray clouds, heavy with rain.

"She's going to die," I say. "On Friday."

"I ... I don't think you should do anything about it," Gael says, reluctantly. "At least not yet."

"What?"

He shrugs. "Yeah, so *okay*, your great-great-grandfather proba-bly used his powers," he admits. "But maybe there *were* conse-quences, and we just can't see them. Things that wouldn't appear in the paper. There's got to be a reason why our families were so serious about us never using our abilities." He makes a frustrated clucking sound at the back of his throat and nods up toward the darkening sky. "Hell, I'm sitting here terrified of those clouds over there, terrified that they're full of lightning, just gearing up to strike us dead for what we're doing up here. And that's just *talking*, Luke! What happens if we start to actually *use* our powers?"

After a moment, I shrug. I have absolutely no idea.

I let out a deep sigh.

"If you want to break the rules, we should at least figure out the possible consequences first. We need to be serious about this, Luke."

"Well," I say, "we also need to be fast. Because I really don't think I can just let Mia die."

I close my eyes and stare into the darkness behind my eyelids.

"I did that once," I murmur, once again trying to call up a memory of my dad's face, and once again getting nothing but a muted impression. I open my eyes. "I can't do that again."

He has no response to this.

Neither do I.

———

After a couple of minutes, Gael lets out a laugh.

"How could we have not figured this out about each other?" he asks. "We've been friends for so long—since we were, like, what, five years old? How could we not know?"

"We were sworn to secrecy," I say. "We thought our situations were totally unique, so we didn't even think to question it." I smile and shake my head. "Besides, it's not like it's an obvious leap to make. I mean, was I just supposed to *guess* that you had magical paralysis-causing abilities?"

Gael laughs. "You know, I did it to you once," he says. "We were kids, like maybe nine, and we were playing in my backyard. I hadn't had the powers for that long, and I wasn't all that great at controlling it. Anyway, I touched you and froze you in place. When you came out of it, you were totally confused and said you were feeling sick. You went home and I felt like a total asshole for the rest of the day. I told my dad about it, and he was furious."

"I don't remember that," I say.

"Yeah, it was a long time ago."

"I'm guessing Tony Balint has powers, too," I say. "His great-great-grandfather is in that photo. That's how he knew what my sister was wearing. Maybe he has premonitions or something? As for Jim Deacon …" I shrug. "Didn't want to talk about it."

Gael lifts the group photograph and holds it between us. "Look at them, Luke," he says. "Look at how they're smiling. These people don't look like they're cursed. They look like they're blessed. Who are the others?"

I list their names. "There's one from each of the six founding families," I say. "In her notes, Jim's grandmother suggested that maybe the sheer number of Colma's dead somehow managed to give them 'gifts.'"

Gael thinks about this for a time. "There are a lot of people in the ground here," he finally says. "It's, what, all of San Francisco's dead across a half dozen generations? Maybe two centuries' worth?" He grunts. "That makes it more difficult, doesn't it?"

I don't know what he means.

"There are just so many souls. Are they all watching us? Are they waiting for us to do something with the powers they gave us?"

"City of the Silent," I say. "City of Souls." And I imagine a city floating in the sky above us, the huge weight of this imaginary place pinning us to this corpse-filled land.

Gael shivers visibly. "And they're expecting … *what* exactly? They gave us these powers, but what are we actually supposed to be doing with them?"

"Hell if I know," I say. "But I'm guessing *something*."

As opposed to the long, hard torture of nothing.

———

The gray clouds are gone by the time the final bell rings.

Gael meets me in the parking lot in front of the school. He lucked into a parking pass this year.

"Help me do some research," I say. "Somebody wants Mia dead, and I need to figure out why." Gael gives me a horrified look and I shake my head. "Even if I don't stop it from happening, I can at least make sure her killer doesn't get away with it. Justice is a worthy pursuit, right?"

Gael thinks about it for a moment, no doubt trying to figure out if this counts as meddling. Finally, he unlocks his Jeep and points me to the passenger seat. "I'll help you out," he says, "as long as you promise not to do anything stupid—well, nothing stupider than usual."

He drives us to Other Worlds, and I tell him to park so I can see the front door.

"Is this it?" he asks. "Is this your big plan? You just want to sit here and watch?"

"It's a stakeout," I say, "a time-honored investigative tradition." I don't tell him that it's also the only idea I could come up with.

In the first half hour, we watch at least a dozen customers enter and exit the storefront. A couple come out with hunched shoulders, looking vaguely ashamed, while others wave and call out their thanks as they leave.

"Is that her?" Gael asks after a while. He's pointing toward the far side of the Target parking lot. Mia's exiting the Serbian cemetery with her hands clasped behind her head. Once again, she's wearing a flowing dress over her Doc Martens—this one is a beautiful green, changing shade from emerald at the top to mint green at its hem—and she's practically skipping, moving gracefully to something coming out of an oversize pair of headphones.

"Okay, I get it," Gael says. "She's a babe. I can see why you're into her." I look over and see him grinning at me. "But tell me, Luke, can she sing, hit a curveball, and drive a backhoe?"

"Yeah," I say. "And she can speak French, run a cash register, and make me laugh, too."

Gael's grin quickly slides off his face. He's remembering what's coming, I think. He's remembering her fate.

We watch Mia cross the parking lot and enter the store. Even though we're at least fifty yards away, both Gael and I slide down in our seats so she won't be able to see us spying on her.

For the next hour, we keep watch on the front door.

Customers come and go. A breeze rattles the wind chimes in

the store's front yard, and clouds move across the sky, playing tag with the sun.

"Nothing's happening," Gael finally says, letting out a bored sigh. "How long are we gonna stay here?" I look over and see that he's not even paying attention anymore. He's staring down at his phone, playing *Bejeweled Blitz*.

Gael's right. This is getting us absolutely nowhere, and I'm not even sure what I expected to see. Maybe I'd have better luck combing through Mia's Snapchat followers and Twitter feed. Looking for a stalker, maybe. Or someone with a grudge.

Just as I'm about to give up and tell Gael to drive us home, a lone motorcycle rumbles up Junipero Serra Boulevard. It pulls into the dirt on the far side of the road. The kickstand goes down, but the biker stays seated.

"See that guy?" I say, pointing him out to Gael. "He was parked in the exact same spot the last time I was here." It definitely looks like him—same thick beard, same dark sunglasses, same unmoving features.

"What's he doing?" Gael asks, perplexed. "Is he ... is he watching Other Worlds?"

I shrug, and then we sit in silence, both of us watching the watcher.

After a couple of minutes, the biker pulls his phone from his pocket and makes a call. When I look over at Gael, I see that he, too, has his phone in his hand, and he's busy typing something into a search window.

Suddenly, a loud roar fills the air, and a double-flanked parade of bikes rumbles into view. There are exactly fifteen of them, and the scout on the far side of the road joins them in the parking lot in front of Other Worlds.

A big black bike weaves through the tightly packed crowd, ultimately stopping at the head of the formation, directly before Other Worlds' front door. The driver snaps down the bike's kickstand and stands up.

The way that the others sit and wait deferentially makes me think that this is the gang's leader.

After stretching for a moment, the leader flips off a skullcap helmet, and I'm surprised to see that it's a woman. She has thick, braided red hair, weather-chapped skin, and an angry scowl. She makes me think of a Viking warrior. She whips off her mirrored sunglasses, points to two of her bikers—a thin guy with a large purple birthmark on the side of his face, and a linebacker-sized guy with a dark beard—and gestures for them to follow her inside. Then, without hesitation, she walks into Other Worlds.

"Hey," Gael says. I look over and see that he's staring down at his phone. "I googled 'motorcycle gang' and 'Colma.' It looks like there's been a rise in biker crime in the last six months—vandalism, drug possession, drunken fights. It all seems connected to a biker gang called the Devil's Flame."

"What would they want with Other Worlds?"

"There's an article here from just last week, saying—"

Suddenly, a loud bang comes from inside the store—something like a chair being thrown against a wall. Then there's yelling, and some of the bikers in the parking lot smile and laugh at the angry sounds.

I reach to open the car door, but Gael grabs my arm, stopping me before I even realize what I'm doing.

"Are you insane?" he says. "Look at them, Luke," he hisses. "They'd kill us!"

I realize that he's right, and I try to hold still. It feels like my whole body is vibrating, itching to move, to act, to do *something*!

I hear another crash from inside, and my heart stutters inside my chest. Is Mia okay?

Then, suddenly, the front door springs open and the two henchmen stumble backward into the parking lot. After a couple of seconds, their leader follows, moving slowly, like she's reluctant to give up ground.

"You're going to regret this, bitches," she growls, pointing into the store, her voice low and rough with anger. I've heard that voice before. She was the one barking orders at Hills of Eternity, while the rest of the bikers tore up the cemetery.

As the lead biker continues to retreat, Melinda Iverson appears at the door. She's got a shotgun clutched in her hands, pointed squarely at the big woman's chest. I can see Mia standing behind her mom, her hands covering her mouth in horror.

"You should be begging for our forgiveness, you faking little scoundrel," the biker roars. "You should be begging for Big Deek's forgiveness—that perfect saint of a man, up there in heaven, drinking Wild Turkey and shooting pool with the angels—all thanks to you, you and your ungodly lies!" The woman spits on the ground and wipes her mouth.

"Get out," Melinda Iverson says. Her voice is trembling, but there's a steely edge to it. "Get away from me and my family, or I'll put you down right here and now."

The leader looks back at her troops and smiles, raising her arms slightly, like she's getting ready to give the order to attack, and for a time I'm afraid that this is about to get very, very bloody. Then, "Fine," she says, backing down. "We'll go. But hear this: you made a mistake crossing me and my brother. All of your lies are going to come home to roost, and soon. And they've got razor-sharp talons, ready to tear your ass to shreds."

The woman turns abruptly and gets back on her bike. Then, taking her time, she gestures for the other bikers to head out. When she's the last one in the parking lot, she slips her helmet on, blows Melinda Iverson a cold, angry kiss, and rides away.

As soon as she's gone, Melinda Iverson's shotgun droops, and she slumps back against the door frame. Mia comes up behind her and wraps her in a fierce hug. Then, slowly, she helps her mom back into the store. After a couple of seconds, a line of terrified customers comes streaming out.

"What the hell was that?" I ask.

"That was the Devil's Flame," Gael says, holding up his phone to show me an article. "According to news reports, their leader, Anderson 'Big Deek' Mullally, died in a shootout with Mexican nationals last week. It was a drug trafficking situation gone bad. Fifteen people died in the fallout."

"And that was his sister?" I ask, nodding toward the road.

Gael nods. "Brianna 'The Executioner' Mullally," he says. "It looks like she's taken over now that her brother's gone."

The Executioner? Jesus Christ.

We sit in silence, thinking about the situation.

"What do you think this all means?" Gael finally asks.

"It means that the Executioner blames Melinda Iverson for her brother's death," I say. "And apparently she's crazy, crazy enough to do something horrible."

———

This isn't definitive proof of anything—there could be someone else who wants Mia dead, like a drug dealer, or a psychotic ex-boyfriend—but the story I'm starting to see is pretty damn convincing.

And it's a story I'd like to rewrite, if possible.

When I get home, I pore over the Cressman binder again. It's still nothing but photocopied news clippings—including every small, boring, and irrelevant mention of Aaron Louis Cressman. After a couple of hours of intense study, I toss it aside, frustrated. There's nothing new—all of the important information was summarized in Mrs. Deacon's notebooks.

Mia texts me as I'm getting ready for bed.

Missed you today. didn't see you at all … again.

Sorry, I reply, *was busy all day long. We'll do something tomorrow*

I was thinking I owe you one, she says. *You showed me yr mntn, I'll take you someplace meaningful to me … not tomorrow, thgh. but soon.*

In san fran?

Maybe ☺ … but for now, sleep an exciting and dreamy sleep.

G'night, I type.

Then I let my thumbs hover over the screen for a while, wondering if I should tell her anything else.

But what exactly can I say? *You make my heart sing ☺? Watch out for angry biker gangs? I think I'm falling in love with you? You're going to die soon? What kind of witty thing would you like me to carve on your tombstone? Will you go to homecoming with me?*

It's too bad there isn't an emoji for all of that. Maybe a smiling, dazed-looking mushroom cloud, blooming out of a heart on fire, surrounded by never-ending darkness, in a coffin, with wavy lines indicating the echoes of screams underground.

Without that particular emoji, however, there's nothing else I can say.

I type, *Sleep well!*, and leave it at that.

11

My phone rings at 5:50 in the morning, pulling me out of a dreamless sleep.

Who would be calling me? Nobody calls me.

It takes me a while to find the phone. It's on the floor near the foot of my bed, under a pile of dirty clothing. I pick it up and see Mia's silly picture staring out at me from the screen.

"Hello?" I croak. My voice is barely audible, clogged with a night's worth of phlegm.

"Luke?" Mia says, her voice quick and low. "Sorry it's so early, but can you help me out with something? Please? It's … kind of an emergency."

"Yeah," I say thickly. "Whatever you need."

"It's my aunt. She's having one of her spells, and she's wandered off. I need you to help us look for her. I have a list of places to check, but I don't really know the area—"

"I'll meet you at your place," I say. "Give me fifteen minutes, tops."

I hang up, rush my way through a two-minute shower, and get dressed. The house is silent this early in the morning—both Roy and Darla are still asleep. I jump in my car and manage to make it all the way to Junipero Serra Boulevard in a grand total of five minutes.

Mia's sitting on the curb near the front door when I get to Other Worlds. The lights are off in the lobby, and there's a big "Closed" sign in the front window.

She stands up when she sees me getting out of my car. She's clutching her arms tight against her chest, and there's a piece of paper dangling from her closed fist.

I give her a huge hug when I reach her. It looks like she could use it.

"She does this," she says, staying there in my arms for a handful of seconds. "My aunt gets confused and wanders off. She should be fine, though. She's almost always fine." This last sentence seems more for her benefit than for mine.

For the first time since I've met her, she seems fragile, not at all like the wild spirit who dragged me up to the school roof. When we're in the car, she shows me her piece of paper.

"My mom's with the police right now, trying to get their help, but she gave me this list of places where my aunt's been found before." I take the list and read through each location. Most seem to be spots in the nearby cemeteries. "I was thinking you could drive to each of them in turn. I'll keep my eyes open. Maybe we'll see her on the side of the road somewhere."

"No problem," I say. I start the car and head out into the almost-empty streets.

"She wasn't in her bed when my mom got up this morning," Mia explains, her eyes glued to the window. She's talking pretty much on autopilot now, trying to fill the void. "She hears voices, you know, thanks to her schizophrenia. Sometimes they guide her. Sometimes she tries to hunt them down."

Mia's quiet for a while, watching out the window as I turn from Mission Road into the vast expanse of Cypress Lawn Cemetery. The list specifically mentions the monuments at the back of the property.

"Usually, someone finds her pretty quickly," Mia says. "But a couple of times she's been gone for several days. My mom's found her injured, and dehydrated. She even had to be hospitalized once. She really can't take care of herself. Not alone. Not without us."

I drive slowly through Cypress Lawn, guiding us first around the perimeter, then through the small lanes connecting one side of the cemetery to the other. Mia cranes her head, frantically trying to scan each corner. Near the back, she tells me to stop. We get out and walk through the more intricately landscaped areas. Mia makes her way around each monument, calling out her aunt's name.

"Adeline!" she calls. Then, when there's no response, she calls out her nickname: "Lena!"

When we reach the back of the property, Mia shakes her head and turns around. "She's not here," she says. "Let's move on."

"You said she hears voices," I say. "What exactly does she hear?"

Mia pauses and looks down at the neatly manicured lawn. "It's confusing, how she explains it," she says. "It's all so vague, like she's unsure of the words that she's using. She tried to describe it to me once. She told me that sometimes it's just an indistinct murmur that she feels compelled to try to decipher, a voice that's always outside her head—always there, coming from nearby, or from a distant room, but never something that she can actually understand. And sometimes it's the voices of the dead that she hears. They talk to her, sharing secrets and making accusations, telling her where to go."

I nod. I want to ask her more questions, but she starts walking again, moving faster. I catch up to her just as she's getting into the car.

Before I can even get settled in the driver's seat, Mia resumes talking. Her voice is a pained and turbulent rush. "Schizophrenia is awful," she says. I look over and see her eyes glittering, wet with tears. "And the most horrible thing about it is, you can see the madness progressing. Always. Day by day. It's like living inside a slow-motion car crash—something you can walk around, and analyze, but never, ever, *ever* actually stop." She shrugs, raising her hands helplessly. "My … my aunt is losing more and more of herself each day. She used to be so funny and loving, but now she's just confused and lost and broken. It's horrible. I can't imagine, in her more lucid moments, how terrifying it's got to be for her, knowing full well what's going on."

She shakes her head and looks down at the list. "Next is Home of Peace," she says. "Then Greenlawn."

"You're doing a good thing," I say as I start driving. "You came back here. You're helping. I'm sure both your aunt and your mom appreciate it."

"Yeah, well, I know how this ends, and it doesn't end well," she says, her voice small and unsteady. "My mom saw it happen to her mom; it runs in the family, all the way back to my great-great-grandmother, Joanne Seidel."

I nearly drive off the road.

"Whoa! Easy!" Mia says, bracing herself as I regain control.

One of the six founding council members.

I can see Joanne Seidel's face in my head. She was the woman standing next to Raphael Silva in the photo—the happy, smiling woman, two smiles left of my great-great-grandfather.

"Other Worlds is real, isn't it?" I blurt out, my thoughts smashing together inside my head. I'm smiling when I look over at Mia. She, on the other hand, looks startled and confused.

Maybe this isn't the best time for this confrontation, but I can't stop myself.

"Your aunt has real psychic abilities, doesn't she?"

"W-What?"

"You never said that you didn't believe in supernatural phenomena. In fact, you were very careful to *not* say that. That's because you know that it's real."

She stays quiet, looking out the windshield, but the fear in her eyes tells me all I need to know.

"Don't worry," I say. "I have my own secrets. You can trust me to keep yours safe."

———

We drive circles around Home of Peace and Greelawn, then move on to Holy Cross. The day gets brighter and warmer as we make our slow circuit, and the traffic on the street gets denser.

As we drive, I tell Mia about my death visions, about what my dad had taught me, and about what I learned about the six founding families. Mia's eyes remain locked on the passenger-side window the entire time, still looking for her aunt.

When I'm done, she stays quiet for a while. Then, suddenly, she lets out a loud, boisterous laugh.

"*No shit?*" she asks.

"No shit," I say.

And she turns toward me, smiling. I smile back.

"What exactly are your family's powers?" I ask.

"My aunt can contact the dead," Mia says. "She can touch someone, concentrate, and get in contact with their dearly departed. It can be either a blood relative, or someone close to them in life. That's how she does her 'psychic channeling,' which is what my mom calls it in the description for the 'premium package' at Other Worlds." She puts air quotes around her mom's terminology, signaling her disgust. "My grandmother had the ability, too. Probably my great-grandmother as well, although we aren't entirely sure about her. According to family lore, she went crazy and killed herself, ranting about 'all of the voices in the world, screaming out of the endless void.'"

"Did *you* get the powers?" I ask, trying to be delicate. "Did it pass down to you?"

Mia presses her lips together. "No," she says. "At least, not yet. The powers don't seem to hit until our late teens or early twenties, around the time when schizophrenia tends to kick in, and the two seem to be a package deal. So I'm just kind of waiting around. The suspense is rather brutal," she admits. "It's basically waiting to find out if I'm going to live or die."

I bite my cheek. Unfortunately, I could give a pretty definitive answer to that question.

"Your aunt is your grandmother's oldest daughter, right?" I ask.

Mia nods, and I continue. "Maybe it goes from eldest daughter to eldest daughter, similar to how it works in my family—from eldest son to eldest son. If that's the case, then you're out of the line of succession."

Mia lets out a low "huh" as she considers this. "My aunt didn't have any kids," she finally says, her voice low.

"Then maybe that's the end of it," I say.

"Maybe," she replies, but she doesn't sound convinced.

I've been driving slowly through Holy Cross Cemetery, circling some of their nicer monuments. We pause for a couple of minutes near the center of the grounds, and take our time peering in every direction, into every possible corner. There's nothing. We've scoured the entire property and haven't seen any sign of Mia's aunt.

"Where to next?" I ask.

"Olivet Memorial Park," she says. "In the back, near the trees."

I turn the car around and head out, turning left onto Hillside Boulevard.

"So … you can see how people are going to die, huh?" Mia says.

I brace myself for the obvious follow-up question—*How am I going to die?*—but instead, she says, "I don't think I'd want to know what's going to kill me. There's just so much that's out of our control—and death's the big one, right? It's the thing we've all got to face eventually. So instead of dwelling on it, and freaking out, I think I'd want to remain clueless. We get what we get, so we should just try to make the best of things while we're here."

Even if we're here for a ridiculously short time?

I open my mouth, and I can feel myself forming the start of a sentence: *I've got to warn you. . . .* But I don't actually say anything.

I can tell that Mia's watching me, curious, and I turn away, trying to hide my emotions.

Just keep driving, I tell myself. *Just get her to where she needs to go.*

———

Olivet Memorial Park is near the foot of San Bruno Mountain, not far from where I took Mia on our weekend expedition. The lanes leading to the back of the cemetery are blocked off to traffic today, so we leave the car in the parking lot and continue on foot.

Olivet is a bit crowded for my taste—the gravestones here are much more densely packed than on the Cressman grounds—but it's very well maintained. And it's peaceful, far removed from the sounds of the freeway.

Mrs. Rosen will like it here, I think, *remembering that this is where her husband has decided to have her buried. There's no bad piano playing here, and no students who refuse to practice.*

As we make our way through the cemetery, Mia cranes her head back and forth, peering down each row of headstones, like she's expecting to find her aunt collapsed in the grass somewhere.

"So your aunt's the one with the powers?" I say. "I always thought it was your mom who did the readings."

"It is, a lot of the time," Mia says. "My aunt's not exactly reliable. Most of the time, she's just too disconnected from reality to give a good reading." Mia shrugs, then pokes her head around the base of a monument. "So she does the 'premium' work, while my mom does the more abbreviated type of thing. If someone has a specific question to ask a loved one, and if they're willing to pay the premium price, then my aunt gets called in. Otherwise, my mom goes to work."

"She fakes it?" I ask bluntly.

Mia shoots me a frustrated look. "Well, if you want to be *simple* about it, yes. But most of the time, people don't want anything specific out of a reading. They just want to feel a connection. They just want to believe, for a short time at least, that the bond they had with someone isn't totally lost. At Other Worlds, they can believe that. It's an act of comfort, like therapy. Even when she's just drawing a vague picture with her tarot cards, my mom's providing hope and optimism, and maybe even giving people motivation to improve their lives." She continues checking each row of graves in turn. "Yeah, it's sketchy at times, and she does some things that I'm not into—and, honestly, I'm pissed off at you for making me defend her—but she works her ass off, and in the end, she does a surprising amount of good for people."

"Okay, I guess that makes sense." Then I pause for a moment, considering my next words. "But it's a dangerous game, isn't it?" I ask. "Doing what she does, your mom could easily make enemies."

Mia stops five rows away and gives me a confused look.

"I was driving by your shop yesterday after school," I explain. "I saw all of those bikers. It looked like a Tarantino movie."

"Yeah, well, that was one of the sketchier things my mom did," Mia says, letting out a loud sigh.

"What happened? What did they want?"

"A couple weeks ago, they came to my mom to get advice. Their leader—Big Deek, they called him—wanted to talk to his dead father. He wanted to know what his old man would do in a certain situation, if he thought that a rival group would seek retribution for ... for *something*. They were all very careful about what they said. They made sure that they didn't mention any crimes directly." Mia shakes her head and runs a frustrated hand across her brow. "I knew it was a mistake, nothing but bad shit, but my mom ... I guess we needed the money or something, and these guys—Big Deek and his sister—they seemed like true be-lievers.

"My aunt was in her bedroom talking to herself, completely incoherent, so my mom went ahead and performed the reading herself. I don't know exactly what she told them, but they left happy, confident. My mom, on the other hand, left the room pale and sweating." Mia pauses for a moment. "Anyway, things went wrong, Big Deek ended up dead, and his sister blames my mom."

"So they're threatening her?"

"Yeah," Mia says. "I'm guessing that they'd leave us alone if we just gave them money—they seem like the type who'd take cash over principles any day of the week—but my mom says that we've got nothing left to give."

"Have you tried going to the police?" I ask.

"No," Mia says, shaking her head. "My mom refuses. She's been in trouble before, and she's scared the police would just use this as an excuse to go after her. Anyway, my mom thinks this'll all blow over."

Or maybe not.

"Is that it?" I ask Mia. "Just the bikers? Or do you have other enemies as well? Someone who'd want to hurt you?"

"Enemies?" Mia looks perplexed.

I shouldn't have asked that. I might be changing the future with my stupid, clumsy questions.

"No, no enemies," she says. And then, suddenly, she flashes me a bright smile. She touches her lower lip and tries to pull off a coquettish look. "You *have* met me, right? I'm an absolute delight, you stupid prick. Who'd ever want to hurt me?"

And with that, she laughs, turns, and heads deeper into the cemetery.

———

The back part of Olivet Memorial Park is hidden by a long grove of trees.

"Take the left side," Mia says. "I'll take the right. We'll meet up in the middle. Try to stay quiet, and don't yell out if you see her. We don't want to scare her away."

The grounds aren't nearly as well maintained back here, and my clothes catch on loose brambles as I slowly make my way back toward the middle of the cemetery.

There are signs that people have been here before, but nothing that looks recent. I come across a small clearing where a ratty old sleeping bag has been spread across the ground; there's a pair of abandoned socks, and a Heineken box filled with empty beer bottles sitting at its side. I continue on, peering into every shaded corner. I find a soccer ball, a pair of discarded jeans, and at least a week's worth of local newspapers, but no sign of Mia's aunt.

When I make my way back to the middle of the grounds, Mia isn't there yet. I'm about to call out when I hear her voice. It's a low, desperate whisper.

"Please," she says. "It's me. It's Mia. I love you. You love me."

I creep forward, holding my breath and trying to stay as quiet as possible. I don't want to interrupt whatever's going on.

"Adeline, *please*," she pleads, and her voice sounds as if it's coming from just up ahead.

I crouch down low and peer out from behind a wild rhododendron bush.

Mia and her aunt are facing off in a small clearing next to the cemetery's back fence. Mia's aunt is just a couple of feet away from a gap where the chain links have been snipped apart, forming a mouth just big enough for her to slip through. She's facing Mia, but her body is half-turned toward the opening, ready to dart through to the other side.

"I wouldn't lie to you," Mia says. She's holding out her hands. "I love you, and I just want to help. I want to help you feel better."

Mia's aunt is wearing a dirt-stained dress, and there are tear tracks etched into the grime on her face.

"If that's true," Mia's aunt says, "if you are who you say you are, then I'd hurt you, I'd only hurt you." I'm surprised at how scared she sounds. Back when she ran into me in front of Other Worlds, her voice had been a dreamy, melodic singsong. Now, it's a broken quaver. "I'm full of curses, and I'd only taint Mia—too much by a lot and, for God's sake, much too near. A gift I don't want to give, a Christmas that no one should have."

"It's me, Adeline," Mia says again. "You're talking about *me*, and I don't think that you're a curse. Never. Not at all. You're a blessing to me, you're loved … and I need you to trust me, okay? We'll get you healthy. We'll get you happy and sleeping well, but right now we just have to get you home." She smiles warmly, and puts her hands over her heart. "Trust me."

Mia takes a step forward and her aunt flinches back, getting ready to flee. But instead of running, Mia's aunt's shoulders slump, and, finally, she leans forward, giving in.

"I'm sorry," she says. "I'm so, so sorry."

Mia steps forward and wraps her aunt in a tight hug, holding her close.

I give them time together, letting them have this moment.

Then, when it seems right, I step out of my hiding place and help them back to the car.

On the ride back to Other Worlds, Mia and her aunt stay quiet. They both sit in the backseat, and when I look in the rearview mirror, I see that Mia's aunt has her head resting snugly against Mia's shoulder. Her eyes are closed, but there's a tiny smile on her lips. They both look so tired.

I don't say a word.

12

It's noon when I drop Mia and her aunt off at Other Worlds, but I don't even think about heading back to school and trying to catch the last couple of classes of the day. Screw my attendance. I have more important things to worry about.

I park up the road from our cemetery and walk the final stretch home, hoping that Uncle Roy won't catch me playing hooky. I get lucky—he's in the back of the grounds, and I manage to make it up to my room without being seen.

I sit on the floor and pull the picture of the council members from my backpack. I focus in on the woman second from the left: Joanne Seidel, Mia's great-great-grandmother. Now, I recognize the shape of that face, the warmth of her smile—there's definitely a hint of Mia there, even if she is a different age and a different color.

Should I save your great-great-granddaughter? I ask her. *Your friend Aaron wouldn't have hesitated.*

I put the picture aside and pull the stolen Cressman binder into my lap.

There has to be something here, something I missed earlier.

Even a tiny hint—something to indicate how my great-great-grandfather had managed to make all of those changes, avert all of those deaths, without any destruction. I flip back the cover and start scanning pages.

Going through the binder is a mind-numbing chore, and after an hour of frustration, I stand up, letting it fall from my lap.

When it hits the ground, an envelope slides from the back of the book, coming to rest against my foot. It must have been tucked into the spine, needing a big jolt in order to come free. I pick it up and sit down on the edge of my bed.

The envelope is an amber-tinted white, and *Katherine Deacon* is spelled out on the front in faded fountain pen ink. The paper feels old and brittle, and when I flip it over I find a photograph paper-clipped to its back. The picture is black-and-white, and it shows five people in funereal garb gathered around a freshly installed gravestone.

I set it aside and open up the envelope. Inside is a letter written out in graceful, looping calligraphy. My eye immediately goes to the signature at the bottom of the page, and I catch my breath. *Mary E. Cressman.* My great-great-grandmother.

Dear Katherine,

Thank you so very much for the kindness you have shown me and my family during these trying weeks. Your support has helped us beyond measure. Aaron's death was a truly devastating blow. He'd seemed so moody and preoccupied in the weeks leading up to his final plunge, but I'd been hoping it would prove to be nothing but a brief period of darkness. After all, these last years have found him happy and content beyond reason, thanks in no small part to the friendship and camaraderie he found with your husband and the other council members. Their bond was something truly special. It made him happy, and tied him to the world.

I've found reading the reports in the newspaper exceedingly difficult. The way that the witnesses describe Aaron's last hours—wandering through the streets, talking to himself, causing a scene—is absolutely horrific.... What must have been going through his head? What brought him to the bridge over Colma Creek and, finally, to the decision to throw himself into the surging waters?

These questions haunt me.

As you can see, my thoughts still circle and rage ... but in these weeks you have proved my savior. Your letters and company have brought me through the worst of it, I believe. There _is_ light out there, somewhere beyond the horizon, and for showing me that, you have won my eternal gratitude.

With love and appreciation,
Mary E. Cressman

When I finish reading, I go back to the start of the letter and read it through a second time, and then a third. I'm not quite sure what to think. My dad had never told me that my great-great-grandfather had committed suicide.

What pushed him over the edge? Was it something to do with

his powers? Was it something he saw, some tragedy he couldn't prevent?

I put the letter down and turn my attention back to the photograph.

At first, I don't recognize where it was taken. All I can see is a group of black-clad figures facing a stark white gravestone. There are three men and two women, and one of the women, wearing an ankle-length black dress, is bent over the grave, placing a bundle of flowers in the dirt. The grave looks like it's already started to sprout grass, which means that the actual burial would have taken place weeks earlier; this gathering is just to mark the installation of the tombstone.

I flip the picture over and find a couple of handwritten lines. I recognize Mrs. Deacon's script from her notebooks: *D. Balint, A. Deacon, G. Schossler, J. Seidel, and R. Silva visiting Cressman Cemetery. Last known gathering. Council disbanded soon after.*

I turn the picture back over and study the land around the grave. The trees in the background are smaller, and the land looks better maintained, but this is indeed one of the oldest parts of our property.

My great-great-grandfather's grave. I haven't been back there in years.

I tuck the picture into my pocket and head outside, pausing to make sure I can still hear Roy working in the distance. Then I jog toward the heart of the cemetery.

I go down A5, then turn left, cutting through a line of trees, and I find myself wading through calf-high grass. Most of the gravestones back here are from before Ordinance 49B, when the Cressman Cemetery served the local community and nothing more. Nobody visits them nowadays, and they're at the very bottom of the list when it comes to upkeep and maintenance.

Considering the state of some of the neighboring tombstones, I'm surprised to find my great-great-grandfather's marker in relatively good shape. It's a large, pale white granite stone, and the chiseled lines making up his name and dates are still deep and strong. As are the words, *Beloved husband, father, and friend.*

I sit down in the grass and stare at the stone for a while.

Back here, in this forgotten part of the cemetery, it is freakishly quiet, and I close my eyes for a moment, basking in the feel of the warm sun against my face.

I pull the picture from my pocket. The scene is chilly and filled with sadness—the five remaining council members mourning their lost friend. I focus on the woman putting the flowers on the grave, trying to figure out if it's Joanne Seidel, Mia's great-great-grandmother, or Ginger Schossler. Her back is turned, however, so it's hard to tell. Then my eyes wander across the photo, and I notice something at the base of the tombstone, right above ground level. It's something I've never noticed before.

I move forward and part the grass with my hands. It's there, carved into the granite: a second inscription, lost in the weeds.

YOU DID WHAT YOU THOUGHT WAS RIGHT,
AND DIED A MARTYR FOR COLMA.
YOUR SACRIFICE WILL NOT BE FORGOTTEN.

A martyr. Dying for Colma.

And a shiver runs down my spine.

Is that how he did it? Is that what prevented the destruction that my dad had warned me about?

According to his wife's letter, witnesses had seen Aaron Louis Cressman wandering through the streets, talking to himself. Maybe he was trying to psych himself up, trying to talk himself into doing something he knew he had to do.

Maybe he *had* to jump.

After all, my great-great-grandfather had made dozens of changes to the fates of dozens of people. Maybe, after a while, he hit some type of tipping point, and he saw new and horrible consequences looming on the horizon. But perhaps he discovered that he could stop it all with a single act of self-sacrifice.

And maybe that was a price he was willing to pay—forfeiting his own life in order to save the lives of others.

But how did he discover this, and how many changes was he able to get away with before the bill finally came due?

Suddenly, I get the sense that I'm not alone in the cemetery. I'm being watched. I spin around, shoving the picture back into my pocket. "Uncle Roy?" I say, trying to come up with a reason why I'm here instead of at school.

But there's no one there. I'm all alone.

It's just me and my great-great-grandfather's grave.

———

My phone dings as I'm getting ready to head back to the house. It's Gael.

?????dude, you skipping today????? don't tell me you ran back to Portland.

Just researching things. trying to figure things out … you know … the Mia situation.

It takes him a while to respond to this message. *Don't do anything rash!!! Amy's parents are out of town. Last-minute research into selling their cemetery … anyway, she's having her first movie night of the year tonight!!! Meet me there, and we can talk about it.*

I'm about to tell him that I don't think I'm up for it, but Gael sends me another message before I can finish mine. *I'm NOT taking no for an answer!! See you there. 8 sharp! Don't even think about skipping!!!!*

———

I get to the Korean cemetery right at eight o'clock, and a lot of kids are already there. There are candles on some of the gravestones, lighting warm circles around picnic blankets and folding chairs. There's loud laughter as flashlight beams weave back and forth between freshly filled plots. There are no campfires, however, nothing that might leave evidence for Amy's parents to find.

Amy's movie-night parties are a highlight of the Colma social scene. Her family has a large portable screen that we drag out and prop up against the largest mausoleum, and there's an old video projector that provides the picture. These parties are always spontaneous and fun, and back during sophomore year, she threw them every month or so, whenever her parents were out of town.

I remember the first one she threw. There were just twelve of us, and we'd sat around the bright screen watching one of the first X-Men movies. I heard way more laughter than movie dialogue that night, and word had spread like wildfire. At the last movie night of the year, there'd been at least forty kids, eager to party and usher in the school-free summer months.

I remember being impressed by the size of the crowd, thinking that it surely couldn't get any bigger than that. In my absence, however, it seems like movie night has only grown. It's early still, but I'm guessing that there are at least seventy kids here now, ranging from freshmen to seniors. I even spot some recent graduates manning a keg on top of one of the cemetery's nicer monuments.

I guess a lot of people would find this pretty morbid—partying and watching movies in the middle of a sea of graves—but for us it's a point of pride, a big, joyous middle finger pointed right at the dark heart of the universe. It's proof that even growing up here, surrounded by death, we can still live normal lives.

Plus, there's always plenty of beer and pot, and that helps lighten the mood.

When I arrive, there's a large crowd gathered around the video projector, trying to decide on a movie. After a loud, laughter-filled debate, they finally settle on an old classic: *Heathers.*

I scan the crowd around the projector for Gael, and when I don't see him, I head back into the grounds, moving from candle to candle and blanket to blanket.

"Luke!"

I spin around and see Gael sitting on a blanket with Cole, Amy, Erin, Heroji, and a girl I don't recognize. Both Gael and Erin wave me over.

"Well, well, well," Erin says, "look who decided to show up." She smiles, and when I sit down, she hands me a Heineken. "We were afraid your new crush would have you working a séance or something."

I ignore her.

"Lighten up, Erin," Gael says, shooting me a meaningful look. "Mia seems pretty cool to me—a little bit odd, but hell, who here isn't?" Cole laughs and makes a ridiculous kissy face at him. It won't be long before the two of them wander off and start making out.

"Can we talk, Gael?" I ask. Erin gives me an annoyed look as I put my beer bottle down and walk away.

"Do you think your dad would be able to tell us anything about our powers?" I ask. "Like, why we're not supposed to use them?" There's a smile on Gael's face when he joins me, but it disappears as soon as I mention his dad.

"No. He told me never to say anything, and if he knew that I blabbed…" He shakes his head back and forth violently. From what I've seen, Gael and his dad have a very strained relationship. "Besides, I'm pretty sure that he knows exactly as little as we do. His dad told him what he told me, and he's not exactly the investigative reporter type." I groan in frustration. "You said you did some research today, right? Did you find anything new?"

"Maybe," I say. "But nothing we can actually use."

Now is not the time to tell Gael about my great-great-grandfather's death, and my theory on why he threw himself into Colma Creek. I don't want him putting me on suicide watch.

"We'll figure something out," he says, staring up at the dark night sky. Then, suddenly, he snaps his fingers. "That kid, Tony Balint—he's from one of the founding families, right? We can talk to him, see if his family told him anything."

"Yeah," I say, "that makes sense. We'll try him tomorrow."

Unfortunately, I'm not very optimistic about this. What are the chances that Balint's heard anything that we haven't? It seems pretty clear to me that there was a coordinated effort to kill this information several generations back.

"Meanwhile," Gael says, "Erin's been wanting to see you." He nods in her direction. "You should take the night off, man. Go and keep her company."

I glance back over and see Erin watching us. When she sees me looking her way, she flashes me a smile and pats the blanket at her side. Gael gives me a shrug and heads back over to Cole.

I stew in silence for a few seconds, weighing my options; then I give up and rejoin my friends.

———

"What were you two chatting about?" Amy asks when I sit back down. "Are you guys keeping secrets from us?"

Gael casts me a quick glance. "We're just planning your birthday party, Amy," he says, covering for us. "You know, figuring out how many strippers to hire, that type of thing."

"As long as Channing Tatum and Ricky Whittle are in the mix, I'll be happy," she says.

Erin downs the rest of her beer, tosses the empty bottle over the nearest gravestone, and plucks a new one from the case at her side.

Amy gives her a sour look. "And just for that, Erin, you get to help me pick up trash later."

Erin takes a sip of beer and sprays it in Amy's direction. Then she breaks down laughing. It's all so silly and her laughter is so infectious that not even Amy can resist joining in. I'm guessing that Erin's on her third or fourth beer of the night.

"Jesus Christ, Erin," Amy says, shaking her head. "Don't be such a beer bitch, *bitch*!" She throws a bag of chips at Erin and everyone keeps laughing.

I manage a smile, but my mind feels heavy. I take a sip from my beer and somehow manage to drain half the bottle.

Eventually, the talking and laughter die down, and Gael and Cole move away, as do Heroji and the girl he's with. Amy and Erin keep on chatting, but I turn my attention to the movie.

A young Winona Ryder and Christian Slater are busy hooking up and killing their jackass schoolmates. The lead Heather is a very eighties blonde, and I remember that the actress who played her, Kim Walker, died of a brain tumor at thirty-two. Gene Siskel, Mary Shelley, François Truffaut, and Johnnie Cochran all died of brain tumors. None as young as Kim Walker, though.

She doesn't look much older than Mia.

How far am I willing to go? I ask myself. *What am I willing to risk in order to do the right thing? Would I climb up on my great-great-grandfather's ledge? Would I be willing to gamble with my own life?*

After a few minutes lost in my own head, I look over and realize that it's just Erin and me on the picnic blanket now. She sees me looking and flashes me a smile. Then she scoots to my side, leans her head against my shoulder, and lets out a deep sigh.

Surprised, I look around. Gael is sitting with Cole in the row of gravestones behind us. He's watching Erin and me with a big, goofy grin on his face. He's always thought that we should get together, and he's always made fun of me for never giving it a try.

He flashes me a big thumbs-up. With my hand behind Erin's back, I return the gesture, but with my middle finger raised instead of my thumb. I can hear Gael laughing.

Erin lifts her head.

"I'm sorry I was such a bitch at Deacon's party," she says. "I've been all over the place, you know?" Then she puts her head back down, and she's quiet for a little while. "I was so sad when I heard about your dad. I wanted to talk to you about it, but I didn't know what to say. I liked him. He always seemed so genuine whenever I saw him, not at all like my parents. No matter what's going on at home, even if they're fighting or ignoring each other, they always try to make everything look perfect. It's kinda like my dad's business, I guess, like facial reconstruction. Everything you see is just a fake surface spread across dead meat." She leans back and smiles at me. Her eyes are swimming, and I'm guessing that she's even drunker than I realized. She's never this thoughtful and unguarded when she's sober. "I'm really, really sorry your dad had to die. It fucking sucks."

I nod, feeling sad not just for my dad, but also for Erin, for the fate I know is waiting for her at the end of her too-short life.

I reach out and brush the hair away from her temple, trying to see her death again. I've seen this vision at least a half dozen times before, so it isn't much more than a hazy memory.

She's in a car, driving down an empty road. She's in her mid-thirties. It's nighttime, and snowflakes are beginning to gather on the windshield. She's reading something on a futuristic tablet while her self-driving car pilots itself. There are warning lights flashing on the dashboard, but she doesn't see them. Then, suddenly, the car veers sideways and she's thrown against the door. The last I see, the car is spinning off the road.

It's a careless accident, only a couple decades away.

I can't let her die. This realization hits me hard and fast.

I don't know what'll happen if I act. I don't know if there'll be consequences, or if I'll eventually have to kill myself, but I should be willing to take that chance in order to save a friend.

Besides, my great-great-grandfather had made a lot of changes before it ever caught up to him. I should be able to make a small change here, a gentle nudge.

Erin deserves a future. So does Mia.

"It's so stupid," I say. "My dad died in a dumb accident. It shouldn't have happened. He grabbed for a gutter and it gave way. It's like what happened to my sister's biological parents." I make myself look deep into Erin's eyes, and I keep going. "They were driving home in the snow. They had to hit their brakes suddenly, and the tires locked up, sending the whole thing spinning into a tree. There was an antilocking mechanism in the brakes that was supposed to keep that very thing from happening, but it didn't work. Some kind of mechanical failure." Some of this is true, but a lot of it isn't. Darla's biological parents did die in a car accident, but it was in the middle of summer, and no one knows why it actually happened. "My dad shouldn't have died. Darla's parents shouldn't have died. Things fail." I force a laugh. "Think about it. Think about those self-driving cars that they're testing everywhere now. I mean, that's totally insane, right? You're in a thin metal box going sixty or seventy miles an hour, with trees and cliffs all around, and now you're supposed to take your hands off the wheel and trust in a computer to keep you safe? Maybe read a book or take a nap? No freaking way! When things like that fail, people die. You have to look out for yourself."

Erin's eyes are wide, and she looks troubled. I think I've done it—I think I've planted a fear that might just save her life.

"I've gotta go," I say, and I lean in to give her a hug. "Thanks for saying those nice things about my dad."

Wrapping her tight, I touch the back of her neck.

This time, Erin's death is a full-on vision.

I'm in a cozy bedroom. It's early morning. There are birds chirping in the bushes outside. There's the smell of honeysuckle in the air, and I get the sense that we're someplace warm, someplace near the equator. Erin is lying in bed next to a man I assume is her husband. They are both old, in their late seventies maybe. They are both sound asleep. I watch her take a breath, roll over onto her back, and smile. This is her last breath. She dies smiling.

When I pull out of Erin's arms, I let out a relieved laugh.

I did it. I saved her!

Erin gives me a confused look. I kiss her on the cheek, then stand up and leave.

———

It's only on the way home that I start to freak out.

What have I done?

I've changed the future, messed around with someone's fate. I've gone against my dad's rules. But still, the world remains pretty much the same. So far, at least.

It's coming, my dad says inside my head. *Wait for it. Just wait.* I can imagine him saying this, but I still can't remember his face. It's just a disappointed blur over a frowning mouth.

No! I feel confident and angry. *I'm done waiting. I'm done living in a haze of indecision.*

If I have to choose between sitting on my hands and watching people die or acting—being strong and making a difference—then I choose to act.

And everyone who disagrees with me can just shut the hell up.

PART THREE

FROM BAD 2
WORSE

13

I wake up filled with nervous energy, thinking *I saved Erin!* over and over again as I shower, brush my teeth, and get dressed.

I check my phone before heading downstairs, pulling up CNN. I'm looking for news of some type of catastrophe—an unexplained explosion, a school full of children suddenly falling dead, a wormhole ripping through a city—but there's no sign that what I did had any global effect. It's all just the normal doom and gloom stuff, and I'm starting to think that I got away with it.

I saved Erin! And I did it without breaking the world!

Maybe my great-great-grandfather just took it too far. Maybe he tried something too big, only to have it backfire, and *that's* why he had to kill himself. If I stick to small changes, maybe everything will be okay.

I'm smiling when I get downstairs.

"It looks like someone's in a good mood," Uncle Roy says, staring at me over the lip of his coffee cup.

"Yeah," I say. "I think I had good dreams last night."

"Well, don't forget that you promised to pick up the final sprinkler parts when they came in. Can you do it before school? I want to get them installed before noon."

I nod and pour myself a cup of coffee from the freshly brewed pot. "Not a problem," I say. "Anything for the family business."

Then I get going. I need to talk to Gael about last night, and I know that he has jazz band practice early on Thursday mornings.

Then I'm going to have to talk to Mia.

And isn't *that* going to be an interesting conversation: *Hey, Mia, I don't want to freak you out or anything, but someone's going to try to kill you tomorrow night. Don't worry, though. I won't let it happen. We can work together and bring your future killer to justice.*

Yeah, I'm not exactly sure how she's going to take that news.

On my way to the Home Warehouse store, I consider my new situation.

I shouldn't go crazy. I should just make a couple of changes here and there, fixing things before they have the chance to go wrong. If I limit myself to that, I figure I should be able to keep myself from falling into the Aaron Louis Cressman trap. It's a limited superpower, I guess—we're not talking about Iron Man catching an asteroid before it hits New York City—but still, I feel giddy at the thought of using my powers to make an actual difference in the world.

The sprinkler parts are waiting for me at the customer service desk when I arrive, and I'm in and out of the store in a matter of minutes. When I get back to my car, I notice Gael's older sister, Karen, in front of the Target at the other end of the parking lot. She's holding her young baby, Toby, in one arm, while trying to steer an overloaded shopping cart with the other. I toss the sprinkler parts into the backseat of the Focus and run to give her a hand.

"Thank God!" Karen says. "This could have ended with a baby *and* my groceries scattered across the parking lot!"

I'm surprised when she hands me Toby instead of the shopping cart. I know absolutely nothing about holding babies. "Just support his head there, Luke," she says, motioning for me to cup the back of his head with my hand. "That's it. You got it!" Then she turns and starts to push the cart toward her car.

Karen is Gael's favorite sibling. She's three years older than him, and she was the most supportive when he came out to his family. In fact, she was practically giddy at the thought of having a gay brother, acting like it was the absolute height of glamour. I remember Gael complaining about that. "It's not like being gay makes me more awesome or anything," he told me. "That's just who I happen to like. It's countless *other* things that make me awesome."

"Gael told me you were back," she says. Her voice is bubbly, and she sounds too well rested to be a new mother. "He was so bummed when you decided to go off to school—moping around for weeks on end—but now everything's all right again. You know, my husband and I go back to the homestead every Sunday night for a Silva family dinner. Now that you're back, you should come over and tell us all about your Portlandia adventures." Then she lets out a laugh. "Do you remember the water balloon fights that you guys used to drag me into when we were kids? I remember the one that somehow managed to spill into our living room. Man, were our parents *pissed*."

Conversations with Karen, I remember now, tend to have few pauses, shooting off in random directions at a hundred miles an hour.

When we reach her car, she parks her shopping cart at the trunk and starts to unload it. Toby squirms and his neck settles against my exposed arm, and suddenly I find myself dropping down into darkness.

No! Not Toby. I really don't want to see how this baby is going to die, sixty, seventy, eighty years from now.

But then my stomach drops. When my vision emerges from the darkness, I see that he's still just a baby, basically no older than he is right now.

"*Why?*" Karen is sobbing somewhere off to my left, a shadow in the corner of my eye.

Toby, however, is right in front of me, his small body nearly motionless inside a tiny isolation chamber at the center of a dark hospital room. He's hooked up to a ventilator, and there are at least a dozen monitoring sensors dangling off of his arms and legs.

He looks so small and fragile.

"Goddamned tropical virus—why couldn't it have been me instead?" Karen sobs. I focus my attention, and I can see her collapsed into her husband's arms. He, too, is crying, holding on to her tightly as she sobs against his chest.

An alarm sounds from the monitoring equipment, and in a flash a half dozen hospital workers appear. The beeping from Toby's heart monitor stutters, then transitions into a flat monotone. Scrambling, a doctor cracks open Toby's isolation chamber and starts applying pressure directly to his tiny chest.

Then, after twenty seconds of frantic work, the doctor stops.

And Karen starts wailing, her keening voice filled with unimaginable anguish.

"—reminds me," Karen says, her cheerful tone jolting me out of my vision, "if you do decide to come to dinner, you should make it this weekend. Next Tuesday, Joseph, Toby, and I are headed out on our first family vacation. The Caribbean! I can't wait! White-sand beaches, swimming in the warm water, snorkeling!" She does an excited little dance and buckles Toby into his car seat.

The Caribbean. And then I remember her sobbing voice cursing a tropical virus.

That's where he's going to catch it. That's how he's going to die!

This time I don't even hesitate. "The Caribbean? But, Karen, I just heard there's a highly infectious disease running wild down there. I saw it on Twitter. They're about to put out a travel warning. It's hitting kids and old people the hardest, and there's no vaccine yet."

Karen's face immediately goes pale. "I … I hadn't heard," she says, and her eyes fill with worry. There's a long pause—a nearly unprecedented event for Karen. "Maybe … maybe we shouldn't go. I can get a refund on those tickets if I cancel them now. No, *definitely* we won't go. I'll call Joseph and we'll reschedule. Maybe we'll go somewhere else, maybe skiing."

Distracted, she turns and heads for the driver's seat. I push the cart aside and make my way to the passenger-side door. I open it, lean in over Toby's car seat, and give him a kiss on the forehead.

This time, the vision comes quickly and easily. I'm looking down on a wrinkled old man sleeping suspended in a futuristic-looking tank. There's a boxy machine at its side, and I can see a robotic arm mixing something and feeding it into an intrave-nous tube.

The room is filled with a gentle orange light, and there's a crowd of people surrounding the old man's tank. Near the front, a man dressed in white gestures for people to move in closer. Well-wishers touch the tank. They whisper words I can't hear, and a couple of them kiss the glass next to the old man's face.

I don't even pick up on the transition between life and death for Toby. It just happens. The man in white says, with a simple smile, "It is done," and I find myself floating back down into the parking lot.

Toby's round, full-moon face is staring up at me. I give him a pat on the leg and close the car door.

"Thanks again, Luke," Karen says. She's still preoccupied as she pulls her car out into traffic.

"It was my pleasure."

And it actually was.

There's a tiny worry in the back of my head—I've made two changes now, in less than twelve hours—but in this instance I don't think I had much of a choice. I just saved an innocent baby's life!

I don't want to die soon—and I truly hope it doesn't come to that—but maybe, for Toby, that's an acceptable risk to take.

I have to start thinking this way. I have to start figuring out what, exactly, my life is worth.

———

Cora Bell is waiting for me when I get back home.

Her Tesla is parked in the turnaround in front of the cemetery, and she's leaning back against its hood. She has a bouquet of lilies resting at her side, and she smiles warmly when she sees me approach.

"My uncle's inside, if you need something," I say, "but we've decided not to sell. This cemetery is a part of who we are."

"I'm not here about that, Luke," she says. "I'm here for you. Let's have a little one-on-one conversation." She picks up her flowers, turns, and motions for me to follow her down the main path into our cemetery.

"We're not going to change our minds," I say when I catch up to her.

She nods. "I understand. I mean, I'd still like to buy your property, but that's not why I'm here." She tilts her head to the side and looks at me intently. Then she smiles. "What I really want to know is, do you have supernatural powers, Luke?"

My legs freeze in place, and Cora Bell watches my reaction carefully.

"Don't worry about it," she says, amused. "I'm not a threat or anything. I'm just trying to figure things out. Colma's a magical place, isn't it, Luke?"

"What … what exactly have you heard?"

"I've heard plenty," she says, "and I've learned a lot more on my own." She nods toward the heart of the cemetery, and we move from A5 to A4 and continue down its length. "I have a man named Mark Balint working for me. Last summer, he showed me this amazing thing that he can do—he calls it 'ghost-walking,' but a lot of people would call it astral projection. He can leave his body and travel anywhere, incorporeal and unseen, viewing things at a great distance."

My eyes widen involuntarily at the name. Mark Balint must be Tony Balint's dad—and everything that happened with Darla now makes sense. Tony must have used his "ghost-walking" abilities to spy on her.

"Mr. Balint confided in me that his powers were hereditary, passed down from generation to generation. Once I knew that, it was a simple matter of research—connecting the dots, news report by news report, all the way back to the founding council members, the kings and queens of Colma, if you will. That's where this all started, isn't it, Luke? Your great-great-grandfather and all of his friends? They all had abilities, didn't they?"

"I don't know what you're talking about." My voice is unsteady.

"*Don't give me that shit!*" she growls, suddenly turning on me. Her eyes are cold and angry. "You're just a kid! You have no idea what's going on here or how important all of this is!"

After this outburst, Cora Bell closes her eyes and takes a deep breath. She holds herself perfectly still for a couple of seconds, and when she finally opens her eyes again, she's calm and in control.

Her anger's not gone, though, I think. It's still there, only buried, crammed deep down inside. She's like a volcano, ready to explode.

"Tell me what your powers are, Luke," she says calmly. "And tell me what your friends can do. Mia Chevalier, Gael Silva, Jim Deacon, all of them."

I take a small step back.

"That stuff's not real," I finally manage. "Ghost-walking, magical powers—that stuff only happens in comic books."

She stares at me for a while, and it's obvious that she doesn't believe me.

"I've been working with Mr. Balint at Coriolis Solutions. We've been running tests, pushing him to his limits." She shakes her head. "This is a very dangerous game you're playing, Luke, with high stakes that you can't possibly understand."

She stares daggers at me, and I try to remain strong. There's no way I can trust this person, no matter what she might know.

When she sees that I'm not backing down, Cora Bell turns abruptly and hurls her bundle of lilies down on the nearest grave. Her jaw muscles are clenched tight, and her lip is starting to curl. She stares down at the scattered flowers, then abruptly shakes her head like she's trying to shock herself out of a bad dream.

"I'm just trying to do what's right," she says. "Seriously, you've got to trust me on this. I'm just trying to avoid catastrophe."

She moves toward me, and I take an automatic step back. Then she pauses and we stare at each other for a while.

Finally, she says, "You have my card, Luke. I can help you, and you can help me. Call me when you're ready."

Then she turns and leaves, her stride strong and purposeful as she recedes into the distance.

I watch her go.

Am I doing the right thing? I've started using my powers to do good, but maybe I *should* also start talking to scientists. Not her, obviously, given how deranged she seems, but maybe an academic institution somewhere, a university. After all, I could be sitting on a whole new branch of physics here.

But who can I trust?

Cora Bell already has a ghost-walker working for her. What exactly is she having him do? I probably shouldn't be trusting either her or any of the Balints until I can figure that one out. Spying and corporate espionage would be a breeze for someone who could travel unseen and walk through walls. And what happens if a corrupt government gets their hands on that? What happens if they grab me and start using *my* powers? I remember the movie *Minority Report*—I could end up floating in a government tank somewhere, reporting on the future, detecting pre-crime.

Maybe *that's* why Colma's five remaining council members turned their backs on their powers. Maybe they saw nothing but a bleak and depressing future if they kept playing the hero.

These are depressing thoughts, and they help reinforce my decision to stay silent.

I crouch down and start gathering Cora Bell's lilies back into a bundle. I'd assumed she'd just randomly thrown the flowers out of frustration, but when I glance up, I see that they've actually reached their destination. Her daughter's gravestone is a simple marker, still in pristine shape:

LILY BELL

JUNE 5, 2003—MARCH 3, 2018

GONE TOO EARLY.

DEARLY MISSED.

She was just fourteen years old. She didn't even make it to Mia's age.

I stand up and go, leaving the flowers where Lily's mother left them.

I check my phone as I head back to the house. With my chores and my encounters with Karen and Cora Bell slowing me down, I probably won't have time to catch Gael or Mia before first bell.

I can warn Mia at lunch, I decide. I'll fix her future and save her life over heat lamp–warmed pizza and vending machine soda. Such a ridiculous setting for such a serious conversation.

My phone buzzes. It's a message from Gael. *Where r u man, shit's getting crazy here, Amy says Erin's dad just DIED!!!!*

14

Amy fills us in at school.

She, Gael, Heroji, and I meet up at her locker in the break between first and second periods. She looks flustered and confused as she starts telling us the story, and her face is ashen.

"Erin called me before school this morning. She was sobbing—it was so awful. Her dad was on a business trip in Miami, doing some type of celebrity reconstruction work. Anyway, he was walking through the hotel lobby when he collapsed. His heart just stopped." Amy looks like she can't believe what she's saying. "I saw him at Erin's place just a couple of days ago, and he seemed absolutely fine."

"God," Heroji says. "That's messed up. First Luke's dad—*sorry, man*—and now Erin's. And I always thought my dad was the one in danger, locked up in prison with murderers and skinheads and corrupt guards."

"Yeah," Amy says. "My dad can be a real asshole, but I'm planning on giving him a big hug when he and my mom get home tonight."

Gael nods, like he's thinking about doing the same thing.

"When did it happen?" I ask.

"The call from the hospital woke Erin up early. Maybe a little after six?"

So, he probably died six or seven hours after I changed Erin's future. Six or seven hours after I saved her life.

I never actually saw Erin's dad's death vision—maybe we shook hands once, years ago—but the timing seems too close to be a coincidence. It has to be cause and effect. I changed her future, and her dad died a sudden, unexpected death. One plus one equals two.

This is all my fault. This is what my dad warned me about.

———

I meet up with Mia at lunch. My head is pounding, so I just let her talk.

"That poor girl," Mia says.

I nod.

She casts a glance around the cafeteria, then leans in close and whispers, "Did you see it coming, Luke? Did you have a vision?"

"No!" I say defensively, my voice a little bit too loud. Then, calmer, "No. I only met him a couple of times. I didn't see it."

I look at Mia. Her eyes are wide and soulful. She's trying to be sympathetic, I can see, and my heart aches to know that she genuinely cares about me.

And who dies if I save her? I wonder. Her mom? Her aunt?

Or maybe it'll be Gael, or Amy, or Erin, or Heroji, or Darla, or Uncle Roy. Or maybe it'll be all six of them. Maybe that's what I'll get if I continue to meddle.

And then there's Toby, I realize, Gael's nephew. If adding thirty-five or forty years to Erin's life had killed her dad, then what does giving an additional *eighty* years to Toby call for? Does it even work that way?

The risk had seemed worth it when it was just *my* life on the line, but I definitely don't want to be gambling with the lives of others.

"Hey, guys," Gael says, stepping up behind me. He gives Mia a nod, and I realize that they haven't actually met yet, so I introduce them.

"I've heard a lot about you," Gael says. And that's true. He even knows when and how she's going to die.

He turns toward me and his voice takes on the sober tone that everyone's been using today. "I just wanted to let you know that we're going to be walking over to Erin's house after school—you know, to check on her? You guys should come along."

I nod. "Yeah. That sounds good."

It's the least I can do.

After Gael leaves, I notice Mia squirming in her seat. "Maybe I shouldn't go," she says. "I don't know your friends at all. It would be weird for me to just show up."

"You can be there for me," I say.

Mia thinks about it for a moment, then nods. "Okay, Luke," she says. "For you."

I close my eyes for a second.

I don't deserve someone as good as her.

And she doesn't deserve to die.

———

Erin lives about a half mile from Mission Hills High. Amy, Heroji, Gael, Cole, Mia, and I meet up in the parking lot after the final bell, and we walk to her house, cutting through Cypress Lawn Cemetery.

No one talks much, and Mia sticks close to my side. When I look over, she grabs my hand and gives it a squeeze.

"We should have brought flowers," Heroji says, when we're about a block away. "That's what you're supposed to do when there's a death in the family: flowers or a casserole."

"We're fine," Amy says. "Everyone will be bringing that stuff. We just want to let her know that we're here for her. That's all."

When we arrive, there are a half dozen cars parked in front of the house, and it looks like every light in every room is on. Amy rings the bell, and someone I assume is an aunt answers the front door. I can see an end table covered in flowers just inside the entryway.

"You must be here for Erin," the woman says, a bittersweet smile on her face. "She has such thoughtful, considerate friends."

"Can we see her?" Amy asks.

"Of course," she replies. "We're planning services right now. There's still a lot to do, so please don't take too long."

When Erin gets to the entryway, she immediately steps outside and closes the door behind her, joining us on the front porch. She's wearing jeans and a sweatshirt, and her hair is pulled back into a tight ponytail. She looks strange to me, and it takes me a minute to realize that I've never seen her without makeup on.

"Jesus Christ, this sucks," she says as soon as the door is closed. "I've been cooped up in there with my mom and aunts all day long. It's driving me nuts. Does anyone have a cigarette?"

Heroji pulls a pack of American Spirits from his messenger bag.

Erin grabs a butt, casts a careful glance back toward the front door, then gestures for us to follow her around to the back of the house. When we're out of sight, she accepts Heroji's lighter and draws flame into her cigarette. She takes a long drag, then lets it out with a loud sigh.

"You should hear them talking," Erin says. "All of my aunts are just going on and on and on about how he was such a great man, such a good provider, the absolute *best* father." She rolls her eyes, mocking them. "They hated him when he was alive, constantly bitching about his business trips, telling my mom to leave him."

There's an old playset in Erin's backyard, and she collapses into a creaky swing.

"We're so sorry, Erin," Amy says. These are the first words any of us have actually managed to say to her. "We're all here for you. Whatever you need, just tell us."

Erin stares at us in response, her eyes moving from Amy, to Gael, to me, to Mia, to Cole, and then on to Heroji. Her gaze lingers on Mia for a moment but continues on with nothing but a tiny eye-roll. Then she lets out a loud, hard laugh. "Jesus Christ, this situation is so absurd. But it is what it is. I'll be okay."

She swings back and forth a couple of times, holding her legs at an awkward angle in order to keep them from hitting the ground. Then she drags her feet in the dirt and brings herself to a stop. Her eyes are fixed on the wooded patch of land at the back of her yard.

She takes the cigarette from her mouth. "You know," she says, "I forgot about this, but before we got the phone call this morning—at maybe five a.m.—I woke up and sat bolt upright in bed."

She nods up toward her window on the second floor. "It wasn't like how I normally wake up, all slow and groggy; I was just suddenly totally awake. I got out of my bed and moved to the window, and I looked out toward—" She lifts her hand and points toward the wall of trees about fifty feet away. "He was there. My dad. He was wearing a business suit, and his briefcase was dangling from his hand. It was still pretty dark out, but he was waving up at me, and I could see that he was laughing." Erin lets out a short laugh of her own. "I guess he was waving goodbye?" she says. "It didn't seem strange to me at the time, and I don't even remember going back to bed. The next thing I knew, the phone was ringing, and I could hear my mom sobbing."

"Well, that's … fucked," Gael says, looking perplexed. "Was it a dream?"

Erin shrugs. She takes a drag on her cigarette, and blows out a thin jet of smoke.

"Erin!" her aunt calls. "We need your help picking out flowers!"

"I've got to go," she says.

As she gets up from the swing, Amy darts in and gives her a hug. Erin looks confused for a moment, then accepts it blankly. Heroji is next in line, but she shoos him away, gesturing back toward the house.

"You guys should go," she says. "I think I'll be at school tomorrow. If not, next week for sure."

"We'll see you then," I say, pushing aside my worry and guilt.

She smiles a little, and her eyes play over us as a group. "Well, I feel about one percent better now. Maybe two." Then, immediately regretting being so flippant, she backtracks. "I'm sorry, guys, just … just imagine I didn't say that. Imagine I said something nice instead, okay?"

"I'll call you tomorrow," Amy says.

Erin nods, ditches her cigarette, and heads back inside, ready to help pick out flowers for her dad's funeral.

———

"Did that seem weird to you?" Amy asks as we head back to the school. "It was like she was angry and yet … somehow amused? And then there's that dream she had—yikes!"

"People react differently to grief," I say quietly.

I remember going through sorrow, anger, confusion, and guilt after my dad died. It still hits me when I least expect it, over and over again.

"In Haitian voodoo, there's a certain amount of absurdity to death," Mia says, and I'm surprised to hear her speak. So far, she's been silent around my friends. "The *loa*—or god—of death is called Baron Samedi, and he has a wicked sense of humor. He loves rum and tobacco, tells jokes, and swears nonstop. When you die, he digs your grave, then escorts you into the afterworld." Mia pauses and considers this for a while. "Actually, that seems about right to me. So much of life is ridiculous. Maybe someone should be laughing at its end … at the final punch line." And she smiles. "I wouldn't mind meeting that guy when I die. Maybe I'll bum a smoke off of him and tell him a dirty joke."

Amy lets out an amused chuckle. "Do you actually believe in all of that?" she asks. "I mean, do you practice voodoo?"

"Nah. But my dad's Haitian, and he grew up surrounded by all of that stuff. He used to tell me stories about his mom and grandmother, the things that they'd do to please the loa. It's interesting, but I don't really believe in it." She shrugs. "You've got to give them credit for the whole voodoo doll thing, though; sticking those pins in is just so satisfying!"

"I could use a couple of those for Mr. Ramirez," Heroji says, and he makes a couple of stabbing motions with his hand. "And one for Coach Stadler, too! Stab, stab, stab—right in the balls!"

Gael, Mia, Cole, and Amy all laugh, but my thoughts are still back with Erin. She had looked so lost and confused sitting there on that swing.

I did that to her. I killed her dad.

And I didn't see it coming.

Is that how this works? If I change someone's fate, are the consequences totally out of my control, just a shitstorm of chaos and destruction waiting to rain down on a completely random bystander?

If so, once it's all said and done, the results are my responsibility.

I pause in the middle of the road, and Amy, Heroji, Gael, Cole, and Mia keep walking, not noticing the stunned look on my face as I fall behind. Mia's chatting and smiling, smack-dab in the middle of my group of friends. They're all smiling.

If it was just my life, I could handle it. I'd save Mia and die willingly—reluctantly, of course, but convinced that I did the right thing.

But if I live while others die? There's just too much chaos in that equation.

All of the blood drains from my head as I come to an abrupt realization: I'm going to have to let Mia die.

It's nearly six o'clock when we get back to the parking lot, and I pull Gael and Mia aside.

"I need to talk to both of you," I say, in a low voice. "Can we go somewhere private?"

We get in Gael's Jeep, and I tell them about each other's familial powers as Gael starts to drive us back to my house. There's stunned silence for a moment; then they both start talking.

"So you can, like, talk to dead people?" Gael asks, his voice filled with awe.

"Not me," Mia says, "at least not yet. But my aunt can. She's a conduit—the dead talk through her. And before you ask, they know they're dead, so it's not like Bruce Willis in *The Sixth Sense*. It's weirdly undramatic."

I'm sitting shotgun, while Mia's in the backseat, leaning forward between me and Gael. "And you can paralyze people?" she says to Gael enthusiastically. "That's pretty freaky."

Gael makes an embarrassed sound. "Well, it only lasts for a couple of minutes. And it's not like I actually *use* my powers. My dad told me to pretend like they don't exist."

"So did mine," I add, feeling a knot forming in the pit of my stomach. "He told me that changing someone's death would have dire consequences."

Mia nods. "Well, my aunt uses her powers all the time, but she always downplays what she's doing, and besides, I don't think what she does ever makes a huge impact on the world—nothing life-or-death, for sure—so maybe there aren't any real consequences to her actions. Most of the time, she's just giving comfort to the grieving."

I look out the window. The knot in my stomach grows larger, becoming a cold, hard boulder. "Actually, that's what I wanted to talk to you guys about."

Gael turns back toward Mia, then shoots me a hard look, clearly wondering if I've told her about her fate.

"I … I killed Erin's dad," I say.

Both of them are silent. They have the same expression on their faces: deep concern mixed with the barest hint of repulsion.

"I've known how Erin was going to die for years now. It was going to happen in a self-driving car accident when she was in her thirties. And last night, well, I just decided … I couldn't let it happen. So I told her how dangerous those cars could be, and boom, her future changed, and now she's not going to die until she's super old."

Neither of them says anything, and I can see that Mia's brow is furrowed, like she's trying to work her way through a difficult math problem.

"It felt like I was doing such a good thing," I continue. "It was so liberating, and it made me feel so happy. But now … with her dad …" I pause. "I must have done that to him."

"You never saw his future?" Gael asks.

"No, but six hours after I save her life, he just happens to drop over dead? That's no coincidence."

"You can't do it again." Mia sounds adamant. "Your dad was right. If something like that can happen, it's too dangerous."

A part of me is furious that I didn't warn Mia earlier. I could have called her this morning, while I was still happy and confident about what I was doing, before I heard anything about Erin's dad's death. Before I realized—

"You won't do it again, will you, Luke?" Mia asks.

I glance over at Gael and see an iron-hard look in his eyes.

"That's the thing," I say. "I already did it again. This morning, before I heard about Erin's dad."

"Jesus Christ," Mia says.

"I ran into Karen, Gael, and well …" I can't continue.

"What did you do, Luke?" Gael asks, suddenly frantic.

"I held Toby, and I saw his death … and it was going to be *soon*. Like, just a couple of weeks away. I scared Karen into changing her Caribbean trip, and Toby's safe now. He's got at least seventy years left. I saw it. It's a good death now, Gael."

He's silent for a time, but I can see his jaw muscles working, and his knuckles clenching against the steering wheel. Finally, he asks, "And who's gonna pay the price for that, Luke? Is Karen going to die? Or me? Or my parents?"

"I don't know," I admit. "I don't know how it works. I'm looking for answers." I turn toward Mia in the backseat, feeling frantic, needing to assure her. She's staring daggers at me. "My great-great-grandfather—he knew some things. If we can figure them out—"

"And how the hell do we do that, Luke?" Gael asks, his voice full of simmering bile. "I told you to wait until we could figure out a solution, but you couldn't do it. You just had to charge right ahead!"

"We can talk to Tony Balint and his dad," I say. *Or we can go to Cora Bell,* I'm about to add, but before I can even mention my encounter with her, Gael turns the corner onto the road leading to my house.

I'm surprised to see a truck crashed into a tree at the side of the road. It's a surreal sight, like something out of a news report: *crumpled metal and smoke, a wheel still spinning, the back left side of the vehicle tilted into the air.*

It takes me a moment to realize that this isn't just some random truck wrapped around the trunk of a tree. It's Uncle Roy's!

"Pull over!" I yell.

Gael slams on the brakes, and I've got the door open before the Jeep even has a chance to come to a full stop. I leap over the corner of the Jeep's hood and slide down into the ditch, falling on my ass once before managing to make it to the driver-side door. The door is warped, crumpled in where it should be flat, and I have to pull hard at the handle a couple of times before I can get it open.

Darla's pinned beneath the wheel.

Her face is smeared with blood, and she isn't moving. The now-deflated air bag is sitting in her lap. She's all alone. There's no sign of Uncle Roy.

Her left arm had been pinned against the door, but now it dangles free. She's wearing a yellow long-sleeved shirt, but everything from the elbow down is a glossy red, and there's a sharp point jutting out where bone has broken through her skin. I lean in and lower my ear to her mouth, desperately listening for sounds of life. Thank God, she's still breathing, but it sounds shallow, and there's a short, liquid gurgle at the end of each exhalation.

"Call 911!" I yell back over my shoulder. "Get an ambulance here!"

Darla moves slightly, grumbling beneath her breath; then her lips purse and she coughs a little. I'm hit with the overwhelming stench of alcohol. The cab of the truck smells of oil and smoke, but there's also the strong scent of booze and pot radiating up from Darla's body. I look over at the passenger-side seat and see a broken bottle of vodka.

Was she driving drunk and stoned? That's not like Darla at all.

Her grumbling stops, and her body falls still. I reach in and press my fingers against the side of her neck, sliding them back and forth, desperately searching for a pulse. After a painfully long time, I find it. It's there—slow but steady.

"They're coming!" I hear Mia call from somewhere behind me. Her voice is rushed and loud. "It'll take them a couple of minutes, but they'll be here soon."

As if on cue, I hear sirens sounding in the distance.

"Be okay," I whisper, pressing my face against Darla's shoulder. "Please, please, *please* be okay."

Then, suddenly, the sirens dwindle, and the light around me starts to fade.

My vision of Darla's death is different this time.

Instead of a cramped hospital room, filled with breathing machines and her old, cancer-riddled body, I find myself in a dimly lit hallway. The floor is dirty, littered with dried-up leaves and trash. There are a couple of sleeping bags on the hallway floor, and a small, dirty man is hunched up in a corner. Darla is in front of me, sitting with her back against the wall, her head lolled back and her eyes cast up toward the ceiling.

I barely recognize her. If I weren't touching her neck back in the real world, I would never have guessed that the human being in front of me is my little sister.

She looks horrible. She is far too skinny, and her too-long hair is bunched in kinks on her shoulders. Her skin is sallow, and her many layers of clothing are all stained and dingy. But for all of that, I can tell that she is still young. In her twenties.

She groans, sitting there on the floor, and her arms flop down to her sides. There's surgical tubing cinched around her right bicep, and an emptied syringe juts from the vein at her elbow.

I'm almost too stunned for the possibility to even register: heroin.

This just seems wrong. *She* seems wrong. This is not the Darla I know.

I watch as Darla's junkie body twitches and her eyes roll up inside her head. A man walks by but doesn't stop, doesn't even seem to notice. Then Darla's shoulders drop and she collapses to the floor, sliding down onto her back.

She groans, uncomfortably, then her chest shudders, and she vomits. A thin line of bile spills from the side of her lips, but the rest stays lodged inside her throat. Her body convulses a couple of times as she chokes on it. Then she falls still. Her eyelids, mercifully, drop closed before her eyes have the chance to go lifeless and dull.

And then a hand is on my shoulder, pulling me back from the

open door of Uncle Roy's truck. Two paramedics crowd in, while a third one leads me away from the scene.

"We're here now," the paramedic says. She's a woman, and she's angling me away with the quick confidence of someone who's done this countless times before.

"We've got everything under control," she says in a calming voice. "Everything will be okay."

No. Nothing's under control.

And nothing's ever going to be okay again.

15

The paramedics let me ride in the back of the ambulance.

I sit at Darla's side, and I don't stop watching her. I'm almost afraid to blink.

Her body is so still on the cot. She is stable, but sedated and oblivious, and I can't help flashing back to that *other* image I have of her now—the death I've created for her.

Payback, I guess, for what I did for Toby—for my arrogance, for my stupid belief that I'm some kind of superhero.

Darla's never been much of a partier. Just a couple of cigarettes now and then. She even gave me shit once when I snuck into the house stinking of alcohol. Now she's getting blind drunk?

Did I cause that as well? Is that how this works?

Did I do more than just change Darla's future? Did I change her present, too, her very nature, putting her on the path toward that future? Did I turn her into a junkie with just a few words to Karen?

I reach out and touch her hand.

I'm sorry, Darla, I think. *I screwed up.*

Then, casting my eyes up and addressing something else—God, karma, whatever—I beg for the chance to make this right.

The paramedics rush Darla to the OR as soon as we pull up to the hospital, and I follow in a daze. As soon as the admitting nurse sees my pale face, she rushes to my side and leads me back to a private waiting room.

"Is there anything I can do for you, dear?" the nurse asks as she sits me down in an armchair. "Is there anyone I can call?"

"My uncle," I say. "Can you call my uncle? Please?" She nods, a sympathetic look on her face, and I give her his number.

After a couple of minutes, Gael and Mia crowd through the waiting room door. They stand there for a moment, staring at me; then Mia rushes over and wraps me in her arms.

"We followed the ambulance," she says. "Gael blew through a couple of red lights, but they managed to lose us."

"She'll be okay, man," Gael says. My face is pressed into Mia's shoulder, but I can feel his comforting hand on my forearm.

"I changed her future," I say. "I *destroyed* her future."

"What?" Gael asks.

But before I can tell them what I saw, the door crashes open and Uncle Roy storms in.

"Where is she?" he demands, his eyes wide, frantic. His face is pale and he's sweating heavily.

"They're checking her out in the OR," I explain. "It was a pretty bad accident, but the air bag saved her." I can see a wave of relief rush across Roy's face. "She's got a broken arm, some broken ribs, and the paramedics were treating her for a punctured lung. Other than that, we have to just wait and see what they find."

Roy lets out a huge sigh of relief, then collapses into the nearest chair.

"How did you get here so fast?" I ask, after a moment of silence. "I just gave the nurse your number, like, five minutes ago."

"We called him," Mia says. She and Gael settle into the chairs next to me. I suddenly realize how uncomfortable they look. They want to be here for me, I know, but they seem totally out of their depth.

"And I ran every light," Uncle Roy admits. His shoulders slump, and he suddenly looks absolutely exhausted, dropping his head into his hands. "And I scraped up your car, Luke. Sideswiped a pylon out front. It's just the paint, I hope. Sorry."

"Don't worry," I say, trying to comfort him. "Darla would be impressed. That's got to be, like, faster than the fastest video game lap she's ever run."

He sighs, still too stressed out to laugh.

"What was she doing?" he asks. He drops his hands from his head, holding them out in a pleading gesture. "How did this happen? She wanted to borrow the truck after school, but I didn't even think to ask her where she was going."

I shrug. I don't know what to say. I'm sure he'll find out about the alcohol soon enough, but I don't want that weighing on him just yet.

After a couple of minutes of silence, Uncle Roy gets up and starts moving again, his initial relief giving way to growing anxiety.

"Did they say how long it would take?" he asks.

"No," I say. "They want to be careful. They want to make sure everything's okay."

"I hate hospitals." He stops pacing for a moment and gives me a funny look. "It was like this on the day you were born. Your mom went into labor early, and we were waiting while they checked her out. Your dad looked ... well, he looked worried, like he thought that he should be doing something, but didn't know what. Then he got up out of his seat and stormed across the room. He grabbed the doctor attending to your mom and told him that you were in danger, that ..." Uncle Roy pauses here and shakes his head. "I don't remember the words he used. Something medical—endro-something-something-something in extremis, exacerbated by yadda yadda yadda ... I don't know. He just started spouting this stuff, and the doctor took a step back. He stared at your dad for a while; then he called in a nurse. He requested something, and they rushed your mom into an operating room."

Uncle Roy pauses. He turns and moves to the door, putting his hands on either side of the tiny window in its center.

"And that's how you were born," he finishes.

I've never heard the whole story of my birth before. Whenever I asked him about it, my dad had just told me that there had been unavoidable complications that had led to my mom's death. After that, I never pushed him for more information. The pain on his face had been all too obvious, stopping me cold.

"And then what happened?" I ask.

Roy turns and looks at me. For a moment, his face is set cold and hard—an unemotional wall. Then it breaks, and his lip trembles. "Everything was fine for a while," he says. "We celebrated your birth—well, your grandparents and I did—but your dad stayed at your mom's side. Then ... then your mom just dropped unconscious. The doctors rushed her back into the OR, but they couldn't save her."

I look over at Gael, then at Mia. Their sad faces look back.

"After you were born," Uncle Roy continues, "but before your mom passed away, one of the doctors came up to me and asked me where your dad had gone to medical school. I told him that he ran a cemetery, and that he'd never gone to medical school, that he hadn't even finished college. The doctor didn't believe me. 'No one could have seen those complications coming,' the doctor said. He'd looked it up. 'It was a one-in-five-thousand chance on top of a one-in-ten-thousand chance. Even the best-trained medical professionals would have missed that possibility, unless they were very smart, very well educated, and extremely lucky.'"

Or unless they'd seen it coming.

Realistically, the only way that my dad could have known that I was in danger is if he'd had a vision of my death. Touching my mom's belly, did he see me dying in a hospital operating room? Did he hear a doctor spouting out those medical terms as my tiny, unborn heartbeat sputtered and stopped?

And did he then go against the rules that had been passed down to him from his dad?

Is this the great lie of my life—that it never should have happened?

"Sometimes," Roy continues, "I had the feeling that there was a touch of magic about your dad." A smile spreads across his face, breaking through the thick pall of anxiety. "Like … in the hours before his death, he was so very, very moody. He went upstairs and started reading an old book up in the attic. When I found him, I asked him what he was doing, and he looked up, pale as death, and said something odd. He said, 'I'm reminding myself of … of consequences. And responsibility.' Then he went out to clean the gutters and he died. It was almost like he knew what was coming."

"He was looking at a book?" I ask, surprised. "What book?"

Roy shakes his head. "It was a journal, a big black journal … handwritten. I don't think I'd ever seen it before." Then he shrugs. "I guess it's still up there in the attic."

I turn to Mia and Gael and wonder if they realize what this might mean.

The next half hour passes in anxious silence. Uncle Roy heads back to his chair, buries his head in his hands, and stays that way for a long time. Gael gets up and goes to the bathroom. Mia goes to a vending machine in the hallway and returns with soda and snacks for all of us.

I spend my time thinking. My dad had used his powers to save my life. And yet, still, he warned me—constantly—about the consequences of doing just that, hammering home all of his rules.

Maybe that's because he knew firsthand just how important those rules were.

In saving my life, did he manage to doom my mother? Was that the trade-off? My mom's life for my own?

He always claimed that he'd never seen a vision of my mom's death, but maybe that had been nothing but a lie to protect me. Maybe my mom's death had been something completely different until he'd taken my fate into his hands and played God.

I wait for my dad's voice to pipe up in the back of my head— denying this theory, explaining or defending his actions—but nothing comes. Even though I still can't see his face in my mind, I can see his disembodied lips pressed together into a firm, sad line, refusing to budge, glued shut with pain and regret.

I feel a knot forming in my throat, and suddenly I'm choking back tears. I feel Mia's hand on my forearm and look over to see her sympathetic eyes.

I let out a sob, then stand up and turn away, moving to the door to stare out the tiny window.

———

The doctor has a smile on his face when he opens the door and steps into the waiting room. The smile makes Uncle Roy's tense shoulders drop in relief.

"Darla's going to be fine," the doctor says. "The puncture in her lung is small. We were able to reset her fractured ribs, and she's on oxygen right now. The tear should knit itself back together on its own, and we'll be monitoring it for the next couple of days. Other than that, she has a hairline fracture in her right tibia—we've immobilized that in a temporary cast; she has some deep muscle bruising all throughout her chest and shoulders; and she might have some neck damage—possibly some whiplash—but we won't know anything more about that until the swelling goes down. Her most serious injury is the compound fracture to her left radius and ulna, in her forearm. We have that immobilized at the moment, but she'll probably need a couple of surgeries in order to get that set properly. Some pins and metal plates will be needed."

As Roy listens to all of this, his eyes start to well up. The list of Darla's injuries is overwhelming. "But she'll be okay?"

"She should be fine," the doctor says. "But she'll be in the hospital for a little while, and she'll need physical therapy once she gets out. Right now, she's sedated and resting comfortably, and all of her vital signs are stable and strong. She'll probably be asleep well into tomorrow, but you'll be able to go in and see her after we get her settled."

The doctor's eyes move from Roy to me, to Mia, and then to Gael. "Are there any questions?" he asks. When none of us say anything, he continues. "Well, if you do come up with anything, just ask a nurse and they'll be able to find me."

Uncle Roy nods. The doctor smiles again and leaves.

"You guys should go home," Roy says. "Get some food and some rest."

"Are you coming?" I ask. "The doctor said she'll be out of it for a while."

"I'm gonna stay here," he says. "In case she needs anything."

"Then I'll go home and get us some food. I'll come back later, and—"

"No, Luke," Roy says, shaking his head. "Stay home, get a good meal, do your homework if you can, and go to school tomorrow. The doctor said that she'll be fine, and she'll be asleep for a while. You can come see her tomorrow afternoon."

"But—"

"That's an order," Uncle Roy says, sounding every bit the soldier he once was.

"Yes, sir," I say, and I smile. "Call me if you hear anything."

"We have to find that journal," I say as soon as Mia, Gael, and I are out in the parking lot. "I did that to Darla, and worse. If we don't figure something out, she's going to die a strung-out junkie in less than ten years' time."

"What?" Gael asks, surprised.

"Yeah. You should be running away from me right now," I say thoughtfully. "I'm like a tornado over here. I destroy everything I touch."

My dad, Darla, Erin's dad—and now I can add my own mother to that list.

Mia and Gael exchange a meaningful glance; then Mia shakes her head vigorously. "Hell no," she says. "I'm not going anywhere. I'll be right there at your side."

"Me too," Gael adds. "We'll do everything we can to save Darla's life."

As for Mia …

After seeing what happened to Darla, I know that I can't do that again. I can't roll the dice and unleash even more chaos. But the thought of actually letting Mia die—I just can't face that.

Maybe there's an answer in Dad's book. My anxious stomach is roiling, filled with fear and doubt, but also some hope and excitement.

Maybe—just maybe—I can still find a way to save her.

16

Our attic is a dusty, low-ceilinged room packed full of boxes. It smells like dried grass and oil, and I haven't had reason to go up there in years.

I head up first, stumbling on the dark, narrow staircase at the back of the house. Once I'm in the attic, I bump my head on the sloped ceiling a couple of times before I finally manage to turn on the string of dim bulbs that lights the long room from one end to the other.

As soon as the lights are on, Mia appears at the top of the staircase. Then Gael.

"A big black book," Mia says, already surveying the room, all business.

It doesn't take us long to find it. It's sitting on a box next to a folding chair in the middle of the room. There's a pillow for lumbar support propped up against the back of the chair, and a battery-powered lantern sitting on the floor at its feet.

"It's like a tiny reading nook," Gael says. "How often did your dad come up here?"

"I don't know," I say. "The only times I ever saw him come up here was when we needed to get the Christmas decorations out of storage."

Gael gestures toward the chair, and I take a seat. Both Mia and Gael settle onto the plank-wood floor at my feet.

I turn on the lantern and pick up the book. There's a Post-it note stuck to its cover. It reads, *For Luke. In times of trouble, I hope this helps keep things in perspective. Our actions have consequences.* It's my dad's handwriting—big, bold, and exactly as I remember it.

I pluck the note from the cover and hold it in my hands, running my fingers across my dad's message. This was up here waiting for me all along, not even ten feet from my bed. When did he do this? Is this the last thing he wrote, right before he died?

Impatient, Mia grabs the journal from my hands and flips back the cover. There's a signature scrawled across the journal's endpaper: *Aaron Louis Cressman.*

"That's your great-great-grandfather, right?" Mia asks. I nod, and she flips through the book. "This looks like a private journal, from 1913 to 1917."

My heart stutters inside my chest. That covers his entire time on the Colma town council. If he ever found an answer, something I could use to save Mia's life, it would be here, in these pages!

"Read it," Gael tells Mia. "Tell us what to do."

Mia skims through the first couple of pages. "It starts with him being recruited to the town council," she says. "Apparently, Able Deacon had some type of prophetic abilities, and guided by visions, he approached Aaron and the other founding council members. He told them"—and here she starts quoting directly from the journal—"'We are each of us blessed with abilities, abilities that set us apart, but which have been given to us by the rotting dead gathered beneath our feet. To protect them. To make this land sacred. These abilities are a sacred trust, and they'll pass down through the generations, from eldest son to eldest son, and eldest daughter to eldest daughter.'"

So Mia's in the clear. Her family's powers will die with her aunt.

Mia hunches over the book and reads to herself for nearly a full minute. Then she glances up. "Man, your great-great-grandfather sounds downright giddy in these entries," she says. "He talks about the other council members like they're long-lost siblings, going on and on about their powers: Raphael's Silva's 'deadening' abilities, my great-great-grandmother's channeling, Able Deacon's gift of prophecy.... And apparently Ginger Schossler could make people forget brief stretches of time, and Daniel Balint could leave his body and go anywhere he wanted, totally unseen."

Gael snaps his fingers. "That must be how Tony Balint spied on Darla," he says. "He used his family powers!"

I just nod. Then, "Does it say anything about repercussions?" I ask.

"Hold on," she says, delving deeper into the book, flipping page after page after page.

After nearly five minutes, she looks up and fixes me with an intense stare. "They resolved to use their powers to better the world, but yeah, after a while, they started seeing consequences. Especially when it came to Aaron's powers. He used his visions to save Ginger's uncle from a fall that would've killed him, and then the very next day, an old shopkeeper in town was struck by lightning. He stopped a kid from drowning, and someone was shot in a hunting accident." Again, she starts reading aloud from the journal, quoting my great-great-grandfather's words. "'Abe suggests that there will always be some sort of trade-off for using our powers. With small changes—freezing someone for a moment, wiping out a memory—we can count on the trade-off being minuscule, but as soon as we start changing people's fate and altering the shape of the world, the consequences of our actions grow. And it is all so frightfully hard to predict! Never just a life for a life, but instead a push for a pull. Opposing forces. This puts us in a tough spot. If it's not a one-for-one trade-off, then how can we know what to do?'"

Gael grunts. "So … what *did* they do?" he asks.

"They kept going," Mia answers. "At least Aaron did. He foresaw a shootout in a bank, and he had your great-great-grandfather, Raphael, step in and stop it. As a result … a mother and her young daughter were trampled to death by a wild horse." She skims over the next couple of pages, and when she continues, her voice is low, hesitant. "After that, Aaron tried to stop. He couldn't chance it, didn't want any more mothers and daughters dying because of him. But he saw something that he just couldn't let happen. He saw Able Deacon's pregnant wife dying in a trolley car accident. So he stepped in and stopped it."

Mia pauses. She's no longer studying the journal, just fixing me with a stricken look.

"What happened after that?"

"Another vision," Mia says. "He touched Able and saw something horrible."

"What?" I ask, feeling downright panicked at the look in her eyes.

"I'm not sure," she says. And she holds up the journal. "It just says, 'I saw, I saw, my God, I saw,' and then …"

Both Gael and I move closer to the journal, so we can see what's written there, and Mia starts flipping pages. It's the word *fire* repeated hundreds of times, interspersed with barely legible gibberish:

> ... fire fire from the deadest fiery eyes. orange and red BURNING! And I can't see, can't stop, my hands moving and everyone dying in fingers of flame ... and I can't stop seeing it consume consuming and eat eating, and I can't stop it from burn burning. my fire. I can't stop my fire from eating us all ...

As Mia flips through the pages, I can see that this incoherent block of words is spread out over at least thirty pages, broken down into entries marked out in hours and days. It looks like time passed, but Aaron Louis Cressman's mind remained stuck in that incoherent state.

"This is insane," Gael says. "I mean, literally, it looks like he went insane."

I take the journal from Mia and flip to the last page. At the very end, beneath a block of scribbled words, is a pair of neatly printed lines. In contrast to the rest of the pages, these words look downright calm. *I have to kill myself,* my great-great-grandfather writes. *Maybe that will fix this.*

"Did he actually think that that would work?" Gael asks, glancing up from the journal with an incredulous look in his eye.

"Yeah, he did," I say. "That's how he died."

But was Aaron Louis Cressman right, or was this all just a delusional belief, a symptom of his madness? Have I been going about this all wrong? Was his self-sacrifice just a meaningless bit of insanity?

I don't know anymore.

"I bet that this is why the town council disbanded," Gael says. "They saw people die, they saw Luke's great-great-grandfather go insane and kill himself, and they figured that their abilities were just too dangerous to use. So they broke all connection, buried their secrets, and started telling their children not to use their powers."

If only I'd listened, I could have avoided this whole dilemma. Erin's dad would still be alive, and Darla would still have a bright, happy future.

Mia's hand touches my forearm, and I look up, staring into her loving, sympathetic eyes.

And she'd still be dying. Just like she is now.

I look down at my dad's Post-it note. *Why couldn't you give me something more useful than this stupid, fucking journal?* I clench my fist and crumple the note into an angry ball. *Yeah, I messed up, Dad, I didn't follow your rules, but this is your fault, too! You could have told me everything right from the start!*

Suddenly, Mia's hand tightens on my forearm, and I look up. Kneeling next to me, she lets out a loud, pained gasp, and I watch as her eyes spin up inside her head, leaving just white orbs staring out of their sockets. Her entire body shivers, and her lips pull away from her clenched teeth.

Her face looks like a grimacing death mask. Not human. Not alive. She's something else entirely now.

I try to pull away, but instead, Mia's fingers dig in deeper, pinching off the circulation to my hand.

She lets out a long, hissing breath.

"I'm sorry, son," she says, and her voice is different now. I can still hear her natural tone, but it's taken on a different inflection, now at the low end of her range.

It's my dad's voice, I realize. He's speaking to me through Mia.

"What the … ?" I hear Gael say as he scrambles away from Mia's hijacked body. But I remain perfectly still, my eyes locked on her face.

"I thought the rules would work for you, son," my dad says. There's a surprising warmth in his words, and Mia's lips relax, transforming from a grimace into a sad, wistful smile. "I thought that they'd protect you, keep you away from pain, but perhaps I should have talked to you earlier, should have explained … better."

"Explained what?" I ask.

"Explained that you're old enough now to move beyond the black-and-white rules that I taught you to live by. Now you've reached an age of truth and consequences…. *Yes*, it's possible to act on your visions and save lives, and *yes*, perhaps it will be worth it…. But also, perhaps it will be catastrophic!" He shrugs Mia's shoulders. "That's the dilemma you face. Every move you make is rolling the dice with other people's lives. And if you do that long enough, the odds *will* catch up to you. That's a statistical certainty, and that's why I left you the journal." He nods toward the book at my feet. "Aaron Louis Cressman's life is an object lesson, a reminder that things can go wrong. Your great-great-grandfather tried to do good, but his most noble actions led to the deaths of others, and to his own insanity and suicide—haunted, I'm guessing, by a vision of something even worse, something unimaginably bad. Whenever I was tempted to make a change, no matter how good the possible benefit might be, I came up here and made myself reread the journal. And each time, I held back, realizing that the possible consequences could be so much worse than anything I could ever imagine."

"That's what you were thinking about when you came up here on the morning of your last day," I say. "If you saved yourself—"

He interrupts me with a shrug. "Who knows what would have happened? Perhaps you, or Roy, or Darla …"

"And you made that mistake once already," I say, my voice losing strength, becoming nothing but a weak whisper.

My dad leans back and studies me for a moment, somehow seeing me through Mia's blank eyes. Then he smiles.

"Actually, no," he says. "I wasn't thinking about that at all. I consider saving your life my one great victory. And your mother … well, let's just say that your mother agrees with me."

The muscles in my face spasm as soon as I hear these words, and I start to sob. My dad pulls me down off my chair and into Mia's arms, and it's *him* hugging me. I can feel his big, strong presence, somehow here, crossing over from the other side and filling Mia to the absolute brim.

And I can see his face!

Crow's-feet and stubble, a warm and easy smile—it's right there in my mind's eye, waiting for me. It's *always* been there. How could I ever think that it was gone?

"What should I do, Dad?" I ask, whispering in his ear.

"You know what to do," he says. "Your life isn't dictated by rules anymore, Luke. It's about knowledge, responsibility, and a commitment to the greater good." Then he pulls back until we're at arm's length, and he gives me an approving nod.

"I love you, son," he says. "And I trust you."

Then, suddenly, he's gone.

With great effort, Mia manages to pull her hand away from my forearm, and her entire body slumps down, deflating like a balloon spitting out air.

"No, no, not now!" she gasps, and these are her words now—100 percent horrified Mia.

Then she gets up on her feet and stumbles back, shaking her head violently.

She stares at me for a long time, her eyes brimming with tears. Then she turns abruptly, brushes past Gael, and heads down the stairs.

I call out her name, but she doesn't stop, and after a handful of seconds, I hear the front door slam shut as she runs out of the house and into the dark.

———

I tell Gael to stay inside as I search the cemetery.

The night is still and calm, and the moon is a thin sliver up in the sky. I head toward the center of the grounds, calling out Mia's name. I'm not even sure if she came this way. She might have just hit the driveway and kept on running all the way home, trying to get away from me and from whatever happened up there in the attic.

I can feel a huge weight settling into my stomach.

"Mia," I call, one more time. Then I turn and head north, toward a familiar grove of cypress trees.

The angels are waiting for me in their secluded alcove. I sit down at their feet and stare up at their open arms.

I'm surprised to see that the offerings I left over a week ago are still here: three coins, a Coke bottle lid, a folded-up receipt, and a ballpoint pen. The receipt is starting to wilt into a misshapen lump of pulp after being repeatedly soaked in morning dew.

I search my clothes for something new to add to this collection, but all of my pockets are empty. I have nothing to give them.

"They're beautiful," Mia says, her voice thin and ghostly. I spin around and see her at the edge of the trees. She stands still for a moment, shrouded in shadow; then she joins me on the ground in front of the statues, sitting about five feet away.

I can see that her cheeks are streaked with tears.

"I was hiding," she says, "thinking things through. Then I saw you come over here and my curiosity got the best of me." She manages a weak smile. "These are your parents?"

I nod.

"It's beautiful. You did them good."

I don't know what to say.

"I'm sorry I ran away. I was just overwhelmed. I just … you've got to understand, Luke, I spent so long trying to …" Then she trails off into silence.

Her gaze travels from my parents' angels to me, and she blinks, sending more tears falling down her cheeks.

"This … this is the beginning of the end for me," she finally says. "Now that my powers have surfaced, I'm going to go downhill fast. And—*fuck!*—one of the worst things is, I *knew* that this was coming, but still I let you get close, and I'm so sorry about that." She lifts her hands in a pleading gesture, unconsciously mimicking the angels' pose. "I just … I got my hopes up, you know? I told myself that maybe it wouldn't happen to me, and I'd be able to live a normal life. But now it's here, and I can't let you stick around for what's coming next."

"But how could you know?" I ask, surprised. "It's supposed to go from eldest daughter to eldest daughter. And your aunt—"

"Is really my *mother*," she interrupts.

My breath catches in my throat, and the clearing falls silent around us.

Her mother? But how?

And I remember helping Mia search for her wayward aunt, driving her from cemetery to cemetery. Now, in light of this new knowledge, the heartbreak in her voice becomes even more devastating, Mia having to explain—to her mom, her own mom!—that she was, in fact, who she said she was.

Seeing the shock on my face, she pauses for a moment and then explains. "Before you told me, I didn't know anything about the other Colma families, the other powers. But I knew all about *my* family, and I knew about our powers. My aunt—my *real* aunt, Melinda Iverson—told me everything she knows. She told me about how our family powers tend to surface in our late teens or early twenties, but they appear hand in hand with debilitating schizophrenia." Mia grimaces. It looks like there's a bitter taste in her mouth. "*That's* our family's real curse—the schizophrenia.

Hell, for a long time I thought that my mom channeling the voices of the dead was just a minor side effect. Occasionally, she'll be okay for a while—the doctors will try her on a new drug and she'll be coherent for a couple of months—but it never lasts long. She's never been well enough to care for me on her own."

She pauses and considers me for a while, watching me with those deep, pale brown eyes. "It scares the shit out of me, being around her. It's a reminder. Each time I have to calm her down, each time I have to help her eat, or shut down one of her delusional rants, it reminds me of what's waiting for me in the not-too-distant future. And now, with what happened up in your attic, I know for sure that that not-too-distant future is here."

I watch the pain move across her face, from her brow to her eyes, and then to her pursed lips. And I remember the bottle of pills I found in her bag.

"You've been noticing symptoms, haven't you?" I ask.

She sighs. "Yeah, I think so. I wake up and think there's someone moving in the corner of my room. I hear whispering, too, sometimes, and I've started to get confused. I've tried some of my mom's medications, but I don't think they do anything. They just make me feel sick."

I reach toward her, trying to bridge the gap between us, but she cringes away.

"Before, you said that we should be running away from *you*," she says, blinking back tears. "Well, you got it wrong, Luke. You're the one who should be running. Soon, I'll be totally unrecognizable. I've been trying to embrace life, trying to be spontaneous and free while I can still enjoy it, but there's a darkness pressing in around me. And I don't know what I'm going to do."

Before she can react, I crawl to her side and pull her into a hard hug, clenching her tight against my body. She resists for a moment, then gives in, collapsing into my arms. Her whole body trembles as she starts to cry.

"I'm not going anywhere," I say. "Whatever you have to face—doctors, drugs, confusion, whatever—I'll be right there with you. Every step of the way. Okay?"

She lets out a long, ratcheting sob, and then gathers herself together. "Okay, Luke," she replies. Then, in a completely exhausted voice, she says, "Thank you. Thank you for being here for me."

And we stay like this for a while, held in each other's arms, under the silent angels' eyes.

———

I check my phone as we make our way back to the house. It is after midnight: 12:24 a.m.

Friday. The day of Mia's death.

Rounding the corner onto A5, I can see Gael leaning against the hood of his Jeep, waiting to take her home.

Maybe it will be a mercy to let her die. After all, what does the future hold for her? Nothing but confusion, helplessness, and growing horror.

Maybe it's better to suffocate in a coffin underground than fade into insanity. This is a heartless thought, I know, but maybe it's also a kind thought.

I look over and see Mia smiling up at me, and I feel absolutely awful for thinking these things. I pull her into my arms, wanting to make her happy, wanting to make her think that I'll be able to protect her from insanity and death and everything bad in this world—even if that belief is, ultimately, a lie.

17

I have a hard time waking up. Each time I start to surface, my dreams pull me back down.

Mia's there with me—a presence at my shoulder, a voice whispering in my ear.

I find myself walking down a city street. There are tall, alabaster buildings stretching up into the bright summer sky. They have wide, clear windows, and I can see human-shaped figures standing on the other side. They're watching me, even though they don't have faces, just blank flesh where eyes and nose and mouth should be.

"They're dead," Mia says. "And waiting."

There is no sound or movement on the street. I'm the only one outside.

Then we're somewhere else—a dark midnight woods. I'm running, being pursued, and there are voices laughing behind me. There's the sound of a river crashing up ahead. And in a thoughtful voice, Mia says, "We're not here yet."

And I'm in a museum at night, lost in a maze of empty hallways.

And in a car on the freeway, winding through mountains.

And falling through clouds, toward a jagged cityscape, just high enough up to see the curvature of the earth in the distance. It looks like the horizon is on fire.

And each time, it's just me and Mia. I can't see her, but I'm glad that she's there with me, keeping me company.

And then I'm in a garden. There's a cup of coffee in my hand, and it's early morning. I can hear birds chirping in the trees, and traffic grinding in the distance. And I'm happy, yawning away a good night's sleep. My body feels old, and I know that it's the future—my muscles are knotted and sore, and my knee twinges with age.

And finally, I'm not alone.

There's someone in the garden up ahead. A woman facing away from me, on her knees, weeding a recently planted row of flowers. I turn—there's no one at my shoulder—and turn back.

"Mia?" I ask, my voice hesitant.

And she laughs.

But when she looks back at me, there is no smile on her face— just blank flesh where eyes and nose and mouth should be.

And finally, I wake up.

———

I hate that I have to let her die, but I can't risk the destruction. I can't put everyone else in jeopardy. That's my burden, my responsibility—the very thing that my dad had reached across from the other side to warn me about.

But I can make damn sure that the assholes who kill her don't get away with it.

I'll follow. I'll take pictures, gather information. I'll make sure that there's enough evidence to put them away for good.

It's the least I can do. The very, very, very least.

For Mia.

———

I text her before I get out of bed. *That concert tonight—florence + the machine—did you end up getting tickets? are you going?*

She doesn't answer right away, so I get up, take a shower, and get dressed. I'm jittery as I stand under the hot water, as I pick a fresh T-shirt and jeans from my dresser, as I remember the horror of watching her die. *And I'm going to have to do it again,* I think, but in the real world now, standing to the side as she's buried alive, as her lighter flickers underground and her last breath seizes in her chest.

After I get dressed, my phone dings with Mia's response. *Nope. My aunt called me in sick today. She has an important meeting and my mom's totally off her nut—totally agitated, needs looking after. So no school for me today and definitely no time for concerts/fun… probably for the best. I need time to think.*

Okay, I reply, *I'll try to come by after class. Want to be there with you.*

Mia responds with a question mark, an exclamation point, and then a smiley face.

I don't reply. When the time comes, I'm going to have to step aside and let fate run its course. She'll get her concert pass—some-how—and I'll watch her go to her death.

I grab a quick breakfast, then call Uncle Roy as I'm heading out the door.

"You're going to school, right?" he asks without preamble.

"Yeah, I'm heading out right now. I'm putting up the closed sign as we speak." I do just that, letting Roy hear the metal gate swing shut. "It's the sign that has your number on it, so try to keep your phone charged and nearby, okay? But enough with the chit-chat. How's Darla doing?"

"She's … she's resting comfortably. They've got her pretty doped up. A specialist came in earlier this morning and went over the situation with her arm. He showed me X-rays—it looks pretty bad. There'll be surgeries and a buttload of metal plates and pins." He pauses; then his voice gets lower, downright stern. "You didn't tell me about the booze, Luke," he says, an edge to his voice. "They say her blood-alcohol level was off the charts. A police officer visited me. They're not going to charge her with driving under the influence, but only because they think her injuries are punishment enough."

"I didn't want you to worry about that last night, Uncle Roy," I explain. "Don't hold it against her … please. She screwed up. Besides, after this, I'm sure she'll learn her lesson."

He's quiet for a time, and I wonder how angry he is, if he's contemplating grounding her once she heals, maybe never letting her drive again—or, hell, never letting her out of her room again.

I'm the one you should be grounding, I think. *I'm the one who screwed things up.*

"It's … it's not my fault, is it, Luke?" he finally asks, his voice low. "I'm trying to do my best, but maybe I'm just not cut out for this—you know, not parent material."

"No, Uncle Roy," I say, shocked and horrified. "You're great.

You're the best. It's just kids, you know? We're stupid, guaranteed to screw things up."

"Thanks for saying that, Luke," he says, and there's a hint of genuine relief in his voice.

"I'll try to stop by tonight," I say. "There are some things I have to do after school"—*horrible things that make me want to throw up*—"but then I'll stand watch and you can head home and take the rest of the night off. Okay?"

"Okay," Uncle Roy says, and I can hear the start of a smile in his voice.

————

The school day drags on and on and on.

Mr. Ramirez calls on me several times in calculus, and I have to admit my complete ignorance each and every time. I missed two days of class this week, and already it feels like I've fallen completely behind. He gives me a head shake. "Not good, Mr. Cressman," he says. "Not good at all." I have to agree.

Gael meets up with me at lunch. When he sees that Mia's not around, he leans in close and starts whispering in my ear.

"I had nightmares all night long," he says. "Really messed-up ones, too. I think something bad is going to happen." He pauses and looks around. "You shouldn't do it, Luke. I don't think you should save Mia."

"Yeah," I say, letting out a deflated sigh. "It's just too dangerous."

He sits back and gives me a sympathetic look, and I hate the way that this makes me feel. Helpless—like I'm a swimmer lost at sea and my arms are too tired to carry me home.

"I still want to follow her and figure out what's going on," I say. "Take some pictures, make sure her killers get sent to prison."

Gael pauses for a time, thinking. "Wouldn't that count as meddling?" he finally asks. "Using your powers to change the way things happen?"

I shrug. "I'm not changing my vision any," I say. "Mia's still going to die, so, hell, who knows? Maybe this is *exactly* how it's supposed to happen." Maybe I was always right there, just offscreen, watching her die.

Gael nods, the thoughtful look still on his face.

"And then I'm done," I say. "After this, I don't think I'm ever going to touch anyone again. It just isn't worth it, Gael—knowing so much but unable to do a fucking thing! My powers are nothing but a sick joke!"

Then I stand up and walk away. When I glance back, I see that Gael's staring after me, a stunned look on his face.

———

My phone buzzes with a new text halfway through English lit, my last class of the day. I hold my phone low and check it on the sly while Mrs. Trudeau lectures away at the front of the room. It's from Mia.

U won't believe it! Won VIP ticket to concert! Original winner fell through at last moment and they picked my entry to take her place. They even sent a town car with bright red graffiti hearts on its side. Super fancy!!! My mom's so grateful for all the help I've been giving her, she's letting me go. I get to hang out with the band before and after the show—dinner, sound check, everything... OMG SO excited! Exactly what I need to get my head back on straight.

I forget where I am and immediately stand bolt upright in my seat, knocking my desk aside.

"Mr. Cressman?" Mrs. Trudeau exclaims in surprise.

I'd forgotten all about Mia's contest entry.

"I ... I'm sorry, but I have to go," I say, still staring down at my phone. I can feel everybody in the room watching me, but I don't care.

I grab my bag and dart out into the hallway. I read the message a second time, wondering what I should do, how I should respond.

I can't stop her. I can't do anything.

Too bad I only got one pass, she texts, *or you'd be right here with me.*☺

My fingers shake as I try to reply. It feels like I'm going to vomit with each letter I type.

I love you, Mia, I say. Nothing more.

There is a long pause, and then, *I love you, too. The driver's taking my phone away now, security measures, you know, but I'll tell you all about it the next time I see you, okay?*

Then she sends me a heart emoji.

And that's it.

Her last words to me.

Gael has AP history this period, all the way on the other side of the building. I sprint over, covering the length of the school in a matter of seconds.

The entire class is reading silently when I slam through the door. They all stare up at me, startled, and a girl napping in the back row jerks upright in her seat, knocking a stack of books to the floor.

I scan the rows of desks and see Gael sitting near the front. He shoots me a worried look.

"C'mon, Gael," I say. "We have to go. Now!"

"What's going on?" the teacher demands, getting up from his seat. He looks furious, and I'm guessing that he's a take-no-prisoners type.

"It's an emergency," I tell him. "I'd explain, but …" Then I trail off, realizing that there's absolutely nothing I can say.

"His sister was in a car accident last night," Gael says as he gathers up his things and heads for the door. "I'm his ride to the hospital." At this, the teacher sits back down, nodding.

"What's going on?" Gael asks, as soon as we're alone.

"It's Mia," I say. "It's happening … right now! I thought we had more time, but she's already gone, and I need your help. I need you to drive."

Gael nods, and we rush out to the parking lot.

We jump into his Jeep and I start barking out orders. "The concert's at the Fillmore, so head downtown. She messaged me, like, six minutes ago, so if we hurry we should still be able to catch up to them."

Gael pulls out of the parking lot and heads north, toward San Francisco. He's silent for a couple of seconds, concentrating on the road; then he lets out a sudden, violent "Fuck!"

"I'm sorry, man," he says. "We're running on fumes here. We need to stop for gas." Then he cuts the corner of an intersection and turns hard into the Shell by the freeway on-ramp.

"For God's sake, hurry!" I yell as he jumps out of the Jeep and starts filling the tank.

Mia's house is further south than the school, so she and her car can't be too far ahead of us now—a couple of minutes, at the most—but I can still feel her pulling away from me. It feels like there's a tether rooted inside my chest and tied to her heart, and it's growing tighter as she gets farther and farther away.

I hear a roar growing in the distance, coming from down south. Motorcycles.

I turn to see a black town car with bright red hearts painted on its side cruising toward the freeway. There's a pair of motorcycles in front of it, guiding the way, and another dozen or so following in its wake.

My breath stops as the procession nears. Everything around me drops into a slow-motion crawl.

I lean across the driver's seat and yell out at Gael, "That's Mia! The bikers have her!"

Gael glances up and sees the motorcycles driving past. He slams the fuel nozzle back into the pump and jumps into the Jeep.

"Go, go, go!" I say. "For God's sake, don't let them out of your sight!"

Gael starts the engine and pulls out into traffic, eliciting a long, belligerent honk from a Prius he nearly sideswipes.

"What are we supposed to do?" Gael asks between clenched teeth.

"Just stay close," I say. "If they get away from us, we'll never see them again; we won't get any evidence, and we'll never figure out where they bury her. But don't let them know that we're following!"

"Jesus Christ, Luke. I barely passed driver's ed. And I must have totally missed the section on stealth surveillance."

"Just not too close, I guess. And not too far back, either."

Gael lets out a groan, but despite his objections, he manages it surprisingly well. We stay a few car-lengths back, following the motorcycles up onto the interstate.

"They're not going to the Fillmore," I say when I see that they're heading south, not north. Gael stays focused on the road.

Once we're merged into traffic, we're able to fall back even further. When they're all clumped together like this, it's actually very hard to lose track of a dozen-plus motorcycles driving down the freeway.

"The Devil's Flame," I say.

"What?"

"That's the name of the motorcycle gang, right? I *thought* it was going to be them, but I wasn't a hundred percent sure." So, not an ex-boyfriend, or someone Mia stole something from. Just a biker gang looking to get revenge for what Mia's mom did to them: a bad psychic reading that got their leader killed.

The Executioner, Brianna Mullally, I think, remembering what Gael and I saw in front of Other Worlds the other day. She's the one who's responsible for all of this. She's the one who should be thrown in jail forever.

"They must have stalked Mia, found her contest entry on the band's fan page, and faked a response, then rented a car to pick her up. They made it all look nice and authentic."

"But why?" Gael asks. "Why go to all of that trouble?"

"I don't know," I say. "Maybe it's just easier to kidnap someone when they come along willingly. Hell, Mia probably jumped into that car without hesitation. She probably had a huge, excited smile on her face." My stomach drops at the thought.

The bikers continue south. Woodlawn Cemetery appears on the left side of the freeway, and they swerve to the right, taking the interchange onto State Route 1. The traffic gets a bit thinner here, and Gael drops back a little bit further, trying to keep us from being seen.

After a couple more minutes of driving, we hit the coast, and the huge expanse of the Pacific Ocean appears at our side. The water is slate-gray and peppered with orange-bright patches of light. The residential streets on the left side of the highway soon fall away, and there's just a long expanse of scrub grass leading back to a series of jagged hills.

"Milagra Ridge," Gael identifies. "It's fairly isolated out here— no buildings in sight."

Gael falls back further still, and the road curves toward the ocean. When the highway straightens out again, the tarmac up ahead is almost completely empty. No bikers. No town car.

"Where—," I start to ask, panicked. But before I can even form the question, I see Gael pointing to a tiny road branching off the left side of the freeway. Brake lights flare just up its length.

"I'm going to go a little past," Gael says. "So they don't spot us."

We're right at the southern edge of Milagra Ridge, and Gael pulls into the next residential street. The houses here are huge and no doubt massively expensive. Gael makes a three-point turn in the nearest driveway and pulls back out onto SR-1, this time heading north.

Now that the town car is totally out of sight, the tight fist of panic starts to clench inside my chest. Mia's trapped inside that car, out of sight and nearly out of time.

Has she figured out that she's going to die yet? Or does she still think she's going to survive this ordeal?

"Hurry up," I tell Gael. "We can't lose them! They can't get away with this."

"We won't, man," he replies. "We'll find them. We'll make them pay."

We finally make it back to the side road, and after about a hundred yards, the gravel track swings around a jagged hill and disappears from sight.

"Should we park and go in on foot?" Gael asks. "They could be right around that corner. If we keep driving, they're going to hear us coming."

"Hold on," I say.

I get out of the Jeep and move a couple of feet away. Then I close my eyes and listen.

The waves are crashing in the distance—a low, white-noise babble. I can hear the sound of the freeway and the gentle whisper of the wind. Then, suddenly, a peal of laughter comes from the other side of the jagged hill.

I tell Gael to try to hide the Jeep out of sight. Then I move ahead, slowly making my way up the side of the hill, toward the top of the rise. I take the last stretch crouched on my hands and knees, then settle between a pair of boulders, positioning myself so that I can peer out into the hollow down below.

The motorcycles are parked in a semicircle around the graffiti-painted car. Their headlights are pointed inward, illuminating the group of bikers standing at its side, making them blaze in the otherwise dim afternoon light. About a dozen feet away there's a coffin sitting next to a hole in the ground. The coffin's lid is open, and I can see that the lining inside is a shade of pink that was popular about ten years ago.

I slip my phone from my pocket and start filming the scene, zooming in and panning across the group of bikers, trying to capture as much detail as possible.

"This won't bring my brother back, but *damn it* if it won't feel good," Brianna, the Executioner, is saying. Her henchmen are holding Mia immobile, while the big woman towers over her. "Just knowing that I'm leaving your mom tortured, twisting in the wind, with absolutely no idea what's happened to you—that'll be like *heaven* for me. Maybe, after a while, I'll send her a treasure map. With a big red *X* on it that says *dig here*."

Mia cries out, but the Executioner just grabs her in a tight bear hug, swings her around, and walks her over to the coffin. She throws her in, and I hear Mia's body hit the bottom with a loud thud.

"Ashes to ashes, dust to fucking dust," the Executioner growls. Then, with a dark smile, she draws a sign of the cross with her middle finger and gestures for her henchmen to close the lid.

"Don't be stupid, Luke!" Gael hisses in my ear. His hand is on my shoulder, holding me back.

I'm surprised to see him at my side—I didn't hear him approach—but I'm even more surprised to find that I'm already halfway out of my hiding place, gearing myself up to run down to Mia's aid.

"You can't do it!" Gael hisses. "Remember what happened to your great-great-grandfather?"

He's right. Reluctantly, I settle back down into our hiding place. Gael takes pictures while I continue filming.

The Executioner says something to four of her bikers—I recognize the linebacker-sized guy and the one with the purple birthmark on his face. They grab the coffin and lower it into the ground. The hole isn't six feet deep, but it's still deep enough for the coffin to make a loud clunk when it hits the bottom. Gael and I both jump at the violent sound. Then the bikers start pushing dirt onto its lid.

In less than a minute, the hole is completely filled in.

"Rest in agony," the Executioner says, her voice just loud enough to reach us at the top of the hill. She's standing at the edge of the grave, and as she talks, she upends a bottle of beer into the freshly turned dirt. Once it's empty, she cocks her arm back and throws the bottle out into the heart of Milagra Ridge, where it smashes against a faraway rock.

Then she turns and addresses her troops. "This'll show that rich bitch that she doesn't own us!" she yells. "Deek may be dead, but the Devil's Flame burns brighter than ever!"

At this, the bikers erupt in loud, raucous applause, celebrating their victory.

I have no idea what the Executioner is talking about—in fact, her words don't even really register with me. The only thing in my head right now is an all-too-familiar scene: Mia struggling underground, gasping for breath as her lighter gutters and fails.

I lower my phone and close my eyes for a moment.

I touch the dirt in front of me.

I can't save her, I tell myself. *I have a responsibility....*

But I also have a choice. It's up to me to decide what to do, to decide what's important. My dad had made that perfectly clear.

I open my eyes.

The bikers are still hooting and hollering down below. The one that looks like a football player rears back and lets out an earsplitting howl.

The Executioner strides to her motorcycle. She starts it up and rides away, rounding the hill and heading back out to the freeway. The other bikers—some still laughing and cheering—rush to follow, mounting their bikes, revving their engines, and peeling out into the setting sun. The town car brings up the rear.

"I can't do this, Gael!" I say. "I have to save her!"

I bolt out of our hiding place and slide down the hill as quickly as possible. When I get to the bottom, however, I pause. The town car's stopped moving, and the driver—the guy with the purple birthmark—is standing in its open door, cursing loudly. "Fucking thing's locked up again!" he growls.

The linebacker-sized guy stops at his side. He gets off his bike and gestures for Birthmark to pop the hood.

These are the last two bikers in Milagra Ridge, and I'm horrified to see that they're parked directly between me and Mia's grave.

What do I do? Mia's dying—right now, right on the other side of that car!

I don't have time to wait them out, but they're both focused on the engine compartment, so I decide to try to sneak around to the other side. It's a risky move, but I'm all out of options.

I'm about a dozen feet away from Mia's grave when Linebacker spots me.

"Hey!" he calls. "Who the fuck are you?"

I spin around and see both of them staring at me. Birthmark reaches into the waistband of his dirty jeans and comes up with a long-bladed knife.

My heart plummets.

"She's dying," I plead, still inching my way toward the freshly turned grave. "Please, please, please … it's not too late. We can still save her."

"Stop where you are," Linebacker says. He turns toward Birthmark and gives him a frustrated look. "Jesus Christ, man. What the hell are we supposed to do now? This wasn't part of the plan."

"You can do the right thing," I say. "You can do the *human* thing, and let me dig up my girlfriend. Please!"

I hold my breath as the two bikers exchange looks. Then Birthmark lets out a shrill laugh.

"You *really* don't know our boss, do you, kid?" he says. He turns back toward the other biker. "Do you know who took the shovels, man? I think we've got to dig ourselves another grave."

Just then, I notice Gael approaching from the other side. When he's a couple dozen feet away, he calls out, in a conversational tone, "Hey, guys, Brianna gave me this to show you. It's important. She said she needs her top lieutenants on it right away."

"What?"

But Gael doesn't slow down, moving toward them with a surprising nonchalance. He's got his phone in his hand, and he's holding it out like he's trying to show them something.

Birthmark lowers his knife, casts me a confused glance, and takes a step toward Gael. He reaches out to take the phone.

"Who are—?"

Gael touches his hand and Birthmark freezes in place. I see him give the biker a tiny shove, and the man topples over, landing at Linebacker's feet.

"Oh my God!" Gael says, hamming it up. "What happened to him? Did he faint? Is he all right?"

"I … I don't know." And Linebacker leans over to check on his friend.

Gael touches his arm and the second biker topples over.

I'm impressed. Gael's powers are totally badass.

"Save her!" he barks at me. There's urgency in his voice as he crouches down and starts frisking the bikers for weapons. "You're right, Luke—we can't let Mia die. After seeing what we just saw, it's the right thing to do, no question."

I drop to my knees and start digging. There are no shovels nearby, so I use my hands, trying to get down through the dirt as quickly as possible. My palms are scratched and bleeding in a matter of seconds.

"Hang in there, Mia, I'm coming," I say, even though I know she can't hear me, buried down there in the dark.

Gael joins me after a couple of seconds. "I'll have to knock them out again in a bit," he pants. Then we both dig frantically.

It takes about three minutes to hit wood.

"Mia!" Gael cries, and I think I can hear a simple, wordless yell coming from down below.

I gather dirt in armfuls and scoop it from the open grave. Luckily, the lid of the coffin is only two and a half feet belowground. If they'd done a better job and buried her six feet deep, this would have been absolutely impossible.

When I have enough dirt cleared from the lid, I bolt out of the grave and reach back in. My grip slips a couple of times on the polished wood, but I finally manage to grab hold of the coffin's seam. Gael is doing the exact same thing down at the coffin's foot.

Together, we heave, pulling the dirt-covered lid open.

"Jesus Christ!" Mia gasps, inhaling as much air as she can. She drops her lighter and crawls out of the coffin. Her cheeks are wet with tears, and I can see blood on her fingertips, where her nails have cracked.

She lifts herself up onto her palms and looks around. When she sees me, she scrambles to my side and throws herself into my arms. I can feel her body trembling against mine. I hold her close, trying to comfort her.

"What the fuck happened?" I look around and see that Birthmark is back up on his knees. "Where did—" He pats at his belt, then starts looking around frantically.

"Looking for this?" Gael asks, smiling and holding up the biker's huge knife.

Birthmark nods slightly, then starts inching away, a perplexed look on his face. As soon as Linebacker is conscious again, they both retreat, hopping on his motorcycle and speeding away.

"I should have kept them unconscious," Gael says beneath his breath, "but really, what were we going to do with them? It's not like we could turn them in to the police—not without revealing our powers."

Mia's still in my arms, but she's stopped shaking.

"You guys saved me," she says, pulling away. "How did you even know I was here?"

I don't say anything, but I watch as the expression on her face goes from confusion to concern. "Oh, no. You saw me die, didn't you, Luke? Of course. You saw me die in that coffin!"

I nod, and she stays silent for a time. "You saved me," she finally says. "Even after what happened to Darla and Erin's dad, even after what we read in the journal, and what your dad warned you about."

"I ... I just couldn't let you die," I say.

She looks at me for several more seconds, her brow furrowed. Then she throws herself back into my arms. "Thank you, Luke," she whispers. Her lips find mine, and she kisses me passionately.

Somewhere behind us, Gael clears his throat. "I'll just ... I'll just give you guys some space," he says. Then he disappears.

Mia pushes me down to the ground and straddles me, our lips parting just long enough for her to give voice to a joyful, adrenaline-fueled laugh. Then she lowers herself on top of my body, and we resume kissing. Her hands guide mine to her breasts.

I did the right thing, I think, lost in this bright, warm moment, expelling a bashful laugh as Mia's hand slips down to cup my ass and pull me even closer.

I did the right thing. No matter what the cost.

Then, suddenly, I find myself falling head over feet into a dark abyss, a new death vision swimming into focus before me.

I see Mia walking down a hallway. It looks like a college dorm—there are students laughing and running past, and there's loud music coming from every room. Mia stops in front of a door that has her name on it, and she glances back over her shoulder. She looks distracted and anxious. She's only a couple years older than she is now. *Maybe I didn't really save her after all. Maybe I just gave her a little more time.*

Can I bear to see this? Can I handle seeing her die in some new way?

She opens up the door and goes inside.

Her dorm room is dark, but I can see that there's someone sitting on her bed, waiting for her. *Her killer? Is this how she dies, assaulted in the dark, ambushed as she comes home from class?* It's got to happen soon. My visions usually don't last that long—a couple minutes at the most.

Mia turns on the light, and my heart leaps inside my chest.

It's me. *I'm* sitting on her bed.

This future version of me looks tired, defeated. My hair is shaggy, and I have a black eye—a nasty-looking shiner that's starting to turn from purple to yellow. My shoulders are slumped and my eyes look dull.

"Did you find her?" I ask as Mia sits down on the bed at my side. I'm fidgeting with a black pen, but as soon as she sits down, I toss it to the floor.

Mia nods. "I found her," she says, her voice as quiet and flat as mine. "It got … interesting."

She has a quizzical look in her eyes—but they go wide with surprise as soon as I duck down and grab a hunting knife from beneath the bed. I slide away from her and swing the knife around in a quick arc. She makes a low squeaking sound as it impacts her chest with a solid *thud*.

"I'm sorry, Mia," I whisper, standing up from the bed and taking a couple steps back. "I … I had to."

Mia's fingers reach up, grasping for the knife sticking out of her chest. But before they can touch the hilt—or the ooze of blood now seeping from her wound—they tremble and drop down to her sides.

Then she looks up at me, her eyes still wide. There is no pain in her expression. Just confusion and betrayal.

I fall down to my knees, and we both hold perfectly still for a handful of seconds. Mia tries to take a breath, but fails. The sound is a low whistle in her chest that stutters and peters out.

Then she topples over backward, landing flat on her back.

Dead.

"I … I had to," I repeat, my voice low, barely audible. Then, still facing her, I bury my head in one hand while I reach back with the other, holding it up like I'm trying to block my face from view.

I know I'm here, I realize. *I know I'm watching this horrible crime, peering forward from the past.*

Then I'm back at Milagra Ridge, and Mia's kissing me passionately.

I push her off me and roll onto my side, my body trembling with shock. The setting sun has bathed the entire world in a cold violet light.

Good God. I kill her, I think, horrified. *I saved her life today, only to kill her sometime in the future.*

But why?

What happens to us? What happens to me?

"What's wrong, Luke?" she asks, moving to my side and putting a comforting hand on my shoulder. I look back and see the concerned expression on her face.

No, I tell myself, shaking my head violently. *It can't be right. I'd never do that to her!*

But there's another voice inside my head now, a calm, dispassionate voice. *But you* do *do that, don't you, Luke? You stab her. You kill her. You saw it.*

This is followed by a cold, hard laugh that echoes inside my head.

Face it, Luke, you're in uncharted territory here. You saved Mia's life, but at what cost? And for what horrible future?

EPILOGUE:

TWO WEEKS
LATER

It's just the eight of us right now: me, Mia, Gael, Cole, Amy, Erin, Heroji, and Heroji's newest girl, Amanda. We're walking back to Amy's house, carrying bags of chips and cartons of soda. Her second movie night of the year is tonight, but it's only five o'clock, and it's still light out. People won't start showing up until after the sun goes down, and that gives us plenty of time to get ready.

It is a relaxed walk through downtown Colma, and everyone seems to be enjoying themselves. Erin's whispering in Amy's ear, and Amy's laughing loudly. Heroji's got his arm around Amanda's shoulder, and Amanda is smiling up at him adoringly. Cole and Gael are bumping shoulders and talking about music.

We cross in front of Woodlawn Cemetery, and I notice that there's a new sign hanging on the front gate: "Under New Management."

Cora Bell?

Gael shoots me a knowing look. "Things are changing, Luke."

I nod.

Mia squeezes my hand, and I glance over. "But change isn't always bad," she says, in a low voice. "After all, the future isn't what it used to be. I get to live." Then she leans against my side and gives me a tender kiss.

She seems so happy, so relaxed—and I want to be happy for her. If anyone deserves a new future, it's her. Especially if she wants to spend a lot of that bonus time with me.

The bikers have left town, it seems. I considered giving the photos and video that Gael and I took to the police, but Mia stopped me. "There are just too many questions that we can't answer without revealing ourselves," she argued. "We should only come forward if they start bothering us again, okay?" I agreed. Reluctantly.

Darla's been home from the hospital for four days now. Uncle Roy's been lavishing her with attention—waiting on her hand and foot, cooking her food, and *talking, talking, talking*—but I can tell that she's already bored out of her mind. She's set up a makeshift computer stand in her bed, but her broken arm is seriously getting in the way of her elite gamer skills, and she's about ready to throw the entire setup out the window. And most troubling of all, each time I enter her room, it seems like she's popping an oxycodone.

I want to beg for her forgiveness and tell her that everything's going to be okay.

But I can't. That would be a lie.

There are still bad things waiting for us in the future, things I can't get out of my head: *My hand wielding that knife. The way Mia's eyes go wide. The look of betrayal on her face, and the low whistle coming from her chest as she tries to breathe. And then my head collapsing into my hand as I'm racked with grief.*

I keep seeing it—her death—and I drift off in the middle of sentences. I've been kicked out of class four different times, for inattention and insubordination, and the people around me are starting to get worried. I can see it in their eyes.

I feel like I might be going insane.

Is this what my great-great-grandfather went through in the last weeks of his life? Did he see something so horrible that his brain went totally off the rails?

The only thing that gives me comfort is Mia, and the way that she holds me and tells me that everything will be all right. But that comfort never lasts. It seems like every other time I touch her, the vision returns, and I'm forced to live through her death again.

Why? I want to ask her. *Why do I kill you? Do I grow to hate you? Do I go insane and turn evil? Or is this something else entirely? Did I make a mistake in saving you, and this is the price I have to pay to correct my error?*

So far, I've managed to stop myself from actually asking any of these questions out loud. But I wonder if it's only a matter of time before I let it slip.

———

And I wonder if this future is inevitable. Do I have to kill her?

And if not, if I can change things, will that only make matters worse?

Will more people die?

———

When we get back to Amy's place, we crash on the lawn for a while, talking, laughing, and staring up at the cloud-dotted sky.

Heroji points out a cloud that looks like a sailing ship, and Gael points out one that looks like an erect penis; this is greeted with groans, cries of "Gross!" and a smack to the back of the head with a well-aimed bag of chips.

Amy lets out a yawn and gets to her feet. "It's time to get going, assholes," she says. "People are going to start showing up soon, and we've still got to drag the projector out."

"Noooooooo," Erin groans, languidly stretching her arms up over her head. "*You* drag the projector out. I'm busy working on my tan."

"And just for that, Erin, you get to help me rake the leaves, trim the bushes, polish the headstones, and then, if there's time, move all of the graves one foot to the left."

Everyone laughs. Only I remain silent.

Mia stays behind as the others start off toward the house. She reaches out and touches my arm. "I'm not blind, you know," she says, her voice low and sympathetic. "I can tell that you're worrying again, Luke. You should tell me what's wrong. We can fix it together."

I nod, but don't say anything.

Eventually, Mia lets out a low sigh and stands up. She brushes grass off her jeans and turns away, rushing to catch up with the others.

As I watch her go, the only thing I can think about—the only sound inside my head—is the low whistling noise that she makes as she breathes her last breath.

It haunts me.

If it gets to be too bad, there's something I can do. Somewhere I can go.

But only as a last resort. If I can't think of anything else.

The third time I saw her death vision—in the backseat of my car this time, Mia holding on to me as I try to get away from her—I noticed something odd about the way I'm holding my hand. Collapsed on her dorm room floor, my head buried in my left hand, I lift my right palm up, putting it on display. At first, I thought I was trying to hide my face in shame, but the gesture looks awkward, and on third viewing I notice the writing.

There are words written on my palm. A shorthand note, in awkward, shaking script.

And I remember the pen that I was holding when Mia first entered the room. I must have been writing something on my hand.

It has to be a message to myself—to my *current* self—from the room in which Mia dies.

Luke, it says, *talk to Lily Bell!*

Cora Bell's daughter. Cora Bell's *dead* daughter.

———

And that's it.

Message over.